Dancing in the Dark

Dancing in the Dark

ROBYN BAVATI

Woodbury, Minnesota

First U.S. Edition
First Printing, 2013

Originally published by Penguin Books Australia, 2010.
This edition published by Flux, an imprint of Llewellyn Worldwide Ltd.

Book design by Bob Gaul
Cover design by Ellen Lawson
Cover image: Cover photo © Brooke Shaden Photography
          Blue smoke © iStockphoto.com/Auke Holwerda

Flux, an imprint of Llewellyn Worldwide Ltd.

Library of Congress Cataloging-in-Publication Data
Bavati, Robyn.
  Dancing in the dark/Robyn Bavati.—1st U.S. ed.
      p. cm.
  Summary: Passionate about ballet, Ditty Cohen signs up for dance class despite being forbidden to by her Orthodox Jewish parents, then must face the consequences when the two worlds collide after five and a half years of study.
  ISBN 978-0-7387-3477-4
[1. Jews—Australia—Fiction. 2. Family life—Australia—Fiction. 3. Ballet dancing—Fiction. 4. Orthodox Judaism—Fiction. 5. Judaism—Customs and practices—Fiction. 6. Conduct of life—Fiction. 7. Melbourne (Vic.)—Fiction. 8. Australia—Fiction.] I. Title.
  PZ7.B3287Dan 2013
  [Fic]—dc23

                                                    2012035621

                        Flux
                Llewellyn Worldwide Ltd.
                2143 Wooddale Drive
                Woodbury, MN 55125-2989
                    www.fluxnow.com

        Printed in the United States of America

For Aviya, Kada, and Ilai,
and
in loving memory of my father,
who combined a passion for knowledge
with a love of Judaism, a belief in tolerance,
and a sincere appreciation for the arts.

Dear Reader,

Like Ditty, I have always loved ballet. As a girl, I was allowed a "taste" of it—one or two lessons a week—but I was not allowed to learn seriously or attend classes on Saturdays. I accepted this, but there was a part of me that wished I could choose for myself. Given the opportunity, I'm not sure whether I could have become a professional dancer, but I would have liked the chance to try. By creating the character of Ditty, who has to overcome even greater obstacles than I did, I think in some kind of vicarious fashion I fulfilled a dream.

My family were modern orthodox, not haredi, but I have been closely connected with a number of haredi families, and must stress that the family that is portrayed in this book, and the community of which they are a part, is by no means typical of all haredi communities. Similarly, the community portrayed in this story is not representative of the broader Jewish community, which ranges from the ultra-orthodox to the extremely liberal.

For the sake of authenticity, I have included a number of words and terms that are part of the everyday vocabulary of orthodox Jews. These are explained in the glossary at the end of the book.

I hope you enjoy Ditty's story.

—Robyn Bavati

PROLOGUE

I'm lying on my bed, staring at the peeling paper on the wall in my room. Shayne and Gittel are still asleep in their bunks, opposite. The walls close in around me. This room is not big enough for three, and I am suffocating.

My father is waiting to ambush me in the kitchen and I'm scared to go out there. It's past nine in the morning and he's meant to be in *shule*. I can't remember him missing shule before, especially on *Shabbos*.

It's a *mitzvah* to enjoy Shabbos, and my father does everything in his power to keep the *mitzvos*. So last night he tried to act as if it were just an ordinary Shabbos, but when he tried to sing his voice cracked and he could not continue. Ever since then, the whole family has been acting as if they've been betrayed. As if *I* have betrayed them.

Tonight, I'm supposed to be dancing. Miss Mitchell will be wondering why I haven't arrived to warm up for this morning's rehearsal.

Afterwards, she'll advise us all to go home and get some rest.

I don't think I'll ever rest again.

I want to. I want to close my eyes and make my problems disappear. I don't want to deal with the consequences of the past five years. But Miss Mitchell is depending on me, and I can't let her down.

I can't let myself down.

I get out of bed and brush my teeth. I splash cold water on my face and towel it dry. Then I put on my tights and my leotard, and pull my Shabbos dress over the top.

I can hear my parents talking in the kitchen. If I sneak out quietly, they won't know I've gone.

I tiptoe out of my bedroom and toward the front door.

Just three more steps and I'll be out of here.

Two more steps and . . .

"Where do you think you're going?" says my father.

I open my mouth to speak but . . .

"I asked you a question," says my father.

I take another step toward the door.

"Stay where you are." His voice is a command. "If you leave now, if you set foot outside that door, you are not to come back. Do you understand, Yehudit? *You are not to come back.*"

I hesitate. I don't want to stay here, but I don't want to leave and never come back, either. I'm only seventeen. But my father was never one for idle threats.

What will I do now?

Time seems suspended . . .

Memories flash before my eyes . . .

One

• ◆ •

I was twelve years old. It was Sunday morning, a week after my bat-mitzvah, and my best friend, Sara Kesten, had just rung to say that I *must* come over. She had something to show me. She wouldn't tell me what it was over the phone. It was a hot day in early autumn and I ran all the way to Sara's house, sweating beneath my long-sleeved dress and nylon tights, envious of the kids I passed in the street wearing shorts and T-shirts.

Sara was waiting for me on the footpath, and as soon as she saw me she ran toward me. "Ditty, you'll never guess. Never in a million years." She swore me to secrecy and I took a vow of silence, even though it's against the Torah and I knew I shouldn't. I just couldn't wait to see what it was she had to show me.

We went straight inside. Sara's house was so different

from mine. It was empty and silent and immaculately tidy. I followed Sara up the stairs and into her mother's bedroom. I was invading Mrs. Kesten's privacy, and I felt like a criminal.

The room was cold, the bed narrow, and the bedspread a dull mustard color. There was a strong smell of Mrs. Kesten's jasmine-scented perfume.

Sara went over to her mother's wardrobe and opened the door, and my mouth dropped open when I saw the TV nestled inside.

It wasn't that I'd never seen a TV before. The Fischers, my less-religious cousins, actually owned one, though out of respect for my parents it was never ever on when I was there.

We weren't allowed to watch TV. No one in our community had one, and our school, Beis Hannah, the most religious of all the Jewish schools in Melbourne, had a strict "No TV" rule. When parents first enrolled their children, they had to sign a form declaring that they didn't have a TV at home, so I was amazed at Mrs. Kesten.

"How . . . how long has she had this?"

Sara shrugged. "I found it this morning when my mum left for work."

"Have you turned it on?"

"I haven't touched it yet. I will if you will."

We both reached out and touched the screen. The TV fit snugly on a shelf in the cupboard, and there was a DVD player attached to it, beneath the screen. A small pile of DVDs was stacked neatly on a shelf below.

Sara said, "Let's give it a try."

"I don't think we—"

"Come on, Ditty. If my own mother watches it, how bad can it be?"

Then why is it hidden? Why has your mother kept it a secret? But somehow the questions got stuck in my throat.

We weren't sure how to turn it on, but there was a manual lying on top of it. *How to operate your Sony 243 TV and DVD.* Sara opened the booklet and I located the power button. I pressed it, hard, then jumped back, startled by a buzz of static. The TV flickered to life, but there was no picture on the screen, only a haze of grayish dots.

"You've got to put it on Channel 3 to start with," said Sara, looking in the manual, "and you don't need to touch it. You use this to turn it on."

We spent a while fumbling with the buttons on the remote controls, and finally we knew what we were doing. We sat down on Mrs. Kesten's bed to watch in earnest.

There was news on one channel, something with policemen in it on another, football on another, and a program called *Video Hits* on another, with girls who were almost naked thrusting their hips as they danced. We understood exactly why we weren't allowed to watch, but somehow, that didn't stop us.

Half an hour before Mrs. Kesten was due to come home, we put everything back exactly the way we found it, closed the cupboard door, and crept downstairs. Even though there was no one to hear us, we spoke in whispers.

———

It was early afternoon when I got home. Ezra and Hillel, my younger brothers, both had friends over, and about fifteen boys seemed to be chasing each other around the house. The littlest ones came barreling into me as I walked in the door, and I pushed my way past them. I headed toward the room I shared with my younger sisters, Shayne and Gittel, tripping on some discarded toys in the hallway and an odd shoe left lying around.

Shayne was in our bedroom with two of her friends. They were sitting on the top bunk, which was Shayne's bed, dangling their feet over the bottom bunk, which was mine. Gittel's crib took up most of the opposite wall, so there was no room for me.

It was times like these I envied Rochel, who was three and a half years older than I was and had her own room. She used to share with us, before Gittel was born. Then my father suggested we find a bigger house, but my mother didn't want to move; she said that 46 Gordon Street was the ideal location. So another, tiny room was tacked on to the back of the house for Rochel. You had to walk through the laundry to get to it, but who cares? Like my older brother, Pinny, I'd have walked through a bathroom and a garage, and maybe a small war zone, if it meant I could have a room of my own.

I wandered out of my bedroom and into the kitchen. One-year-old Gittel was crouching on the worn green linoleum near my mother's feet, banging metal pots with a wooden spoon.

My mum didn't seem to notice the noise. She was sitting

on one of our shabby, hard-backed kitchen chairs, folding laundry. I sat down and started folding with her, trying to forget what I'd been doing for the last few hours.

"What did you do at Sara's?" It was the first thing she asked.

Normally, I wouldn't wait to be questioned. I'd charge right in, volunteering every detail of my day. But then, normally I'd have nothing to hide.

My mum was looking at me strangely. "Are you okay?" she asked, one eyebrow raised.

I nodded, not trusting myself to speak.

"So...what did you do at Sara's?" she asked again.

"Nothing special."

I wished I could tell her. I wanted to own up, if only to ease the uncomfortable feeling in the pit of my stomach, but I'd promised I wouldn't.

My mum was concentrating on lining up the sleeves of a long-sleeved T-shirt, and I glanced at her covertly, wondering what she would think of me if she knew.

She's a small woman, my mum, and pretty—at least, I'd always thought so. That day she looked tired, though maybe she always did, with seven kids and no one to help her. Her skin was pale—she never wore make-up—and her hair was covered, as always, by a brown, nylon *sheitel*, a wig so coarse it was obviously not human hair. Her own hair might have been gray by now for all I knew. Like all *haredi* women, she kept it covered from the minute she got up in the morning till the minute she went to sleep at night. It had been years since I'd seen it.

My mum was dressed, as always, to blend in, avoiding what she calls "loud" colors. Despite the heat, she was wearing a nondescript calf-length skirt and a high-necked, long-sleeved blouse, in neutral colors. She was also wearing the usual pantyhose and closed-toed shoes that are standard in our haredi community. She never relaxed her standards of modesty, even in the house. Yet despite the fact that she probably looked exactly the same as she always did, she suddenly seemed more vulnerable than usual. I wondered why I'd never noticed the washed-out color of her gray-blue eyes.

To make up for my deceit, I did the dishes without being asked, wiped down the kitchen bench, and swept the floor. Then I took Gittel, and Hillel and his friends, to the park, and when I got home my mother told me what a thoughtful, considerate daughter I was.

That night I lay awake, my conscience heavy. I had never lied to my mother before, and I wasn't used to keeping secrets. My mum had always been my confidante. I told her everything. I couldn't tell her this, though. It would have been disloyal to Sara. Besides, I knew that if I did tell her she'd be disappointed in me, and I didn't think I could bear my mother's disappointment. My mum trusted me, and I had betrayed that trust. I vowed to myself never to betray her trust again.

Two

• ◆ •

I woke up feeling good before reality kicked in, and with it the memory of what I'd done the day before.

As I washed my hands and face, I studied my reflection in the bathroom mirror, wondering if there were any signs that might give me away. There didn't seem to be. I was surprised at how ordinary I looked, how unchanged.

I was small for my age, and skinny, with dark, wavy hair and olive skin. My eyes were not quite green, not brown. Hazel, my mum called them. I peered into them, remembering what my mother had once told me—that the eyes are the window to the soul. If that were true, mine would reveal wickedness, deception.

"Stop hogging the bathroom, Ditty. You've been in there for ages." Rochel was pounding on the door. It was often like this in the mornings. One bathroom just wasn't enough for nine people. I gave myself one last, lingering look in the mirror and opened the door.

By the time I got back to my room, my younger sisters were both up. Shayne was pulling on her tights, and Gittel was standing up in her crib, singing. I took her out and kissed her. Then I got dressed quickly, ate a small breakfast, and walked to school, where the day began, as usual, with morning prayers.

"Ashrei yoshvei baisecha..." *Happy are they who dwell in Your house...* The words were familiar and comforting.

But what, I wondered now, did they actually mean? I knew what I'd been taught—that happiness wasn't something a Jew should strive for, it was a bonus that came from keeping the laws and strictures that had been passed down from one generation to the next in an unbroken chain. If you did that, you felt a sense of security, a feeling of well-being that came from doing what you knew was right.

But the sense of security the prayer promised eluded me, and I stumbled over the words. I, Ditty Cohen, no longer deserved to be happy.

Neither Sara nor I mentioned what we'd done the day before. We talked about anything and everything else, just as we always had. But our secret was never far from my mind. I glanced at Sara, wondering if it was on her mind, too. Her face just wasn't giving much away.

Physically, Sara was nothing like me. Her hair was either

red or sand-colored, depending on the light, and she had a light sprinkling of freckles on her nose and cheeks. Her skin was light, the hairs on it bleached gold by the sun, and her eyes were like a pale blue sky.

If eyes were the window to the soul, I reasoned, they should say something about her. I searched Sara's eyes, looking for some sign of the *yetzer hara*, the evil inclination that is said to be in each and every one of us all the time, tempting us to do bad things. I didn't see it there.

Sara caught me looking. "What is it, Ditty?"

I shook my head. "Nothing," I said.

For the rest of the week, Sara and I spent almost all our time together—before, during, and after school. I was itching to discuss her mother's TV, wondering whether she felt as bad as I did about having watched it, but I wasn't brave enough to ask.

I was pretty sure that the whole incident was a one-off, that neither of us would ever mention it again. I assumed we would go back to spending our Sundays as usual, meeting up with friends, walking round the neighborhood or baking biscuits. We'd pretend we'd never seen the TV, and life would go back to normal. I would not have to keep secrets. I could stop feeling guilty, and ashamed.

———

On Friday, as school finished earlier than on other days, Rochel, Shayne, and I hurried home to help my mother get ready for Shabbos.

As the sun started sinking in the sky, my mother lit two candles and made a *bracha*, a blessing, over them. She covered her eyes and chanted the words in a quiet sing-song. For a few moments, the house was completely silent and the atmosphere in the dining room was transformed by the soft glow of candlelight into something holy.

Rochel, Shayne, and I played word games, and took turns bouncing Gittel up and down on our knees.

Soon, my father and brothers came back from shule, and all nine of us stood around the table. My father blessed each of us in order of age, starting with Pinny. When my turn came, he placed his hands on my head as he said the prayer, and it felt as if all my sins of the previous week were washed away.

I was protected, treasured, safe. I knew that Hashem would look after me because my father had asked Him to, and my father was a pious man.

After the blessings over wine and bread, Rochel, Shayne, and I served and cleared the Shabbos meal—fried and boiled fish, chicken soup with noodles, roast chicken with potatoes, and compote for dessert. In between courses, we sang *zmiros*. My father's voice was rich and deep when he sang the traditional Shabbos songs, and we listened for a while, spellbound, before joining in.

Shabbos was the only time we ever heard my father sing. After the zmiros, he spoke about Shabbos, and how lucky we were to have this day of rest. He reminded us that only the Jews had Shabbos. The *goyim* did not. We were the Chosen People. We were different.

The pride in my father's voice was contagious. I was glad I was Jewish. I had a purpose in life. I had been brought into this world to serve Hashem. My nation would be a shining light to other nations, and we would make the world a better place. If we were not rewarded in this world, we would be rewarded in the next. This world was nothing but illusion. The real world, the eternal world, the true world, was the *Olam Haba*, the World to Come.

This was what my father said that night, as on every other Shabbos, and I believed him. Our lives had meaning, and I felt sorry for people who did not have Hashem in theirs.

Three

•◆•

By Sunday, all traces of the *kedusha*, the holiness of Shabbos, had disappeared.

Once again I went over to Sara's house just after her mum had left for work. Once again Sara was waiting for me on the footpath.

"It's already on," she whispered.

I didn't need to ask what she was talking about.

"I can't watch," I said as I followed her inside. "I can't do it again."

Sara turned and went upstairs, just as if I hadn't spoken. "Come on," she said. "Let's see what's on."

"But . . ." I hesitated at the foot of the stairs. "I don't want to lie to my mum again."

"You don't have to lie. Just don't say anything."

"That's almost as bad as lying."

Sara shrugged. "Even if it is, it's not such a big deal. I mean, lying to my mum wouldn't bother me that much."

"Wouldn't it? Why not?"

"She lies to me. All the time. White lies, she calls them. And when she isn't lying, she's keeping secrets. She kept the TV a secret from me, didn't she? So now I'm keeping it a secret from her. Why should I feel bad about it? I'm only doing to her what she did to me."

"Yeah, well, it's not like that with my mum. She's honest. And she trusts me. And lying is against the Torah," I reminded her.

"Like I said, Ditty, it's not that big a deal. I mean, where in the Torah does it say: Thou shalt not watch television?"

I laughed. "The Torah was written long before TV was invented," I argued.

"Exactly. Oh, come *on*, Ditty."

Once again I found myself weakening, and I followed Sara upstairs.

———

"What if your mum finds out?" I said as I was leaving.

"She won't."

Mrs. Kesten had a small shop in Carlisle Street where she sold Jewish books and gifts. It was open all morning on Sundays, and she never got home before one o'clock.

"Don't worry, Ditty. Nobody knows. No one is going to know."

But *I* knew. Hashem knew. I couldn't hide the truth from Him. Nobody could. He knew all of our secrets.

Even so, it soon became our secret routine. Each Sunday, after Sara's mother left for work, I followed Sara up the stairs, guiltily aware of the buzz of excitement I felt inside.

Entering Mrs. Kesten's bedroom still felt wrong, but I did it anyway. The TV was always there—solid and silent and real. And still forbidden.

We watched whatever happened to be on. In the stuffy confines of Mrs. Kesten's bedroom, TV became our link to the world beyond our small community, a world we had never been allowed to enter.

Sara and I kept the secret to ourselves. There was no one else we could trust with it. The bond between us strengthened. We were more than best friends. We were partners in crime.

———

One Sunday, I was sitting cross-legged and barefoot on Mrs. Kesten's bed, flicking through the various channels. Already, just a few weeks after discovering the TV, we were fussier than we had been, and when there was nothing good on, we flicked through Mrs. Kesten's collection of DVDs. She didn't have much—only a few films, and they were all about old people, with titles like *Driving Miss Daisy*, *Shirley Valentine*, and *On Golden Pond*.

There were only five channels, and that day most of them were screening sports. Tennis on Channel 7, soccer on

Channel 9, and cricket on 10. There was something in Japanese on SBS, and an ancient black-and-white film on ABC.

I was about to turn the set off when the black-and-white film finished and I caught a preview of Act Two of something called *Nutcracker*, which was about to begin. A voiceover explained that the ballet was about a girl named Clara who was in love with a soldier. War broke out and the soldier had to go and fight, and Clara was heartbroken, not knowing when she would ever see him again.

The preview was short, less than a minute, but it intrigued me. I sat back down again.

Sara wandered in with a box of chocolates. We only ate chocolate in Mrs. Kesten's bedroom. Never biscuits or chips, because of the crumbs.

"What are you watching?"

"A ballet. It's about to start."

I moved over to make room for her, and we sat squashed up beside each other on the narrow bed. Sara offered me a chocolate. I murmured a bracha and popped the chocolate into my mouth.

As the music started up, I explained the story to Sara. Then the curtain rose.

At first the stage was dark and empty. Slowly it became lighter and Clara, dressed in a soft, flowing, pale lemon dress, made her entrance. She looked around for the soldier, ran toward him, and began to dance.

Her body was lithe and beautiful and every emotion I'd ever felt crossed her features. I couldn't take my eyes off her.

I knew what she was feeling. It was in every movement of every limb.

When the soldier had to leave, she clung to him, not letting him go. She was dragged across the floor, still holding fast to him. Then he tossed her up into the air as if she were weightless, and just for a moment she seemed suspended there, defying gravity.

I got the shivers watching it.

"Wouldn't you love to do that?" I said.

"Do it?" Sara looked at me blankly. "No, it's nice to watch, but I wouldn't want to do it."

"I would," I said.

Here was a power I had never seen before, a kind of haunting loveliness I had never imagined. Seeing it made me long for something, I didn't know what, and when it was over I wanted to watch it again.

Then there was a close up of a DVD with a cover picture of Clara. A disembodied voice said: " ... *Nutcracker* and other ballets are now available at all ... "

"Shhh ... " Sara cocked an ear and listened, and a second later she was jumping madly up and down.

"Turn it off, Ditty. My mother's home."

Her ears were so attuned to the sound of her mother's key in the door that I was convinced she'd hear it even if there was a thunderstorm outside and the TV was turned up to full volume, which of course it wasn't because we'd never risk it.

I pressed a button on the remote control and Sara closed the cupboard door. We smoothed the bedspread on her mother's bed, tiptoed quietly out of the room, and shut the door.

Sara caught her breath the way she always did when she panicked. There was a creak as Mrs. Kesten climbed the stairs, and we glimpsed the top of her head on the landing just as we slipped into Sara's bedroom. Sara heaved a sigh of relief.

"Sara!"

"Hi, Mum. I'm in my room. Ditty's with me."

Mrs. Kesten poked her head around the door.

"Hello, Mrs. Kesten," I said.

"What have you girls been doing all morning?"

"Nothing much," said Sara.

"Why don't you go outside, stretch your legs a bit?"

We raced down the stairs and out into the street, where we collapsed against each other, laughing with relief.

Four

◆

A loud buzz of conversation was coming from our living room. I pushed the door open and peeked inside.

"Ditty, come in. Come and say *mazeltov* to Aunt Rivka. Shoshi is getting married."

"Really? Mazeltov!" I walked over to where Aunt Rivka was sitting on the couch and bent down to kiss her. "Who's she marrying?"

"Shimon Stern," said Aunt Rivka proudly.

"Of the American Sterns," my mother added.

"Such *yiches*! He comes from a long line of rabbis and scholars. You'll be next, Rochel," she said to my sister.

"Rivka," my mother protested, "she's only fifteen."

"I don't mean tomorrow."

"Well then, there's no point talking about it now, is there?"

Aunt Rivka, my father's sister, was a professional matchmaker. She'd been talking about a *shidduch* for my sister since Rochel was five.

"She'll be ready to marry in a year or two," Aunt Rivka said. "A year or two is not far off."

I glanced at Rochel to gauge her reaction. She was studying the carpet, too embarrassed to speak.

"She's so pretty," Aunt Rivka continued, as if Rochel wasn't in the room. "She'll have no trouble getting a shidduch. You'll see. No trouble at all."

Aunt Rivka was right. Rochel was pretty. She had big green eyes and long brown hair that was so silky it always looked as if it had just been brushed. She was of medium height, slim but not skinny, and she had a fabulous complexion, not a single blemish.

My mum was always telling us what a good example Rochel set for the rest of us, and it was true. Rochel would never have spent a morning doing what I'd just done.

"So, have you set a date yet?" asked my mother. "Have you booked a hall?"

As Aunt Rivka gave my mum the details, my mind drifted back to the heart-wrenching dancing I'd seen. I gazed out of our living-room window, toward the street. Aunt Tamara and Linda were getting out of their car.

"Anyway, I'd better be going," said Aunt Rivka.

"Why?" said my mother. "Stay. Stay and have a cup of coffee."

"No, no. I only came to tell you the news. I've got so much to do at home."

My mother had enough to do herself, with only seven kids, so when Aunt Rivka, who had eleven, said she was busy, my mother didn't even begin to argue.

"Well, mazeltov again," she said, giving Aunt Rivka a hug.

I went over and hugged her, too. So did Rochel and Shayne. I picked up Gittel, who waved goodbye with her fist, and we all walked Aunt Rivka to the door. My mother opened it just as Aunt Tamara reached the doorstep outside.

"Shoshi's getting married," my mother burst out happily, before Aunt Tamara could say a single word.

"Really? That's wonderful." Aunt Tamara smiled broadly. "Mazeltov, Rivka. A big mazeltov to all the family."

"Thanks," said Aunt Rivka. "You have a daughter, too, don't you, Tamara? It'll be her turn soon." Linda, standing beside my aunt, rolled her eyes, and it was only then that Aunt Rivka noticed my fifteen-year-old cousin. She stepped back involuntarily, not quite able to hide her shock.

The rest of us, even Aunt Tamara, were dressed in strict accordance with Jewish law, in modest clothes that covered our elbows, knees, and collarbones. Linda, on the other hand, was wearing three-quarter jeans, a low-cut T-shirt and thongs. Aunt Rivka's lips pursed in disapproval and I knew what she was thinking—dressed so immodestly, Linda would not find a shidduch at all.

I was glad my father wasn't there to see her. He was critical of Linda at the best of times. My mother didn't like what Linda was wearing either, but she didn't comment because Aunt Tamara was her sister. Besides, she was used to Linda and her rebellious streak.

Aunt Tamara herself didn't seem to care too much what Linda wore. She and Uncle Yankel weren't haredi, like we were. They were modern orthodox. Once I overheard my father saying he didn't know what had happened to Aunt Tamara; she was raised exactly the same way as my mother, then somehow she met and married Yankel Fischer and turned into a "liberal thinker." Of all the words my father could use, "liberal" was the most insulting.

After a perfunctory goodbye, Aunt Rivka marched off and Aunt Tamara gazed after her. "She looks good, doesn't she, Zipporah? You'd never guess she has eleven children."

My mother nodded in agreement. "She's the one person I know who never looks tired."

"How old did you say Shoshi was?" asked Aunt Tamara.

"I didn't say. She's seventeen."

"Seventeen! The poor girl ... "

"What are you talking about?" said my mother. "She's in love. She must be. Why else would she agree to marry him after only one date?"

"Love, my foot!" said Aunt Tamara. "What does Shoshi know about love?"

My mother shrugged. "Nobody's forcing her to marry him. And anyway, arranged marriages are much, much safer. And far more likely to succeed."

"Only because the kids have no option. It's archaic, the way these matches are made. It's not the Middle Ages anymore. Young girls today should choose their husbands for themselves."

"How could Shoshi possibly choose for herself? She's only seventeen…"

"That's what I mean," said Aunt Tamara. "She's far too young to get married at all. I hope you won't marry your girls off at seventeen."

"Seventeen, eighteen… That's the way it's done in our community. It's what they expect."

Linda looked at me and rolled her eyes. We'd heard this argument before. It was a subject our mothers never agreed on.

Shayne disappeared into our bedroom and Rochel went out to visit a friend. Linda and I decided to leave our mothers to their quarrel, and we went outside.

Even though Linda was three years older than me, and only nine months younger than Rochel, it was me she got along with the best. She was more like a friend than a relative, and I was closer to her than I was to any of my cousins on Aunt Rivka's side. I was glad Rochel had left. It meant I could have Linda all to myself.

It was quiet in our back garden. None of the boys were around just then, so I tucked my skirt up under the elastic of my underpants and started to practice one-handed cartwheels. Linda clapped and cheered wildly, and we both ended up lying on our backs and laughing, looking up at the sky.

When we wandered back inside we found our mothers chatting happily together. My mum was sitting in her usual position on the couch and had resumed her Sunday task of darning socks, a job so automatic that she barely watched what she was doing.

"Maybe Ditty can come back to our house for the rest of the afternoon?" said Linda.

"To do what?" asked my mother.

"Hang out with me."

"Yes, good idea," Aunt Tamara agreed.

"Thanks, I'd love to," I said, before my mother had a chance to refuse.

I hardly ever got to go to Linda's. My father didn't like me going there. He always said that the modern orthodox were a bigger threat to the continuation of the Jewish people than the Jews who didn't pretend to be religious in the first place, and he hated the thought of us being exposed to the secular influences of Linda's home.

The Fischers were the only people we knew who weren't haredi. Not only did they own a TV—which had pride of place in the living room—but they also bought secular newspapers like *The Age* and *The Herald Sun*, whereas we only got *Torah News*. And they had a computer, which was not so bad in itself—we had computers in our school—but their computer had access to the Internet, which my dad said was just like inviting Satan right into your home.

To make matters worse, Aunt Tamara and Uncle Yankel sent Linda, their only child, to Sinai College—a modern orthodox, co-educational Jewish day school, which, as far as my father was concerned, was almost as bad as sending her to a government school, maybe worse.

"I don't know…" said my mother.

"Pleeease!"

"Don't worry, Zipporah," said Aunt Tamara. "I'll see she doesn't do anything unsuitable." So my mother agreed, and soon I was sitting next to Linda in the back seat of Aunt Tamara's luxury car.

———

The Fischers lived in Caulfield, in a spacious, three-bedroom house they'd bought when Linda was small. We climbed the stairs to Linda's bedroom and Linda decided to give me a makeover. It wasn't the sort of thing I could do at home. Make-up isn't expressly forbidden, but in our community wearing it is considered frivolous and vain.

Linda sat me down in front of the mirror and drew my hair back into a ponytail. "You're so striking, Ditty," she said. "Not classically pretty, like Rochel, but..." She searched for the right words. "Really attractive."

"No, I'm not. I'm small and skinny."

"Skinny's good," she answered. "Lots of girls would kill to be skinny."

Linda, too, was skinny, but she was also tall. She must have inherited the tallness gene from her dad, because Aunt Tamara is short like my mum. Also, Linda had a small but conspicuous bust, whereas I didn't. I hoped I'd never develop big breasts. I was sure they'd be really uncomfortable.

Linda's make-up case was enormous, with so many different shades of eye shadow and about fifteen kinds of lipstick. I looked longingly at the mascara, eyeliner, powders, and blush.

"Your eyes are hazel, Ditty," she said. "Did you know that? Green will make them look brighter." She looked from my face to the contents of her make-up bag and back again, and picked out browns and tans and a kind of heavy, plum-colored lipstick, which she threw back in. "You need something more subtle," she explained, choosing a lighter shade. "Here, this one is brilliant."

When she'd finished doing both my make-up and her own, we stood looking in the mirror, grinning like idiots and making faces at each other. Then Linda decided to experiment with different hairstyles. Her own hair was straight and chestnut brown. It came to just below her shoulders. Linda straightened my wavy hair with a hot ceramic rod, then used the same rod to put curls into hers.

"You're really good at this," I said. "You could do hair and make-up for a living."

She tilted her head to one side while she considered the prospect. "Yeah, I could, but I'd rather be a singer." As if to prove her point, she put on some music, held an imaginary mike, and sang along, her voice strong and powerful.

In between blasts of song, she showed me her iPod playlist. Linda had so many tracks, and knew the most amazing dance moves. She taught them to me, and complimented me on how quickly I picked up the steps and how well I moved.

"You're a natural, Ditty," she said. "You should have dance lessons. Jazz or hip-hop, or ... "

"Ballet?"

Linda looked at me, impressed. "What do *you* know about ballet?"

"Not much," I admitted, my secret still too new to share.

Five

• ◆ •

"You can do it, Ditty. Just a little further, now. Keep the control and watch the angle of your head, that's it."

And I'd done it. I'd just accomplished my first back-bend without using my hands, arching back till only my head and feet were on the floor, my arms straight out to the sides. The girls in my class gave me a round of applause and Miss Smith beamed. From my upside-down position, the world looked weird, but in a good way.

"Well done, Ditty," Miss Smith said as I was leaving the hall.

Of all the teachers at Beis Hannah, Miss Smith was my favorite. She had done competitive gymnastics when she was younger, and almost made the Olympics. She'd come to our school when I was eight, and since then I'd been her model pupil. I'd received a glowing report from her the previous year, which I still remembered, word for word:

Yehudit is an enthusiastic and talented gymnastics student, with a great deal of natural ability. To maximize her potential, it may be worthwhile sending Yehudit to extra lessons outside of school hours.

My mother smiled when she read that. My father gave a grunt and turned the page.

"Miss Smith thinks I should do extra gymnastics outside of school," I'd said to my dad. "What do you think?"

"I don't know why you have to learn gymnastics inside school, let alone outside," he replied.

"Miss Smith thinks I should."

"Miss Smith is a non-Jewish gymnastics teacher. What can Miss Smith know about being Jewish? You were put on this Earth for a purpose, Yehudit. You have a mission in life, to be the best Jew you can be, to do mitzvos, to bring the *moshiach* into the world, not to run around standing on your head and playing games."

Still, I got to do gymnastics each week at school, and on sunny days I could practice at home in our back garden. I'd practiced a lot. I'd learnt to do backbends, headstands, walkovers, and handsprings. None of the other girls in my class could do them. They weren't very interested, and didn't make an effort. I couldn't understand how Miss Smith put up with them.

"How can you stand teaching a class as bad as ours?" I asked her now.

She shook her head and laughed. "One Ditty Cohen makes it worth it," she said.

I was late back to our regular classroom and had missed the first few minutes of *Halacha*, Jewish Law, which was taught by Mrs. Teitlebaum, a large, round woman with an untidy sheitel. She frowned at me, but continued talking about *hilchos shabbos*, the laws of Sabbath.

" ... shouldn't walk on the beach on Shabbos because you might make footprints in the sand," she was saying, "and you shouldn't walk across a field because you might squash a blade of grass. The slightest oversight can detract from the kedusha, the holiness of Shabbos."

Mrs. Teitlebaum's voice was so monotonous that my mind drifted off. I found myself thinking about gymnastics instead, and soon my thoughts turned to ballet. There was just something about it. It was even better than gymnastics. It was like gymnastics with soul.

The walls of the classroom disappeared as the memory of Clara and the soldier filled my mind, and they were all I could see. But the picture was vague. The details had blurred. The blonde ballerina in her soft, flowing yellow dress had started to fade, and seemed almost like a figment of my imagination now.

But I knew she was real.

"Just pick one," said Sara.

"I can't decide." I flipped through the books piled on

the table in front of me, wishing I had the time to browse through them properly, but it was getting late. My mum didn't keep tabs on where I went—my parents weren't strict in a general sense, only in a religious one—but she liked me home before it got dark. If we didn't leave the library soon she'd start to worry, whether or not she knew were I'd been.

It wasn't that Elsternwick library was out of bounds. Not exactly. We were allowed to go there, but only under supervision, and only when we couldn't find what we needed at school. Our school had two libraries—a Jewish one and a secular one. The secular one was very small. All books were censored, and most didn't make it into the school library in the first place. Those that did were vetted, so that you'd come across lines, paragraphs, and sometimes whole pages that were covered in blank white paper.

Some of the girls had held the pages up to the light to try to see through to the words underneath, and a few claimed to have managed it. According to them, the bits we weren't allowed to read were those that mentioned God or religion, or the bits where boys touched girls. Also, the secular library had no books with pictures of children who weren't dressed modestly, so of course there were no books about ballet.

In the public library, there were so many books about dance I didn't know which to choose. I turned the pages hungrily, devouring the pictures.

"I *wish* I could take lessons."

Sara was standing beside me, trying to hurry me along. "Maybe you can."

"No. There's no way my dad would let me."

"How do you know?" she said. "You haven't asked."

I thought of my father, with his black suit and black hat, his knotty beard and long gray *payos* hanging loosely by his ears. For him, life was all about Torah, and he wasn't the sort of person you could argue with.

"Sara, you don't know my dad."

"At least you have a dad," she said. "At least he cares." Her voice turned thick, like she was trying not to cry, and I realized, too late, that I'd reminded her of her own father.

Sara's dad had abandoned her, right after he and Mrs. Kesten got divorced, though it wasn't something we ever really talked about. In our community, divorce was rare, and the word itself was whispered as if it might bring bad luck.

Sara was the only person in my class whose parents were divorced. She'd lived with both her parents in Sydney, but after the divorce she and her mum moved to Melbourne and her dad moved up to Queensland. Sara was nine at the time, and she hadn't seen her father since.

She'd showed me a photo of him once. It was taken when Sara was about five, and she was sitting on his knee. Her dad looked tall, with sandy hair just a shade darker than Sara's.

"This is the only photo I have of him," she'd said. "My mum doesn't know I've got it. She threw the others out."

"Why would she do that?" I asked her.

"She hates him. I mean, she *really* hates him."

That was one of the longest conversations we'd ever had about her dad. Sara didn't talk about him much. But I knew she thought about him. She'd told me how she used to wait for letters, phone calls, anything. He hadn't been in touch with her at all. Not once. Not even for her bat-mitzvah. I thought she'd given up hoping, because most of the time she just pretended he didn't exist.

But Sara was right. My own father was pretty wonderful compared to hers. I had no right to complain.

Where have you been, Ditty?" my mother asked.

"With Sara." If I mentioned the library to my mum, she'd want to know what I'd been doing there, and I didn't want to tell her. But I hated the way my secrets kept piling up.

"That poor girl," said my mother. "It must be so lonely for her, spending all that time by herself while her mother's out working. What did she ever do to deserve that good-for-nothing father?"

It was a rhetorical question and I didn't even try to answer. I shifted my schoolbag from one shoulder to the other, feeling the telltale weight of the book I had borrowed.

"It's good that you spend time with her," my mother said. "It's a mitzvah, Ditty. A real mitzvah."

Getting away with my deceit was one thing. Being praised for it was somehow worse, and for a second I thought of owning up—to everything. But there was a shriek from the next room, and a second later Hillel was crying. My mum rushed out to see what was wrong.

Hillel had tripped on a saucepan Gittel had been playing with and hit his head on the corner of the coffee table. By the time my mum came back into the kitchen and Hillel's cries had subsided to a muffled sob, Rochel, Shayne, and Ezra were already at the table, waiting for dinner, and the moment for confessing had come and gone.

———

Later, when dinner was over and Hillel and Gittel were both in bed, Rochel and I stacked the dishwasher and washed and dried the pots while my mum made *challahs* for Shabbos, singing as she kneaded the dough. Pretty soon I was humming along with her, and for a while I forgot about my secrets.

A few minutes later, Rochel joined in the singing too, and the three of us sounded like a choir. We harmonized well together, and we kept on singing until we heard the click of the front door opening and the sound of my father and another man talking.

My father poked his head around the kitchen door. "Reb Saunders is here," he said. "The *shiur* will be starting soon."

We couldn't sing anymore after that—it's against Halacha for men to hear women sing—but that didn't bother us. We were used to it. Reb Saunders had been coming to our house every Thursday night for years. He was the most respected rabbi in our community, and once a week he gave a shiur, a lesson, to my father and some other men from my father's *kollel,* while the rest of us tiptoed around the house, careful not to make a noise that would disturb them.

When we had finished cleaning up the kitchen, I moved softly past the dining room on the way to my bedroom. I put on my nightie, and when I was sure that Shayne and Gittel were asleep, I opened my schoolbag and took out the library book I'd borrowed. I slipped it between my nightie and my dressing gown and folded my arms across my body to secure it there. Then I crept down the hall and into the bathroom.

I locked the bathroom door, sat down on the lid of the toilet seat, and placed the book gently on my lap. The picture of shiny pink ballet shoes on the cover shimmered in the bathroom light and I caressed it tenderly, half expecting to feel the slip and slide of satin on my fingertips.

I opened the book with infinite care. *Ballet for Beginners*. The book was full of photos, mostly of children aged about eight to fourteen. The younger ones were demonstrating the simpler exercises and the older children were demonstrating the more advanced ones. There were also written, step-by-step instructions.

I pored over this treasure greedily. I read every word and studied the pictures. I pointed my foot with the whole leg rotated outwards, like the girl in the photo. I did something that was called a *plié*, and something else that was called a *tendu*. Then I did the splits. I'd done the splits before, in gymnastics, but the dance students in the book did it differently. They made it look more graceful. They pointed their feet more, and made their arms look soft and rounded.

The green linoleum floor felt cold against the bare skin of my legs and feet, but I soon got used to it. Besides, I was too engrossed in the book to care.

I practiced the exercises in the book until Rochel and

Pinny came banging on the door, arguing over who would use the bathroom next. Then came a loud shushing as my mother reminded them about Reb Saunder's shiur. I put my dressing gown back on, slipped the book under it, and opened the door. The two of them tumbled inside, arguing more quietly now.

As I drifted back toward my room, I felt like I was floating. The ballet exercises had left me with a feeling of ... not just satisfaction, but a kind of ecstasy. They had also given me an appetite, and the smell of baking challah was divine. I stood in the hall taking deep whiffs of it. No point going into the kitchen. I wouldn't be allowed to eat any until the following night.

I padded silently back to my room, hid the book under a stack of jumpers in my section of the wardrobe, and climbed into bed. I said the *shema* out of habit, not really concentrating on the words of the prayer. Then I lay awake, imagining that I was one of the dancers in the book. I could almost feel my perfectly positioned head and erect posture, the arch of my foot and the graceful sweep of my arm.

Six

•◆•

The following Sunday I was helping my mother fold my brothers' T-shirts when the doorbell rang. I got up to see who was there. Linda was standing on the doorstep, but I hardly recognized her. It wasn't her face that was so different. It was her clothes, and hair.

I'd seen Linda in clothes that weren't *tsnius* before. More than once I'd seen her in jeans. So had my mum, and although she didn't exactly approve of Linda's jeans in our house, she was used to it. She wasn't used to this, though. Linda was wearing very short denim shorts, frayed at the edges, and a tiny black top that left the whole of her shoulders and her midriff bare. To make matters worse, she had dyed her hair jet black, and was wearing black nail polish and a nose stud.

"Aren't you going to let me in?"

"Of course." I gave her a hug and moved aside to let her pass. I wanted to get her to my room before my mother saw her, but my mum was standing right behind me.

"Hello, Aunt Zipporah!" Linda called.

My mother glared at her. "It's a good thing Pinny isn't home," she said. "Don't you think you should be wearing some clothes?"

Linda shrugged. "I am wearing clothes."

"Does your mother know you're dressed like that?"

"Of course she does," said Linda.

My mother shook her head and went back into the living room, and Linda followed me to my room.

"Does your mother really let you dress like that?" I asked her.

"*Let* me? How's she supposed to stop me?"

Come to think of it, Linda had always done pretty much whatever she liked. I looked at her bare skin and shivered. It was late autumn now, and there was a chill in the air. "Aren't you cold?"

"Not particularly. And if I was, do you think that would stop me?" She gave me a sly, mischievous grin, and I was too stunned to reply.

We listened to a CD of Hassidic songs, and we sang along. Rochel and Shayne came and joined us, and we closed the bedroom door to make extra sure that none of the boys could see us dancing. After a while, I told Linda that maybe she should leave before my father came home.

"Don't worry, Ditty," she said. "I'm not scared of Uncle Yitzchok. Anyway, my parents said they'll pick me up."

But my father and Pinny came home before her parents arrived. Pinny flushed bright red when he noticed Linda. He looked quickly down at the floor, but didn't say a single word. My father, on the other hand, was not so reticent.

"Have you seen what that girl is wearing?" He was loud enough to be overheard by the next-door neighbors and maybe the people a block away, as well.

"Lower your voice, Yitzchok," said my mother. "She'll hear you."

"I don't care if she does. It's not tsnius, Zipporah. It's a disgrace." This was more or less what my mother had said herself, but her saying it was different because Aunt Tamara and Linda were her blood relatives, not his.

"Don't you think you're overreacting? It's not as if she's killed anyone, and she isn't on drugs."

"She might be a bad influence on Yehudit," said my father.

I knew that even if my mother agreed with him, she wouldn't give him the satisfaction of knowing it.

"Maybe Ditty will be a *good* influence on her," she replied.

———

When Linda's parents arrived, Aunt Tamara took my parents' side. Or at least, pretended to. "You should know better," she said to Linda.

Linda was always so unfazed, even when she got told off. "Sorry, Mum, I couldn't help it. I came straight from work. I didn't have a chance to change."

And that was it! Aunt Tamara accepted Linda's cheery,

half-hearted apology. But she turned to my mother, just the same. "I'm sorry, Zipporah," she said. "She should know better than to come here dressed like that."

"I don't know how you let her dress like that at all," said my mother.

"Well, life can't be all rules and regulations," my aunt replied. "If you dictate every little thing to your children, how on earth can you expect them to develop their own opinions? Besides, I doubt she'll dress this way forever. It's only a phase she's going through. There are worse things."

"Yes," agreed my mother, sighing. "I suppose there are."

The crisis seemed to be over, and the four adults sat down at the kitchen table with cups of tea and homemade scones. Rochel and Shayne had taken Gittel for a walk, and Ezra and Hillel were out in the garden now that their friends had gone home, so it was fairly quiet.

Linda and I went back to my room and Linda showed me how to take photos with her new mobile phone. Hardly any of the kids in our community had a mobile phone. Aside from the possibility of connecting to the Internet and accessing unsuitable websites, it was considered an unnecessary extravagance. Even my parents hadn't bought one, though they'd talked about it.

We played around with Linda's phone for a while, and then we headed toward the kitchen for a brownie break. My mum had made the most amazing brownies for Shabbos and I was pretty sure there were still a few left over. We were only a few steps short of the kitchen when we heard our parents arguing, and we stopped to listen.

"No, Yankel, I don't blame Linda," my father was saying, "but what can you expect from a modern-orthodox education? 'Modern orthodox'—pah! It's a contradiction in terms. You can't be modern *and* orthodox."

"I'm well aware of your views, Yitzchok," said Uncle Yankel, "but the fact is, Sinai College is—in policy and practice—both modern and orthodox."

"How can you call it orthodox when it's co-educational and over half the children there are from homes where they don't even keep Shabbos? I've never understood how you can send your daughter to a school like that."

"I send her there," said Uncle Yankel, beginning to seethe, "because I want to broaden her mind. I want to give her a good, solid Jewish education and a good, solid, secular education. Not that I should have to explain myself to you, Yitzchok. I wouldn't presume to tell you where to send your children to school. And if you must know, we chose a co-ed school for Linda because we don't want her growing up to think that boys are a different species—"

"But you're responsible for your daughter's education, her spiritual welfare. How can you take that responsibility so lightly?"

"I don't take it lightly," said Uncle Yankel, "but I want her to know that there's a whole world out there. I don't want to narrow her focus. I want her to choose."

My father laughed bitterly. "Don't you want her to make the right choice?"

Uncle Yankel gave an exaggerated groan. "It wouldn't be a choice," he said, "if she only had one option."

"You're wrong, Yankel. It's the parents' job to mold their children."

"You can mold them up to a point," Uncle Yankel replied, "but there comes a time when they want the freedom to make up their own minds. You can teach them, you can guide them, but in the end it's up to them. Not everyone's cut out to lead the sort of lifestyle you lead, Yitzchok. Not everyone wants to be so sheltered, so . . . restrained."

"*Restrained?*"

I tiptoed closer to the kitchen door where I could see my father, his face red with anger.

"*Restrained?* I am not raising my children to be restrained, Yankel. I am raising them to be free—free from the corruption of secularism, free to follow the path Hashem intended."

"But don't you want them to know there's a world out there? Don't you want them to have a choice, a *real* choice?"

"No, I don't," said my father. "I want them to live as Jews are supposed to live. And it isn't what I want, Yankel, it's what Hashem requires."

The atmosphere in our house remained tense even after the Fischers had gone. I ventured into the kitchen, hoping my mother wouldn't go on about Linda's appearance. She did, though.

"She's getting worse."

"Worse than what?"

"Don't pretend you don't understand me, Ditty. You

know very well what I mean. Black nail polish. That thing in her nose..."

"What's wrong with black nail polish?"

"Oh, Ditty! Don't argue so much."

"Tell me," I said, "where in the Torah does it say, 'Thou shalt not paint thy nails black'?"

"Don't be so rude," said my mother, and she told me exactly where it said "honor thy father and thy mother," instead.

I'd only wanted to stick up for Linda, but somehow my good intentions had backfired. I couldn't believe I was picking a fight with my mum.

My father overheard the tail end of the conversation and knew immediately that we were arguing about Linda.

"So," he said, "what has your cousin been telling you now?"

I shrugged and said nothing.

"Whatever it is, don't listen. Think for yourself."

My father was always telling me to think for myself. But after what he'd said to Uncle Yankel, I was starting to wonder whether what he really meant was, "Think like me."

Seven

• ◆ •

Tensions were still running high a few days later when Aunt Tamara came round with tickets for Linda's school musical, which was an annual event. The boys never went—they weren't allowed to hear *kol isha*, a "woman's voice"—and Gittel was still too young. But Rochel, Shayne, and I looked forward to it every year.

My parents had never really liked the whole idea, but as my mum wanted to remain on good terms with Aunt Tamara and Uncle Yankel, they allowed us to go. This year Sinai College was putting on *Oliver!* and Linda had a starring role. The school had hired out the National Theatre, which Aunt Tamara said was old and shabby now, though it had once been glamorous. Shabby or not, I couldn't wait to go.

On the night of the musical, Rochel, Shayne, and I brushed our hair and put on our best Shabbos dresses. Then at twenty to seven, Aunt Tamara and Uncle Yankel came to collect us. Linda wasn't with them; she had to be at the theater an hour earlier than the rest of us.

When we reached the theater, it was ten to seven and already dark, but the streetlights were on and even from a distance I could see that the theater was swarming with people. The large glass windows were lit up, and the first thing I noticed, even before we went inside, were the eye-catching posters of dancers mid-flight, reaching heavenward and soaring through the air.

The posters were ads for the National Theatre Ballet School, and as I studied them, a procession of older teenage girls walked past us and made their way around the outside of the building. Their backs were ramrod straight, their hair swept up into neat little buns and gelled into place, and they walked with a kind of unconscious elegance.

I asked Aunt Tamara for my ticket, and told her that I was going to the bathroom and would meet her inside. Then I followed the girls, and watched as they entered a door at the back of the building.

I stood gazing after them even after they'd disappeared and the door had closed. Soon it opened again, and a lot of other girls, my age and younger, came out. These girls too had their hair pulled into buns, and, like the older ones, were dressed in track pants or jeans. When their jackets fell open, I caught a glimpse of the leotards beneath them. Then I remembered that Linda's musical was about to start, and I ran inside.

Linda had the part of Nancy. She wore a blonde shoulder-length wig and a torn skimpy dress, and she stole the show. I was thrilled by her, amazed by her. I mean, I knew she'd be good, but I didn't realize she'd be *this* good. As I watched, I wondered what it would be like to be up there on the stage, what it would be like to perform. I imagined it was me up there instead of her, all eyes on me, my heart racing.

When it was over, Linda got a standing ovation. After the show, she was bombarded with praise. She was so ecstatic she couldn't stop grinning. Neither could I.

As we drove away from the theater, the songs from the musical mingled in my head with thoughts of the ballet students I'd seen earlier. I must have passed the National Theatre countless times before, but I had never paid it much attention. Now I knew it housed a ballet school, and in the weeks that followed, the image of the girls with their straight backs and long necks stayed with me day and night.

———

I paid another visit to the library. I returned *Ballet for Beginners* and took out *Improving Your Ballet* instead. At night, I practiced in the bathroom—*tendus* and *pliés*, *dégagés* and *relevés*.

The bathroom was old and badly in need of renovation. There was a spidery crack along the mirror, a gray concrete strip of wall where two tiles were missing, a chip in the old pink bathtub, and a shower with a smoky glass door that never quite shut. But it was large, and it was private—more private than any other room in the house.

I tried to increase my flexibility. I was pretty flexible already, but I could see that I still had further to go. Soon, I could do the splits without twisting my hips the tiniest bit.

One night I was so engrossed in mastering the correct positions that I didn't notice how much time had passed.

"Ditty, stop hogging the bathroom."

Shayne was practically knocking down the bathroom door, and I could hear Rochel telling my mother that I must have caught some terrible disease because I was always on the toilet.

"Hurry *up*, Ditty," said Shayne. "I can't hold it in."

For hours each night (and during my more tedious classes during the day), I imagined I was a ballerina. The only person who knew about my growing love of ballet was Sara. When we went to the library together, I headed straight for books on dance, while she made a beeline for the romance section. She was almost as passionate about love stories as I was about ballet.

I continued to teach myself as much as I could through books and the occasional snippet of ballet on TV, but what I really, badly wanted was a teacher. I started to dream of real lessons, but it didn't occur to me that the dream could ever become a reality.

———

Then one Monday, a couple of weeks after *Oliver!*, there was a Staff Conference Day at Beis Hannah, which meant that I had the day off school. Sara had gone to help her mother in the shop, so I was on my own. I walked up our street to Glenhuntly Road, thinking that I might stop at the kosher ice-cream shop.

I don't know why I changed my mind, but instead of turning left toward the shop, I crossed the road and stood at the tram stop outside Elsternwick station. Before long, a number 67 tram arrived and without really thinking, I climbed on board. The tram turned right into Brighton Road and I rode it a few stops to the corner of Carlisle Street and started to walk. I hadn't consciously decided where I was going, but after about ten minutes, I found myself standing outside the National Theatre, looking up at the familiar posters of dancers leaping through the air.

I peered in through the double glass doors. The theater seemed deserted. I made my way around the back to the school and tried the door. It was open so I gave it a push, and the next thing I knew, I was standing inside.

My heart was pounding in my chest and I wondered what I was doing there. Would someone think I was trespassing and tell me to leave? There was a faint smell of dampness in the building, and the sound of a piano tinkled somewhere down the hall. The office door was on my right and I hesitated, wondering whether I should knock, and what I might say if I did.

Before I had a chance to decide, a white-haired, officious-looking woman hurried out, practically bumping into me, and I stammered an apology.

She just smiled and asked me politely whether I'd like some information about the ballet school. I nodded. She went back into the office and came out a moment later with some forms.

"Why don't you have a look at the timetable?" She thrust the pages at me and hurried down the hall.

According to the information sheet, there were classes in jazz, tap, and contemporary dance as well as ballet. It looked as though there were five—no, six—studios in all.

"What are you interested in learning?"

I jumped, startled. I'd been so absorbed in the timetable I hadn't noticed her returning.

"Ballet," I found myself saying.

"What grade are you in?"

"I'm in Year Six at school."

"What grade in ballet?"

"Oh, I ... don't know."

"Well, where did you learn before?"

"I didn't ... I mean, I've never learnt before."

She cocked her head to one side and looked me up and down. "How old are you?" she asked me.

"Twelve."

"Hmm ... you'll probably have to start in Grade Three or Four, but I'll go and get Miss Mitchell, and you can talk to her about it. It'll be up to her."

Miss Mitchell was a tiny, thin woman, probably in her early fifties. She was wearing a black leotard with track pants on top, and soft, pink ballet shoes with a heel. Her hair was pushed back off her face with a sports band and she looked as though she might have been in the middle of teaching a class. But she gave me an encouraging smile as she introduced herself.

"Twelve's quite late to start," she said, "but you can give it a go. We can start you off in Grade Three, and if you pick it up quickly, we'll move you up to Grade Four. I'd like to put you with girls your own age, but most of them have already been learning for five or six years and I don't think you'd cope."

I nodded, thinking how clumsy I'd look next to girls who'd been dancing all their lives, and wondering once again just why I'd come.

"Would you mind starting off with eight and nine-year-olds?"

I shook my head, not wanting to admit that I wouldn't be allowed to have lessons.

"You can try it for a week," she said. "After that, if you decide to continue, you'll have to get the right shoes and uniform, but don't buy anything yet. First, see if you like it. Wear a leotard if you have one. Otherwise, shorts and a T-shirt will do. Oh, and by the way, the first week is free. I'll look forward to seeing you in class, then."

And she was gone.

A minute later I was outside the building again, staring at the white paint of the closed metal door. I couldn't quite work out what had happened inside.

———

When I got home, no one even asked me where I'd been. Rochel and Shayne were out, and Pinny and Ezra were doing homework in their room. Hillel was still at kinder, and my mum was in the laundry, trying to get stains out of Hillel's clothes. Gittel was in there with her, playing with a bucket full of plastic clothes pegs.

I offered to help my mother with the housework and was soon standing at the kitchen sink, peeling potatoes. I was quieter than usual, but my mum was too busy with Gittel to notice. A part of me wanted to tell her about my day, but what could I say? That I'd been out among the goyim on my own? What if someone had seen me going into the ballet school, or coming out again? I shuddered when I thought of the risk I had taken.

Could I go back the following day? That teacher, Miss Mitchell, had said it was free. But it would mean more lies, more deception. It wasn't practical. It wasn't honest. It wasn't realistic. I couldn't return. Wouldn't return.

But this was my chance—maybe my only chance—to find out what a real ballet lesson was like. How could I pass up the opportunity? I knew I would never forgive myself if I did.

Eight

• ◆ •

I wore the only pair of shorts I owned—a pair of bike shorts I'd bought to wear under my uniform when we had gymnastics at school. I had my school tights on beneath the shorts, and a white, long-sleeved T-shirt on top. My hair was drawn back into a ponytail because I didn't quite know how to make a bun.

I didn't look much like a dance student, and my face burned as I sensed the other students watching me. They were neat and tidy in navy leotards and pale pink tights, and I felt awkward and messy beside them. And unlike me, they didn't seem the least bit self-conscious about wearing such immodest clothes.

The first few minutes of the lesson were every bit as embarrassing as I'd imagined they would be. But when the music started and the barre exercises began, I forgot what I was wearing and the fact that I was two or three years older than everyone else.

The barre work lasted for about half an hour. It included some of the steps I'd seen in books—*tendus* and *pliés, rond de jambe à terre, and rond de jambe en l'air*—and finished with stretches. Miss Mitchell smiled when she saw how easily I slid my leg along the barre, and a moment later she came over and pushed down gently on my hip. "Don't lift your hip. That's better." She smiled again when she saw how effortlessly I did the splits. The weeks of nighttime practice in the bathroom had paid off.

"You're lucky, Ditty," she said, as we moved to the center. "You have a great natural range and flexibility. Some people work for years to achieve that and still don't manage it."

All in all, the class wasn't as hard as I'd thought it would be. Everything seemed to come easily, naturally. Except the part when you had to lift your leg and hold it still. I wondered if I'd ever be strong enough to do it properly. I watched the other girls with envy, wishing I too had started learning when I was six years old.

"Did you enjoy it?" Miss Mitchell asked me after the lesson.

I nodded, and her face lit up. "You're built for it," she said. "You've got the ideal body type. I hope you decide to stay."

———

I didn't even have to lie that day. On weekdays I often went to Sara's after school, so when I came home late, my mum just assumed that's where I'd been.

I was desperate to tell her that I'd been to a ballet lesson, that I'd loved it, that I wanted to go as often I could. It was hard keeping quiet about it when it was all I could think of.

I had two whole days to wait before the next lesson, and once or twice I came close to confessing. But in the end, I didn't dare. I didn't want to risk being told I couldn't go. And when I arrived at the National that Thursday afternoon, I knew I'd made the right decision. The movements seemed to ripple through me as my body flowed to the music, and my spirits lifted. I felt vulnerable and vibrant and intensely alive, bursting with feelings I hadn't known existed, couldn't name.

Suddenly, it was over. The trial week was over.

I longed to continue. I knew that I'd be good at ballet if I got the chance, and I wanted that chance. I wanted it more than I'd ever wanted anything. It was time to confront my parents, time to ask them if I could take classes.

———

I picked at my food, barely noticing what was on the plate.

"What is it, Ditty?" said my mother.

This was it. I'd put off asking as long as I could, but the next lesson was the following day.

I took a deep breath and plunged in. "What would you say if I told you I wanted to learn ballet?"

The question lingered in the air. There were only six of us at the table. Hillel and Gittel had already eaten and gone to bed, and Rochel wasn't home yet. My father, unusually, was eating with us, before going to the kollel with Pinny and Ezra. He looked surprised at the question, but remained silent because he'd already made the bracha over the washing of hands. He dried his hands, said the blessing for bread, took a bite, and chewed thoroughly. It was only after he'd swallowed that he allowed himself to speak.

"Ballet lessons," he mused aloud. "And what sort of preparation would that be for the Olam Haba?"

I could have kicked myself. I should have asked my mother before he came home. I should have got her on my side.

"Yitzchok," I suddenly heard her say, "not everything is preparation for the World to Come. Maybe Ditty needs a hobby." I said a silent prayer of thanks to Hashem for steering my mum in the right direction. "Yes," she continued, "it would be good for her to do some exercise. But ... ballet?"

My heart was alternately leaping and sinking as I tried to anticipate her train of thought.

"No," she said at last, "it's not modest. Besides, there could be boys in the class."

"No, there ... I don't think there would be. Boys don't like ballet, do they?"

"Hmm ... maybe not, but we can't take the risk. You could try swimming, though. There are separate hours for men and women at the St. Kilda swim school."

"Yes," my father agreed. "Swimming would be better. You can save a life with swimming."

This was not the way the conversation was supposed to go. "But I'm not interested in swimming. I want to learn something that interests me. Something I might be good at. Something I might really love."

I glanced at the others, hoping they might back me up. But no one said a word.

"No," said my father, "your mother is right. It isn't tsnius. A *Yiddishe* girl does not go on the stage."

"Who said anything about the stage? I only said I want to take lessons."

My father shook his head. "I think not, Yehudit."

"But, why not? I mean, who's to see? It's not like I'd be doing it out in the street. And think of the benefits. Ballet is really good for posture, and it builds strong bones—"

"I said no, Yehudit."

"Some parents *want* their children to learn…" The words were out of my mouth even before I knew I'd spoken. There was a ringing silence in the kitchen, and everyone was staring at me. I knew I'd made my father livid. From across the table, I could feel the heat of his anger.

"*Some* parents? Who are these parents, Yehudit? They are not Jewish parents and they do not have Jewish children. Goyim, as you very well know, are not required to live as we do."

"Even other Jews don't live like we do."

Once again the words were out, and it was too late to take them back.

"Which other Jews?" my father hissed. "Jews who want to forget they are Jewish?"

"You sound as if you hate them."

"*Hate* them? God forbid I should hate another Jew. I fear for them, yes, because they forget their Jewish heritage and are tempted by the secular world. They are like children—they don't know any better."

I fiddled with the food on my plate but I couldn't let the subject go. "But there are really religious Jews who have secular hobbies..."

Now my father had had enough. He stood up and banged his fist down on the table. The dishes shook and the saltcellar slid a few centimeters before falling over.

"I said *no*, Yehudit. The subject is closed."

———————

Tears of disappointment pricked my eyes as I lay in bed. It was *so* unfair. Until now, I'd been a good daughter—at least, I'd tried to be. I helped with the housework when I could. I read to Hillel and Gittel, and took them to the park. I often helped with the baking for Shabbos. What was wrong with wanting to do something for myself for a change?

Why shouldn't I dance? Maybe it wasn't a mitzvah, but it wasn't a crime, either. I'd had two ballet lessons already and it hadn't hurt anyone. It was *so unfair, so unfair, so unfair...*

I finally fell into a restless, troubled sleep, and woke up exhausted. I poured out my heart to Sara on the way to school, and she tried to be sympathetic. But how could an unfair father possibly compete with an absent one?

"Ditty," she said, "you're lucky you have a father who cares."

And deep down, I wasn't entirely convinced my father was wrong. It was hard to believe he could be wrong about anything, hard to believe he wouldn't be fair.

Maybe I should learn to be happy with what I had—a large family, friends, Torah, Shabbos, and Hashem—because after all, I was not put on this Earth for my own benefit. I was here to serve Hashem. I was part of *Am Yisrael*, the nation of Israel, the Chosen People. We were a people with a special mission in life who, through our dedication to keeping the commandments, would bring the moshiach, the Messiah, into this world.

But a voice in my head said, *Do you even want the moshiach to come?* For the first time in my life, I wondered whether belonging to the Chosen People wasn't more of a burden than a privilege.

———

That Sunday there was another dance program on TV, this time an act from *Swan Lake*. I came home from Sara's wanting to dance, my head full of ballet.

I tried to talk my mother around. "It's not fair," I said. "Other girls take lessons."

"Oh, Ditty," she sighed. "We've already discussed it."

"But—"

"Not another word, Ditty," she said. "I don't want you to even bring the subject up again."

That night I dreamed that I was watching Swan Lake performed on a real lake, in the open air. It was a balmy night and dancers in long white tutus skimmed the surface of the water, gliding alongside real swans that bobbed in the moonlight. The poignant, moving music filled my senses, and suddenly I was no longer part of the audience. I was out on the lake. I had become the dancer. I had become the swan.

I woke up feeling torn. I knew my parents only wanted what was best for me. But what if they were wrong? Could they be wrong? Was it possible that I knew better?

I prayed to Hashem to take away my doubts and my resentment, and make me grateful for what I had. I asked Him to make my parents proud of me, to make me worthy of their pride.

Hashem didn't answer my prayers. I doubt that he was even listening.

Nine

My cousin Shoshi's wedding came and went, but I had spent the evening brooding and couldn't enjoy it. When I got home, I went straight to my room. Gittel was already sleeping in her crib—she'd fallen asleep in the car—and Shayne followed suit as soon as her head hit the pillow. I changed into my nightie and went into the kitchen, hovering uncertainly at the sink, forgetting what it was I'd come in for.

"What's up, Ditty?"

I hadn't heard Rochel as she came up behind me, and I jumped when she spoke. Rochel started talking about how beautiful Shoshi had looked at the wedding, and what a wonderful evening it had been. But I just couldn't match her excitement. All I could think of was ballet and my longing to dance.

"What would you do if you wanted to do something you

knew Mum and Dad wouldn't approve of?" I asked Rochel suddenly.

"Like what?" She'd never been very good at discussing ideas in the abstract. She always wanted examples.

"I don't know. Something. Anything."

Rochel frowned. "I'd talk to them, I think. Try to convince them. Try to get them to change their minds."

"But what if you couldn't? What if they didn't change their minds?"

"I don't know. I suppose I'd … " She stopped talking and looked severely at me. "What is it you want to do, Ditty?"

"Nothing. I just … nothing."

"Because whatever it is, you shouldn't be doing it. Not without their permission."

"But what if they're wrong? Don't you ever think they could be wrong about anything?"

"That's not the point, is it? Wrong or right, they're our parents and it's a mitzvah to respect them. But chances are they're not wrong. Chances are they're right."

Rochel went off to bed, but I remained sitting at the kitchen table, suddenly aware of how alone I was. It occurred to me then that even though there were eight other people living in our house, I couldn't talk to a single one of them. At least, not about this. Not about anything that really mattered.

———

I waited till everyone, including my parents, had gone to sleep. Then I took the telephone into the bathroom and locked the door. It was almost midnight, but I had a feeling that Linda would still be awake. I called her on her mobile, and she answered on the second ring, her voice bright and bubbly despite the time.

Careful to keep my voice down, I told her everything. I told her about Mrs. Kesten's TV and about the two trial ballet lessons at the National. I told her I was desperate to continue.

"Haven't you ever done anything your parents don't approve of?" Linda said. She promised to come over that Sunday to talk about it after she finished work at one o'clock. "Listen, Ditty, don't feel so guilty about wanting to express yourself. It's your life. But I've gotta go, now. My boyfriend's on the other line."

Boyfriend? Linda had a boyfriend? My parents would die if Rochel or I had a boyfriend. I wondered if Aunt Tamara and Uncle Yankel knew.

———

Linda arrived on Sunday, just as she'd promised. She was wearing an eyebrow ring as well as a nose stud, and she'd added some dark-blue streaks to her hair. She had on a pair of jeans and a short velour jacket, and she was carrying a bag—a pink canvas drawstring bag that reminded me of a library bag I'd had when I first started school.

We hugged each other and went straight to my room. Linda pushed the door shut and leaned against it.

"So," I said, "tell me about this boyfriend you mentioned on the phone."

Linda kicked off her shoes and jumped onto my bed, just managing to avoid hitting her head on the bunk above. She hugged her knees to her chest, and looked at me thoughtfully. "His name's Ben, he's eighteen, goes to Melbourne High, and he's got his own band."

"How long have you been going out with him?"

"A few weeks."

"Do your parents know?"

"Of course not, Ditty. There are some things in life parents aren't *supposed* to know. Anyway," she said, "I'll probably dump him."

"Why?"

"Last night I met this guy called Terrence ... but I didn't come here to talk about me," she said. "What's happening with you?"

I shrugged.

"Have you decided yet about those ballet lessons ... whether you really want to take them?"

"You know I *want* to ... "

"Well?"

"It's not that simple. My parents—"

"Said you can't. I know. But are you really planning to spend your whole life doing what they tell you?"

"It's a mitzvah to honor your parents," I said.

"Jeez, Ditty! What's it got to do with honoring your parents? And anyway, what if what's wrong for them is right for you?"

This was starting to feel more like an interrogation than a conversation.

"It's easy for you, Linda. Your parents let you do whatever you want."

"No, they don't. But I try to figure things out for myself. For instance, one Shabbos last year, I waited till my parents left the house. Then guess what I did?"

"What?"

"I turned on all the lights. Every single one of them." She burst out laughing. "It was kind of juvenile, I know. It's the sort of thing a six-year-old would do."

I looked at her in horror, too stunned to speak. "But... why?" I said at last. "Why would you do that?"

"Because I'd never done it before. Because I wanted to see what would happen if I did."

"What... what did happen?" I asked.

"Nothing, of course."

"But... weren't you scared?"

"Scared? No. Why would I be?"

She didn't look scared now, either, but I was terrified on her behalf. Shabbos was a holy day, when it was forbidden to work, to draw, to write, or to drive. Using electricity was also forbidden, so we couldn't even do "little" things like switch on a kettle or turn on a light.

Shabbos was meant for meditation, rest, and prayer. I couldn't imagine desecrating Shabbos myself. Just thinking about it made all sorts of Divine punishments seem not only likely, but certain.

Linda laughed again when she saw the expression on my face. "You take it all so seriously. Don't you realize it's all a kind of conspiracy, a kind of trick?"

"What is?" I whispered.

"Religion. Shabbos. Everything. Think about it, Ditty. We're brought up with all these ridiculous rules. We're brainwashed into thinking that if we break a rule, if we eat a chocolate bar that isn't kosher, or turn on a light on Shabbos, our souls will be damaged forever, but it's not true. I broke the rules and nothing happened. I'm just the same as I was before."

How do you know? I wanted to ask, but I was too in awe of her to speak.

Awe was quickly followed by a less flattering emotion. The truth was, sometimes I felt a little sorry for Linda, and a bit superior. I caught myself and felt ashamed. I was in no position to judge! Still, imagine not understanding the importance of Shabbos, the *holiness* of Shabbos!

"I'm not telling you to do what I did," Linda was saying. "I'm not saying you should start breaking Shabbos. All I'm saying is, you have to decide what's right for you. You know better than anyone who you are and what you need."

"But my parents—"

"Are really strict. I know. Maybe they're too strict, Ditty. And maybe their brand of religion is too rigid for you."

I had expected empathy from Linda, but I hadn't expected her to discount my parents' opinions so completely. To be honest, I wasn't sure I liked it. Our parents had always had different views about religion. They had always argued. But Linda and I never took sides; we'd never allowed ourselves to become involved.

Though, come to think of it, I guess I'd always been at

least a little confused—a part of me envious of Linda and her parents' easy, laid-back attitude to life, another part certain they were wrong. It wasn't an argument I wanted to get into. If Linda was wrong, it wasn't her fault. It was the way she'd been raised.

"What's in the bag?"

"Oh, I almost forgot." Linda tossed me the bag. Whatever was in it felt soft and squashy. "Well?"

"Well what?" I asked.

"Take it. Open it."

I opened the bag. Inside was the uniform of the National Theatre Ballet School—two leotards, three pairs of tights, and a pair of soft, pink leather ballet shoes.

A real pair of ballet shoes!

"Where did these come from?" My voice was half-whisper, half-squeak.

"Carly Weiss."

"Who's Carly Weiss?"

"A friend of mine. She used to take ballet at the National, but she doesn't any more. I knew she'd still have the uniform 'cause she hates throwing anything out. They're yours if you want them."

"They look brand new," I said.

"They are. Carly bought them a week before she decided to give up ballet. I don't know if they'll fit you. Try them on."

They were a perfect fit, and it seemed like a sign. It seemed *bashert*, Heaven-sent.

But maybe that was just the reasoning of the yetzer hara, my own evil inclination. Either way, for the first time in days, I felt alive again. Maybe I *could* take ballet after all. I was tempted, so tempted.

I took off the shoes and Linda put them back in the bag. "You don't have to keep them." She scooped the bag up onto her lap. "I can always give them back to Carly."

"No, I'll keep them." I grabbed the bag and stuffed it into the back of my wardrobe.

Linda laughed. "Jeez, Ditty! Don't look so guilty. It's not as if you want to rob a bank or murder anyone. It's only ballet."

————

When I pointed my feet wearing the pink leather ballet shoes, they looked almost the same as the feet pictured in *Ballet for Beginners* and the other library books I'd borrowed. I wore them at night, when I practiced ballet in the bathroom. Sometimes I wore the leotard and the tights as well, and I stayed in the bathroom for ages, waiting for Shayne to fall asleep before returning them to their hiding place at the back of the wardrobe.

One night I practiced putting my hair up into a bun, and after a few attempts I mastered it. With my hair up, and wearing the uniform and the shoes, I looked a lot like a dancer. At least, I thought so. It was just a shame that no one else could see. What a waste of a uniform! What a waste of a perfect pair of ballet shoes!

"Ditty?"

"Yes?"

"Are you still up?" My mum must have seen the light coming from under the bathroom door. "Are you okay?"

"Yes. I just got up to use the loo."

"You sure? You've been in there a very long time."

I pulled the hairpins out of my bun and let my hair loose again. Then I buttoned my dressing gown down to the ground so that the pink tights I had on were invisible, as were the ballet shoes, which were hidden by large, furry slippers.

"I'm fine," I said, emerging from the bathroom. "I was just going back to bed. Good night, Mum."

"Good night, Ditty," said my mother.

Linda was right about one thing, I thought as I climbed into bed. Ballet was harmless. I wouldn't be hurting anyone by going. Not if no one found out.

I had already managed to get away with going to two lessons that nobody knew about. And if I could do it twice, I could do it again.

Ten

•◆•

I stood in the office, counting out my entire savings in notes and coins. I had a grand total of twenty-seven dollars. It wouldn't be enough. I was sure it wouldn't. Still, it was a start. Maybe I could pay by the lesson, and somehow figure out a way to get the rest. Maybe if I was careful with my pocket-money…

"Never mind, dear," said Miss Johnson. "Our usual policy is one term's payment in advance, but we do make exceptions. Ask your mum to come in for a chat. I'm sure we'll be able to sort out some kind of payment plan. And we can organize the paperwork while we're at it."

"I … uh … don't think she'll be able to come in herself. She's always busy."

"Oh, well, in that case, I suppose I can send the forms home with you. Tell her to give me a call about payment options if she wants to. Otherwise, she can fill out the credit card details or send in a check."

I was getting in deeper all the time, and I hadn't even started yet. When I looked at the three-digit figure on the form, I realized I couldn't have asked my parents for the money even if they'd wanted me to take lessons. I mean, it wasn't that we were poor. My father worked in a bank in the city, but it was only a regular job. It wasn't like he was the manager or anything. And we weren't exactly a small family. There was food to buy and bills to pay. And what little was left at the end of the month went to *tzedakkah*, to charity, to people less fortunate than ourselves.

I came out of the office feeling deflated. It seemed I wouldn't be able to pull this thing off after all.

Miss Mitchell rushed past me on her way to the studio. "Oh, good. You're here. I was beginning to think you weren't coming back." She beamed at me and hurried on, then stopped when she reached the studio door and realized I wasn't beside her. "Hurry up, Ditty. Class is starting."

"I don't know if I'm allowed in."

"Of course you are."

"But I haven't sorted out the payment yet."

"Sort it out next time, then. That's no reason to miss class today."

Soon, I was so immersed in the class that I forgot about the fact that I hadn't paid.

"Place your weight further forward, Ditty," Miss Mitchell said as I stood at the barre. "That's it. Excellent.

"Don't drop your wrist. Keep it in line with the rest of your arm. Lovely!"

I listened to every word she said, and paid attention to the corrections given to the other girls, too.

When the class was over, I changed back into my Beis Hannah uniform and shoved my leotards, tights, and ballet shoes into the bottom of my schoolbag, together with my brush, hairnet, and hairpins. No one ever looked in my schoolbag, so it seemed like a good place to keep them.

I filled in all the forms myself—there were three of them, including the enrollment form, a statement of payment, and an insurance form. I gave a false address and phone number, praying that no one would bother to check. Then I forged my mother's signature on all three forms and asked her for my next installment of pocket money. Added to the money I'd saved, I now had forty dollars.

As I handed the forms and the money to Miss Johnson, I told her my mum would send more cash as soon as she could.

I still hadn't figured out how I'd pay for the rest of the term. What if I couldn't deliver? Then I'd be a thief as well as a liar. Things were going from bad to worse.

But I loved the lessons and Miss Mitchell's calm, softly spoken instructions. Her voice began to take on a life of its own inside my head. It was the first voice I heard in the morning, and the last one I heard in my mind at night.

"Keep the hips level, Ditty. Don't twist. Pull up from the

center. *Stretch the legs but don't lock your knees. Point your feet, Ditty, point them, really stretch them, that's right, more, more, more..."*

I pictured myself doing everything perfectly, my body light and supple. I improved from one lesson to the next, and when I glanced in the mirror to see if I was working correctly, I was secretly pleased with my own reflection.

I was used to seeing a skinny, awkward girl in baggy clothes. But the leotard and tights actually suited me, and for the first time in my life, I felt beautiful.

"What a lovely line you have," Miss Mitchell said. "I'm so proud of you, Ditty. You've made such remarkable progress."

————————

"How's it going, then?" It was the first time I'd seen Linda since I'd started ballet, and I was bursting to tell her all about it.

"The classes are amazing, but..."

"What?"

"I won't be able to keep on going. I can't pay for the lessons, and I can't exactly ask my parents for the money."

"Maybe you could get a job," she said. "And in the meantime, I can lend you some money. I've been working for a while now. I've got quite a lot saved up."

"Really? No, I can't take it."

"Why not?"

"I don't know when I could pay you back."

"Whenever you like," said Linda. "And don't worry if you can't."

"But—"

"No buts," she said. "It's no big deal."

I threw my arms around her and thanked her about two hundred times.

Linda laughed and hugged me back. "Enough bowing and scraping. Any minute you'll be kissing my feet. You're my favorite cousin, Ditty. I'm happy to lend you the money."

Suddenly there was a burning sensation behind my eyes. I wanted to thank her yet again, but I was too choked up to speak.

———

Miss Mitchell continued to encourage me, and I was determined to keep on earning her praise. I spent hours doing dance steps in my head, and on the days I had ballet, everyday life began to recede even before the class had begun. With each step closer to the National, I became lighter, freer. Each lesson was a gradual soaring, and by the time it was over, I felt weightless. I could have sworn I left the studio noticeably taller than when I'd arrived.

Ballet was beauty, and I took pride in executing even the simplest of steps. It was also perfection, but I knew that perfection could never truly be achieved, and there would always be something to strive for.

Dance opened my eyes to other kinds of beauty I'd never paid much attention to before—the different shades of green on the large oak outside our school, the way the forget-me-nots in Harlston Park were more fragrant in the evenings. Happiness broadened my perspective of the world, so that the familiar seemed new.

But it was a short-lived happiness, tinged with guilt.

Eleven

•—◆—•

"You're doing so well in Grade Three," Miss Mitchell said after a month of lessons. "Why don't you come to the Grade Four class as well?"

For a second, excitement bubbled up inside me as I pictured myself whizzing through one grade, and then the next...

But joining Grade Four would mean coming to class on Mondays and Wednesdays as well as Tuesdays and Thursdays. Double the classes! Double the deception!

How could I even consider it? It was hard enough letting my mum think I was at Sara's every Tuesday and Thursday after school. Would she really believe I went there four days a week? And how much would it cost?

"Ditty?" Miss Mitchell was waiting for an answer.

"I really don't think I can pay any more…"

"Oh, it won't cost you any extra. Not when the classes are at my invitation. You've got talent, Ditty. I'd like to see you progress."

Miss Mitchell took my hesitation for agreement. "So I'll see you on Monday in Studio Four."

And she was gone.

I was alone in the studio, my breathing fast and shallow.

What on earth was I doing? What sort of person was I turning into? Was there a shred of honesty left inside me? What was I thinking?

Suddenly I found it hard to catch my breath. I focused on channeling the stream of air—in through my nostrils, out through my mouth. I could do this, I could. I was already in the habit of going to Sara's on the afternoons I wasn't at ballet, and my mum was used to the fact that I wasn't around.

————

I held the tights away from me, and sniffed. The feet had turned gray, and nothing could disguise the nasty smell. My leotards, too, were in desperate need of soap and water. But there was no way I could wash them without attracting my mother's attention. My mum practically lived in the laundry. And when she wasn't in the laundry, she was in the kitchen, with a full view of the laundry door. Even if I washed them in the bathroom sink, I'd still need to hang them out to dry.

Something had to be done, but what? There was a

limit to how long I could keep on smelling of stale BO and unwashed socks. If I didn't solve the problem soon, other people would begin to notice. Maybe some of the girls already had.

"You could wash them at my place, I suppose," said Sara.

"No, I couldn't. Your mum would see them."

Just then I heard my mum and baby sister outside the door. I stuffed the tights under my mattress just in time.

"Hello, Sara," said my mother as she entered the bedroom, holding Gittel. She took a clean nappy from the pile by the crib. "It's been so long since we've seen you. Ditty always goes to your place after school. Why don't you come here instead? We'd love to have you, and you can stay until your mum gets back from work."

I held my breath and waited to see what Sara would say.

She hesitated. "My mum doesn't like me going out after school. She says she wants to know I'm safe at home. But thanks for the offer."

Watching Sara lie on my behalf was somehow worse than lying myself, and I turned away, relieved when my mum had finished changing Gittel and left the room.

"I can't stand the fact that I made you lie," I said to Sara as I walked her home.

"You didn't make me lie. I chose to."

"But . . . "

"Look, I covered for you, that's all. You shouldn't have to tell your mum the truth because of me. You want to dance, don't you?"

"Of course."

Sara was right. I wanted to dance, but I wanted to talk about it, too. That was the hardest part—the silence, the secrecy. When you love something, you want to tell the entire world. I really wished I could tell my mother.

Because I couldn't, I became the model daughter at home. It was me who put Gittel to bed in the evenings, me who read Hillel his bedtime stories, me who watched and listened to them as they said the shema. Each night, after dinner, I helped my mum clear away the dishes, and on Thursdays, while Reb Saunders gave his shiur in the living room, I spent two hours baking cakes for Shabbos.

By the time I'd finished, I was so tired that I fell asleep almost as soon as my head hit the pillow.

I never had a moment to rest. School days were busy. And after school, at ballet, I worked harder than ever. But that didn't seem like work, no matter how tired it made me.

———

One Thursday, Miss Mitchell called me over after class.

"I've been meaning to ask you, Ditty. Can you come to production class on Saturdays?"

It was weird to think that for some people, Shabbos was just an ordinary day. For me, of course, it was a holy day, and going to class on Shabbos was out of the question.

"I can't," I said. "I'm Jewish, and Saturday is our Sabbath, our day of rest."

Miss Mitchell looked a little confused. "We have other Jewish students here," she said. "They come on Saturdays."

"Well, maybe they're not religious," I explained.

"I see," she said, though I wasn't sure that she did. "Well, it's up to you, of course, but unfortunately production class is on Saturday, and if you don't come to production class, I won't be able to put you in the end-of-year concert. There's just no other time to rehearse."

"That's okay," I lied.

Though I hid my disappointment, I couldn't help worrying that Miss Mitchell might think I wasn't serious and start to ignore me. I worked even harder to prove that I was, and far from overlooking me, she offered to coach me after class for twenty minutes twice a week, free of charge.

————

It was getting worse. Each time I loosened the drawstring, a whiff of body odor assaulted my nostrils, even before I'd opened the bag. I bought a can of deodorant, which helped a bit but not enough.

It was Sara who solved the problem in the end. She'd seen a laundromat in Glenhuntly Road with an ad in the window promising to wash and dry within the hour.

I went there one Friday after school and asked the man who owned the place for the best deal he could give me if I came in every week. I guess he saw the desperation on my face because he took pity on me and agreed to do it for a dollar.

I asked him to wait, and I ran to the supermarket and bought a two-dollar wash bag, the kind my mum used to protect delicate things, like bras, in the washing machine. I put my foul-smelling leotards and tights inside it, and the man in the laundromat took the bag and chucked it in with someone else's wash.

When I came back an hour later, the leotards and tights were folded neatly on top of the bag, smelling of lavender. I pressed my nose against a freshly laundered leotard, inhaling deeply.

Every Friday after that, I raced to the laundromat after school. I'd leave my laundry there and hurry home, help my mum get ready for Shabbos, and then dash back to pick my laundry up again, generally claiming I'd left some item or other at school.

"It's not like you to be so forgetful," said my mum, the first time it happened.

"What, again?" she said, the week after that.

By the third week she'd decided my whole personality had changed. "You've become such a scatterbrain, Ditty," she said. "You never used to be like that."

Luckily for me, she didn't seem to notice that I only became forgetful on Fridays. I knew my weekly absent-mindedness only had to last through the winter and that I wouldn't be quite so rushed in the summer, when daylight savings started and Shabbos came in later.

My mother was right, though. I *had* changed, just not in the way she meant. I had a focus now—my life was all about dance, and how I could continue to do it.

I thought about Linda's suggestion that I get a job. A few of the girls in my class at Beis Hannah had babysitting jobs, and I told my mum that I'd like one, too. She promised to keep her ears open just in case, but I knew how busy she was—cooking, cleaning, taking someone to the doctor. I didn't think she'd have the time to think of me. But a couple of weeks later she told me that Esti Kingsley, who lived at the Glen Eira Road end of our street, was looking for a regular babysitter on Saturday nights.

I rang up and grabbed the job before anyone else could. The Kingsley kids, Moishe and Shaindel, were two and four, and they were often in bed before I arrived. If they were still awake, I read them stories before we said the shema, but if they were already asleep, I was free to read or practice ballet.

Now that I had a job, I knew I could pay Linda back, and after that, I'd be able to pay for ballet myself, as well as for the ballet gear I'd need.

———

A month after I'd joined Grade Four, Miss Mitchell told me not to come to the Grade Three class anymore, but to join the Grade Five class instead. The Grade Five class was in a different studio, but the hours were the same. "I'd like to put you in Intermediate Foundation next year," she said, "with girls your own age."

I moved up to Grade Five early in the spring, just after the Grade exams, which were at the end of winter. The class was taught by Miss Moskowicz, who'd been a soloist in the Russian Ballet about a hundred years ago. She was so strict she didn't let you even whisper in her class.

There were two boys in Miss Moskowicz's class—Toby Heely and Christopher Grey. It was the first time I'd ever been in a class with boys, and I was determined not to let their presence throw me. I wasn't supposed to be seen by boys in clothes that weren't tsnius, but it wasn't as if I had a choice, not if I wanted to learn ballet. Modest clothes weren't allowed. And they just weren't practical.

I found a position at the barre as far away from those two boys as I could get. Maybe if I avoided looking at them, I could just pretend they didn't exist.

Grade Five was a lot harder than Grade Four had been, and most of the time I was too engrossed in my own work to pay much attention to anyone else.

On my way back to the changing room, I passed the studio where the Intermediate Foundation class was still in session. The door was open so I stopped to watch, just as Emma Wilson was asked to demonstrate a demanding *adage*. I'd heard that Emma was the best dancer in the entire school, and it was easy to see why. With her long line and perfect turnout, she was truly an extraordinary dancer. I wondered if I'd ever be as graceful as her.

Like me, Emma was in Year Six at school—she was about six months younger than I was—and I was sorry she was in the level above because it meant I'd hardly ever be able to watch her dance. Then I remembered that next year I'd be in her class, and I'd get to see her dancing all the time.

Next year! The thought made me start. Who knew what might have happened by then? I had to take things a day at a time. I couldn't, wouldn't, think about next year. There was no point making plans for a future I couldn't predict.

Twelve

Suddenly, the *Yamim Noraim*, the High Holidays, had arrived. It was time for *teshuva*, repentance, time to ask those we'd hurt for forgiveness, time, as Mrs. Teitlebaum put it, to "take stock of our lives."

"What are the three stages of teshuva?" she asked the class. It was an easy question. I put up my hand. "Stage one: Regret what you've done. Stage two: Resolve not to repeat the sin. Stage three: Do what you can to make amends."

Mrs. Teitlebaum wrote my answer on the board and asked us to contemplate these stages, which together constituted genuine teshuva.

Stage one was easy, because I did regret what I'd done. I'd always regretted lying to my parents, deceiving them. But what good was regret? It was meaningless if I didn't do something about it. That was where Stage two came in.

Resolve not to repeat the sin. Stage two meant that I had a choice—I had to give up ballet or tell the truth.

As for Stage three—well, I wasn't exactly sure how to make amends. But even if I couldn't bring myself to own up to what I'd done, I could still make it up to my parents by being the best daughter I could be.

On Rosh Hashanah, the Jewish New Year, I went to shule with my family and prayed for forgiveness. I made a deal with Hashem. I would stop lying to my parents. I would give up ballet. In return, He would agree not to punish me, because giving up ballet would be punishment enough.

The bargain seemed so simple when I made it. It wasn't until later that I realized I hadn't given much thought to the details. How would I give up ballet, and when? Would I never go back? Would I explain why I was leaving, or simply thank Miss Mitchell for teaching me and say goodbye? Would I never have another lesson? Or would I finish the week?

I realized I had to go back just one more time. I had to say goodbye to Miss Mitchell. I had to say goodbye to my secret dream of becoming a dancer. I had to take one final class and savor each moment, knowing it would be my last. Then that chapter of my life would be over, and I could start a new one.

There was still over a week to go until Yom Kippur. I'd go to ballet on Thursday, and by Yom Kippur I would have said my goodbyes, and come to terms with the fact that I wasn't coming back.

———

"Ditty, where were you last week?" Miss Mitchell asked me. I had missed two lessons in a row.

I should have told her then, as I had planned to. I should have said that I'd loved learning ballet, but that I had lied to my parents about it and now I had to stop. But looking around the studio I'd come to love, with its smooth barres, polished floor, and shiny rosewood piano in the corner, I couldn't bring myself to do it.

"I . . . couldn't come," I said instead. "It was a Jewish holiday. I'll never be able to come on Jewish holidays. Is . . . is that okay?"

"Yes, Ditty, it's fine. But I'd like you to tell me in advance if you know you won't be able to come to class."

"I won't be able to come next Monday and Tuesday, either. It's Yom Kippur, the Day of Atonement, the holiest day of the Jewish year."

––––––––––

The first Yom Kippur service was at dusk. It began with the cantor asking Hashem's permission to pray among sinners and on behalf of sinners. I had never understood this prayer before. I remembered thinking, only last year, that these were good people—they were here to pray. How sinful could they really be? Now I knew better. I was the sinner in this congregation. They were praying for me.

Yom Kippur is more solemn than any other day in the

Jewish year. There was no idle chatter. Not a murmur. Not a whisper. Nobody dared.

When I woke up in the morning, a thick film covered my teeth and my breath smelt bad, but because it was Yom Kippur, I couldn't brush my teeth or wash. Yom Kippur is a day of fasting. We wear canvas shoes instead of leather and spend the entire day in shule.

Standing between Rochel and Shayne in the women's section, I beat my fist against my chest while reciting the litany of sins I'd committed, and I resolved once again to give up ballet. The fact that I hadn't thanked Miss Mitchell or said goodbye was something I would just have to live with.

The day dragged. I didn't eat or drink, and by the time the *shofar* was sounded I was on the verge of fainting. The worse I felt, the more convinced I was that I had atoned for my sins.

––––––––––

"I'm giving up ballet," I said to Sara. "I just don't think I can lie anymore."

It was the morning after Yom Kippur, and Sara and I were walking to school.

"I've made a commitment—to myself and to Hashem. I can't go back on it."

But as the day drew on, I felt myself weakening.

I rationalized. I'd already paid for the rest of the term, which was the fourth and last term of the year, and it would be a waste of money not to take advantage of that. Then there was the fact that I had just been promoted to Grade Five. I hadn't even learnt the Grade Five syllabus yet.

When four o'clock came, somehow I found my feet following their familiar path to the tram stop, my sense of guilt temporarily replaced by overwhelming relief.

I'd made a promise, and I had every intention of keeping it.

I *had* to stop dancing, and I would.

But not just yet.

I would wait until the end of the year.

———

The National Theatre Ballet School put on a production twice each year—one in the winter and one in the summer, when the school year ended. The summer show was coming up, and I was determined to go.

Sara and I bought tickets for the Sunday matinee at two o'clock, and I sat in the audience waiting for a glimpse of the girls in my class. It wasn't long before the Grade Four girls appeared, in long, peach-colored tutus, followed by the Grade Five girls in sheer turquoise dresses over pale blue leotards. The costumes were stunning, the dancing polished and well rehearsed.

Then came the girls my own age, the ones whose class Miss Mitchell had said I would be in next year. There were three who caught my eye—Emma Wilson, Kirsten Marsh, and Frances Hue. I already knew that Emma was an exquisite dancer, so I wasn't surprised when she led the rest of the class in a cheerful *allegro*. Her jumps were higher than everyone else's, her line longer, her feet more pointed. After that she had a solo, and her performance was charming, flawless, and seemingly effortless.

Other than Emma, the main parts went to older students who, to my novice eye, all looked professional already. But then, I had nothing to compare them to. *The Pied Piper* was the first live ballet production I'd ever seen. Like the children lured by the enchanting music the piper played, I couldn't have left even if I'd wanted to. The music, costumes, color, and dance transported me from my mundane world into a world of endless possibility, a world of fairy-tale and fantasy.

Suddenly I understood what all the classes were for, how the hard work paid off and where it could lead. I saw the transformation of what was practiced in the studio to the magic on stage. And though my father had told me a Yiddishe girl does not go on the stage, I knew there was nowhere else I'd rather be.

———

"You were great in *The Pied Piper*," I said to Kirsten. I'd never spoken to the girls who weren't in my class before, and I hoped my self-consciousness didn't show.

"Thanks." She smiled at me, putting me at ease.

"You too," I said to Frances. I'd have liked to congratulate Emma as well, but she'd already left.

The last class of the year was over, and everyone was kissing everyone else goodbye. It would be weeks until they all saw each other again.

"What are you getting for Christmas?" Kirsten asked me.

I was putting my school uniform back on and I laughed at the question. "I don't get Christmas presents. I'm Jewish."

"So! Everyone gets Christmas presents."

"Well, I don't."

"God, you poor thing," said Frances.

"No need to feel sorry for me. I get birthday presents, and Rosh Hashanah presents. Oh, and we have Hanukkah, round about Christmas time."

"What do you get for Hanukkah?" Kirsten asked.

"Hanukkah gelt."

"What's that?"

"Chocolate money. You know, coins."

"That's it?"

"Uh-huh." It sounded so pathetic I was sorry I'd mentioned it.

"That sucks," said Frances.

"Yeah," Kirsten agreed. She was getting the latest mobile phone for Christmas, as well as her own digital camera. Frances was getting an iPod, a Tiffany heart, and a flat iron.

"Are you ... like ... poor?" Kirsten asked me.

"No. Of course not," I said, thinking that even if we were, I'd never have admitted it.

Some of the girls promised to stay in touch with each other over the summer holidays, but most of them were leaving Melbourne. Some were flying to places I could only ever dream of. Places like Fiji, Bali, and Phuket. Others were driving up north to New South Wales or Queensland, but almost everyone was going somewhere. Everyone but me.

Thirteen

•◆•

For one week that summer, Sara and I ran a holiday program for Beis Hannah girls from younger grades. It was
common in our community for teenage girls to look after
younger ones, and now that Sara and I had finished pri-
mary school, we were considered old enough to do it, too.

We'd put up a sign at school, and ten mothers phoned
to register their daughters. The girls arrived at Sara's house at
nine in the morning and stayed till one. We played outdoor
games in Sara's garden, and indoor games when the weather
was bad. We baked cakes and biscuits, and we organized
activities—treasure hunts, clay painting, mask making, and
cake decorating.

We charged a voluntary fee of one hundred dollars, which
everyone paid. After buying art materials, train tickets, and

food, we were left with almost eight hundred dollars, close to four hundred each.

It was more money than I'd ever seen, and I saved most of it. So did Sara. She hardly ever spent any of the money she earned.

"What are you saving up for?" I asked her.

Sara shrugged. "I might go to Queensland one day."

"Queensland?"

"Yeah. I'd like to turn up there and surprise my dad. Remind him that he's got a daughter."

"That'd be brave." I wondered what she'd do if he acted like it was a bad surprise and didn't want to see her. "Do you know where he lives?"

"No," she sighed. "Maybe I could find out, though."

"Maybe," I agreed doubtfully. I couldn't help thinking that it mightn't be so smart to go looking for someone who didn't want to be found. "Have you asked your mum?"

"She wouldn't tell me even if she knew. She thinks I should just forget about him."

Maybe Sara's mum was right, I thought. I mean, if Sara's dad really wanted to see his daughter, then why didn't he pay for a ticket to come and see her?

"It's just… he's my dad, you know? Sometimes, I can't help wondering… what if he's been dying to see me ever since we moved to Melbourne and my mum won't let him?"

"Why wouldn't she let him?"

Sara sighed again. "Because she hates him. Maybe she just wants to punish him."

It seemed a bit of a stretch to me, but I didn't say so. Why make Sara more miserable than she already was?

We were window-shopping in Glenhuntly Road, and I pulled her toward the nearest store. "Look at that gorgeous bag," I said, changing the subject.

"This one's even more divine." She pointed to a white handbag embroidered with flowers and leaves in bright reds, purple, and bottle green. "Can you read the price tag?"

I couldn't, as it had been turned face down. We spent the next few minutes guessing the cost of the bags in the window, and Sara didn't mention her dad again.

———————

Apart from a ten-day break timed to coincide with Hanukkah, Sara's mum worked through the entire summer, and Sara had the house to herself. Sometimes I practiced ballet in the Kestens' living room while Sara read romance books she'd borrowed from the library. At other times we holed ourselves up in Mrs. Kesten's bedroom watching TV.

One day we decided to pay a visit to the Blockbuster in Hawthorn Road. I wanted to see if I could find *Nutcracker* and other ballets and Sara wanted a romantic comedy, the kind we'd seen advertised on billboards outside the Classic Cinema.

Blockbuster was out of bounds for us, of course, and we'd never been inside. We walked fast, and it took us twenty minutes to get there. When we did, we hovered uncertainly on the footpath outside.

"Are you sure no one's watching?" Sara asked.

"As sure as I can be," I replied. Standing on a main road, we were pretty conspicuous. We went in quickly, before we could change our minds.

Even though the place was huge, we found Drama and Comedy quite quickly. But I couldn't see a section for Dance. I went over to Customer Service and asked the middle-aged woman behind the counter. She pointed at a sign down the end of the store that said *Special Interest*.

There were quite a few ballets on DVD, with titles like *Giselle, Sleeping Beauty,* and *Coppélia*. And yes, *Nutcracker*, too. I wondered if Sara would mind watching it again. She was over in the Comedy section, reading the blurb on the jacket of a DVD.

I went and peered over her shoulder. "Look what I found," I said, showing her *Nutcracker*.

She glanced at it and then looked back at the cover in her hand.

"I thought you were giving up ballet. You know, now that the year is over."

I didn't reply.

"Well, aren't you?"

"Yes. No. I mean ... "

"But you said ... "

"I know what I said," I interrupted her.

The truth was, it was bad enough not dancing over the holidays, and when I'd said I'd give up ballet, I hadn't realized how much I'd miss it. "Anyway," I added, "even if I do stop doing it, that doesn't mean I have to stop watching it."

Sara shrugged and we joined the queue at the cashier, where we had to wait five minutes for our turn.

"Can I see your membership card?" the guy behind the counter asked us.

We looked at him blankly.

"You have to be a member before you can take out DVDs," he explained. "You have to join up."

"How do we do that?"

"You need ID and proof of address. Ask your mum or dad to come in and sign you up."

He must have seen the disappointment on our faces, because his voice softened and he added, "You can buy some, though. We've got some great movies on sale, and you don't need to be a member for that."

We went to look at the DVDs on sale, but they weren't the ones we wanted. We left Blockbuster empty-handed and walked back home.

––––––––

Linda came over the following day and we told my mum we were going out. As we ambled down the path toward the street, I told her about our fruitless expedition to Blockbuster the day before.

"Why waste your money on DVDs anyway?" she said. "I've got stacks of them at home. I'll lend you some."

We were heading for Glenhuntly Road, which was past the Classic Cinema at the end of our street. I'd never been inside the cinema before but as we passed it now, Linda glanced up at the billboard on the wall. It was advertising a film called *Billy Elliot* and above the billboard, in flashing lights, were the words *NOW SHOWING*.

Linda stopped and grabbed my arm. "It's *you*," she shrieked. She tugged at my sleeve, dragging me toward the heavy glass doors.

"What's me?" I asked.

"*Billy Elliot*. It's a fantastic film. It was on ages ago and they've brought it back now for this Season of the Arts they've got here. You know, films about art, music, and dance. You've *got* to see it, Ditty. It's your story. It's about this boy whose father won't let him do ballet, and he's dying to learn … "

She pulled me inside and bought two tickets. The film was starting in five minutes' time. I looked around in a panic.

"What if someone recognizes me and tells my parents they've seen me here?"

"Don't be an idiot, Ditty," said Linda. "No one you know will be here, and if they are, they'll be just as paranoid as you are."

I had to admit she had a point, and I followed her inside.

Linda was right about the film. I was riveted from start to finish. I had so much in common with Billy Elliot, I wished I could meet him.

The following week Linda told me that Blockbuster was having a massive sale, so Sara and I sneaked back to the store and I found *Billy Elliot* among the rows of second-hand movies being sold off at two-thirds the usual price. It still wasn't cheap, but I couldn't resist, and I decided to make a dent in the money I'd saved.

Sara and I watched the film while we made our way through a block of Elite chocolate. Sara loved *Billy Elliot* as much as I did, and I was sure we'd watch it a hundred times.

We didn't, though. In the end, we only managed to watch it once—because after that, I couldn't find it. I searched everywhere, but it had disappeared, and I had no idea where it might be. By the time I had accepted the fact that it had well and truly vanished, Blockbuster had sold out of second-hand copies, and I couldn't afford to buy it new.

Fourteen

• ◆ •

When I started Year Seven, it became my job to bring Shayne and Hillel home from school, since Rochel was taking on extra Jewish Studies classes and would be finishing an hour later than the rest of us.

The weather was hot, that first day. I walked home in the heat with Shayne and Hillel and then rushed straight out again. When I arrived at the National, my face was red and my skin was clammy.

I was still wearing my school uniform, an ugly blue-and-white-checked, calf-length dress with sleeves that stopped midway between my elbows and wrists. I was also wearing dark pantyhose—bare legs were against school rules—and I was sweating horribly.

Some of the other girls in my ballet class had also come straight from school, but their uniforms were so short you could almost see their undies, and their legs were bare. Some of them were wearing sandals with regulation ankle socks, and others had ditched their school sandals in favor of thongs. The lucky ones had gone home and changed into shorts or mini-skirts and small, tight-fitting tops.

Emma Wilson was already in the changing room, dressed in a sleeveless leotard and tights and pinning her bun into place. She saw me in the mirror as I walked in, and winced as she took in my long dress, tights, and closed-in shoes.

"God, aren't you hot?" she said.

"Roasting," I agreed.

"Is that your *summer* uniform?"

I nodded. "I go to a really religious school."

Emma shook her head and gave me a pitying look. "That must really suck."

"Yeah, it does."

Emma smiled, and the two of us cracked up laughing. It felt, just for a moment, like we'd been friends for years.

Suddenly I felt torn by divided loyalties. There was a part of me that wanted to stick up for my school, and for my parents who had chosen it. But there was another part of me that felt like I'd just taken a breath of fresh air after weeks of being cooped up inside.

"Can't you change into shorts and a crop top after school?" asked Emma.

"No. I'm not allowed to wear them. My family's really religious, so I have to dress modestly."

"Are you, like, Muslim or something?"

"Jewish."

"Oh!"

"At least I don't have to wear a *hijab*. That's got to be worse."

Just then Kirsten and Frances came in. As I caught sight of the four of us in the mirror, I realized how different I looked from these other girls, and not just because of my clothes. Kirsten, Frances, and Emma were all different shades of blonde. I was dark. They had fair skin. Mine was olive. Just for a second, I found myself wishing I looked like them.

"Maybe I'll go blonde one day," I said to no one in particular.

"Are you insane?" said Emma. "Why would you want to be blonde?"

"Yeah," said Kirsten. "You've got great hair."

"And it suits you," added Frances.

"True," Emma said. "You're really exotic looking, you know."

Did they really like the way I looked or were they just being kind? Either way, I took it as a compliment, though I hoped they didn't think I was fishing for one. All I knew was that these girls had made me feel good about myself, and I liked their company.

Last year, dancing with the younger girls, I'd felt like a bit of an outsider. Now that I was in a class with girls my own age, maybe I'd start to feel like I belonged.

————

"Mum?"

"Yes, Ditty?"

"I…"

"What is it?"

I'd planned to raise the subject of ballet again, in the hope that my mum would persuade my dad to let me take lessons, but now that I had my mother's attention, my courage deserted me. What if she said no again?

"Ditty, what's on your mind?"

"Nothing. I just… do you want me to give Gittel a bath?"

"No," said my mother, looking as if she knew full well I was holding something back. "Gittel doesn't need a bath. She's already had one."

————

Miss Mitchell had placed me in both the Intermediate Foundation and the Intermediate classes, as well as open class and pointe class. I wasn't as skilled as the other girls, but I was catching up, fast. And some of them were envious when they discovered I was more flexible than they were.

Some of the girls were already on pointe. Those who weren't, like me, did all the work on demi-pointe. It was good preparation for pointe work, and strengthened the muscles round the ankles and knees. The work was gruelling and very technical, but I could see that it would make me a better, stronger dancer.

In between telling us to pull up from the center and make sure we keep our shoulders pressed down, Miss Mitchell took to lecturing us before and after class on the importance of grooming. I could see her eyeing the holes in my tights.

"Take a look in the Lost and Found, Ditty," she advised me. "Anything left unclaimed for over six months is up for grabs, and I think you'll find some tights there that will fit you. I'm fairly certain they're in good condition."

"You know, Ditty," my mother said, one Sunday afternoon as we shopped for fruit and vegetables at South Melbourne market, "I bumped into Sara's mother in the supermarket on Thursday morning."

I tried to look cool, hoping that Sara's mum hadn't said anything that might give me away.

"She said she hasn't seen you in a while. I thought you went there all the time..."

"I do," I said, thinking of Sunday mornings, sitting shoulder to shoulder with Sara on Mrs. Kesten's single bed. "But I don't see much of Sara's mum. She's always working. She gets home really late."

"Hmm! I always thought she works too hard. Perhaps she has no choice. I don't suppose that good-for-nothing ex-husband of hers does much to contribute. Goodness! Look at the price of tomatoes..."

Her voice trailed off and I exhaled slowly, thankful for the sudden rise in the price of tomatoes and aware of an urgent need to change my story. But what would I tell my mother instead? Maybe Linda would have some ideas.

When we came home I helped my mum unpack the groceries, and when she started chopping vegetables for dinner, I crept into my parents' bedroom. I wasn't supposed to be in their room without permission—it was out of bounds to anyone over the age of five. It was my parents' inner sanctum, the only place they could get any privacy.

The room looked exactly as it always had—plain and simple. There were no knick-knacks or ornaments in sight. It was neater than the rest of the house, and sort of colorless. No pictures covered the peeling wallpaper apart from a single photo of a famous rabbi who was no longer alive. My mother's dressing table was bare, except for two Styrofoam heads, one of which was bald—my mother was currently wearing the sheitel that belonged there—while the other sported her Shabbos sheitel, the wig she wore on special occasions. There were two single beds in my parents' bedroom, about a meter apart.

I picked up the corded, push-button phone on my mother's bedside table and punched in my cousin's number. Linda answered the phone on the second ring.

"What's up, Ditty?"

Making sure to keep my voice down, I told her about the conversation I'd had with my mum. "What if she talks to Sara's mum again? What if she finds out I'm not even there?"

"First off, don't panic."

"But what should I do?"

"Hmm … don't worry, Ditty. I'll think of something."

Linda's voice was drowned out by a louder one. "Ditty?"

The door to my parents' bedroom opened. I quickly

hung up the phone and flung open the nearest cupboard. My mother walked in to find me staring in fascination at her Shabbos dresses.

"Ditty, what on earth are you doing?"

"I...ah..." I blushed madly. "I'm looking for tampons."

"Tampons?" My mum's voice softened, then. "Well, there's no need to be embarrassed about it. You should have asked me." She opened another wardrobe and took out a box of Carefree tampons. "Is there anything else you need? Do you have enough pads?"

I didn't answer. I had already fled the room.

Fifteen

• ◆ •

"Have you got brothers and sisters?" Kirsten asked me. We were sitting in the changing room, putting on our ballet shoes.

"Yep."

"How many?"

"Six." I was already regretting my answer. In our community, it's considered bad luck to tell people the exact number of children in a family, and when anyone asks my mum how many she has, she just smiles and says "I have several, *Baruch Hashem*." But it was too late to take it back, and the other girls were staring at me open-mouthed.

"It's not such a big deal, you know," I said. "Seven kids in a family isn't all that many. Lots of people in our community have ten or more. Some even have fourteen."

"Fourteen!" said Frances. "Christ, do they even know each other's names?"

"Tell us about them," Kirsten said. "How many boys, how many girls, and how old are they?"

I told them the names, ages, and sexes of my brothers and sisters in order of age, starting with Pinny.

"Weird names," said Frances, "but they're kind of cute."

"They're mostly Biblical names," I explained.

"You mean there's someone called Pinny in the Bible?"

I nodded. "Pinny's short for Pinchas. Rochel is Rachel."

"What about your name?" asked Kirsten.

"Ditty's short for Yehudit. It's Judith in English."

"How do you get Ditty from Yehudit?"

"Yehu*dit, Dit, Ditty*."

Emma walked in while I was still explaining. "I love the name Ditty," she said. "It really suits you."

"Thanks," I said.

"I wish I had an unusual name. Mine's so ordinary. What dancer has a boring name like Emma Wilson?"

"Well, you can always change it," said Frances.

"You wouldn't be the only one," I agreed. "Margot Fonteyn was born Margaret Hookham, and Alicia Markova was originally called Lilian Alicia Marks. Lots of dancers change their names."

"You seem to know a lot about it," said Kirsten.

"I've been doing my ballet research," I said with a smile.

"Do you want to be a dancer?" Emma asked me.

"Me? I only started learning last July."

"Yeah, but you're good. You're obviously really talented."

I tried to hide my flush of pleasure, flattered that someone as gifted as Emma thought I had talent. "Can you imagine a dancer called Yehudit Cohen?" I asked. "I'd definitely have to change my name."

"I don't see why," said Kirsten. "I think your name's theatrical. And it has a nice meaning in English. A ditty is a song. Do you know the Oompah-pah song from *Oliver!*? It's about singing a ditty in the city." She started to sing, and a minute later, everyone in the changing room was joining in.

We were still clowning around and dancing when Miss Mitchell poked her head around the door. "Girls! Girls!" Her tone was mock-angry but her eyes were smiling. "Keep it down and hurry up. You're late for class."

———

At five o'clock on Sunday, Linda came over unannounced. She was dressed to impress—she had (temporarily) removed her nose stud and eyebrow ring and was wearing a boringly respectable skirt and blouse, which I couldn't believe she even owned. She was clearly in suck-up-to-Aunt-Zipporah mode.

We were all sitting at the kitchen table eating pizza when out of the blue Linda said to my mum, "Do you mind if Ditty takes over my babysitting job on weekdays after school?"

I looked up, surprised. Linda didn't have a babysitting job, and there was no way I could take another one.

Then I remembered. I'd told her I needed to change my story, so she was giving me a new one. It was clever, too. My mum knew that Linda always had a job or two, so she wasn't likely to check up on this one.

"I'm getting a heavier workload at school, and I've got exams coming up," said Linda. "I don't want to leave the Riskins in the lurch, and I said I'd try to find a replacement. And Ditty wants to earn more money."

"Do you?"

I nodded silently.

"But you've already got a babysitting job," my mother said. "Why do you want another one?"

"She'd just have to walk the kids home from school and give them dinner and a bath," Linda interrupted, saving me the need to answer. "She wouldn't have to cook or anything. Mrs. Riskin, Adela, always leaves food."

"What does Mrs. Riskin do?" my mother asked.

"She's a lawyer. Her hours are a bit unpredictable, but she's usually home between six-fifteen and quarter to seven."

"Riskin," my mother mused, trying to place them. "Which Riskins are they?" It went without saying that they were not part of the haredi community. If they had been, she'd have known who they were. "Are they modern orthodox?" she asked.

"Yes," said Linda. This meant it was unlikely my mother would ever meet them. It wouldn't occur to her that they didn't exist.

"Well, I suppose everyone has a right to have their children properly looked after," my mother said. "But if Ditty takes this job, who will walk Shayne and Hillel home from school?" It was obvious that Ezra couldn't. The boys' school was right next door to ours but, like Rochel, Ezra finished an hour later than we did.

"Isn't Shayne old enough to bring Hillel home?" I asked. Shayne was already eight and a half.

My mother frowned as she considered this. She was about to say no, but then Shayne piped up. "Yes, I am. I am old enough." My mother smiled at Shayne and agreed.

And so it was settled. I could start working for the Riskins as soon as I liked.

The next day, my mother bought me a mobile phone. I wished I could return it and give her the money back. I didn't deserve it.

"I want you to have it," she said, "just so you can call home if you need me. Take it, Ditty. I'll feel safer knowing you have it."

I vowed not to use the phone unless the situation was really dire, but I was grateful. It meant that my mum would never have to call me at the Riskins' or ask for their number.

———

After that, it was easier to get to ballet on time. While I was fighting for space in the changing room, or warming up, I'd hear about the quarrel Frances had with her mum, the science teacher that failed Emma for not handing in her work on time, or the ongoing war between Kirsten and her younger sister, who actually broke the lock on Kirsten's diary and ratted to her mum and dad about its contents.

The twenty minutes before class started was bonding

time—a chance for us to get to know each other. And though I knew I was different from the other girls, I was starting to think of them as friends.

Sixteen

•—◆—•

Once a week we had pointe class. All year long I'd been envious of the girls who changed into pointe shoes, and I couldn't wait to join them. Now, a few months after my thirteenth birthday, Miss Moskowicz told all the girls in the class who were still on demi-pointe to go and buy pointe shoes, and that meant me.

I'd never entered a dance shop before, since all my dancewear was secondhand. But as pointe shoes wore out quickly and had to be a perfect fit, they had to be new.

Most of the girls in my ballet class bought their uniform and shoes at a shop called Sansha, which was an easy walk from where I lived. It was down the end of Glen Eira Road near Ripponlea station, in the shopping strip where every haredi housewife shopped for food. There were two popular greengrocers in that strip of shops, as well as a kosher fish shop and a kosher bakery. Diagonally across from the dancewear shop was Kraus, one of the few shops that sold local and imported kosher products. And right next door to Sansha was Klein's Kosher Gourmet, a shop selling kosher home-cooked meals.

This was haredi territory, so although I had often longed to go into Sansha, I had never risked it. But I needed the shoes, and buying them close to home would be so much easier than taking public transport to Southgate or Chadstone. So when the winter holidays arrived, I set off to buy them.

I walked up and down the footpath in front of the shop, checking that no one was watching. Then I slipped inside and stood taking great gulps of air, waiting for my heartbeat to return to normal.

I told the sales assistant that I needed pointe shoes, and when she led me to a bench at the back of the shop, far from the prying eyes of passers-by, I finally let myself relax. There was no way anyone from my community would actually come in here.

As my feet were measured, I checked out the interior of this wonderful store. There were racks upon racks of leotards, arranged according to size and color. There were tutus hanging from the ceiling—some plain, others embroidered with silver or gold, with beaded bodices made from costume jewels in bright, rich colors and sequins that sparkled when they caught the light.

And there were shoes—rows upon rows of them stacked neatly on the open shelves—tap shoes that came in black and tan, character shoes with two-inch heels, jazz shoes designed in two different styles, but mostly ballet shoes—flats and pointes and demi-pointes, in soft leather, canvas, or shiny satin. There were ballet flats in white and black for men and boys, and a hundred different shades of pink—baby pink, dusky pink, apricot pink, flesh-colored pink. There was a whole sea of pink along one wall.

The sales assistant went away to find my size, and I gazed longingly around the shop, tempted by things I didn't need—cute little key rings attached to miniature soft satin pointe shoes, handbags patterned with dancing ballerinas, dance magazines from all over the world. Of course, there was no way I could afford to buy them.

I tried on three pairs of pointe shoes before I found the pair that fit. They were even more expensive than I'd thought—about three times the price of ballet flats. I had to buy ribbons as well, and ouch pouches and lamb's wool to cushion my toes. Miss Mitchell had warned us that we might get blisters at first, but I didn't care. I just couldn't wait to dance on my toes.

The sales assistant wrapped up the items I needed and added up the cost. I was ten cents short.

"Not to worry," she said. "My boss won't mind."

I thanked her and put the Sansha bag into the larger bag I'd brought with me. Then I slid the door open and peeped out into the street. From inside the shop, it was impossible to see whether anyone who knew me might be watching. I'd just have to make a dash for it.

I took a deep breath, and ran, and I didn't stop running till I reached my street, deciding then and there that the next time I needed something from a dancewear shop I would go to a different one, no matter how long it took me.

Gordon Street was quiet, and relief flooded over me when I realized that no one had stopped me or called out to me. Now that I had the shoes safely in my possession, I was on a high. I would be dancing on pointe soon. I would be dancing on pointe! I was completely broke now, but I was too happy to care. I wished I could share my enthusiasm with my mother, with someone, with anyone.

I half walked, half skipped along the footpath. In my head I was dancing on pointe, doing *relevés*, *temps levés*, and *bourrées* while hoping that the Kingsleys would be out for longer than usual on Saturday night, because now I needed every dollar I could get.

When I got home, I kissed the *mezuzah* on the doorpost as I usually did before going inside.

The house was buzzing with activity. Doors slammed as kids ran in and out. Pinny was out at the kollel and Rochel was reading in her room, but everyone else—Ezra, Shayne, Hillel and Gittel—had friends over. There were two different Hassidic songs blaring from different rooms, all the lights were on (even though it was the middle of a sunny day), and a radio left on in the kitchen gave a riveting list of the day's disasters to anyone who cared to listen.

I found my mum in the backyard hanging out washing and I offered to help. I whistled as I pegged pajamas, sheets, and towels onto the washing line.

"You're in a good mood today," she said.

I grinned back at her. *I've just bought my first pair of pointe shoes*, I sang in my heart, wishing I could say it out loud.

"Why shouldn't I be?" I said instead. "It's the holidays."

Hillel and his friend Moishe burst through the kitchen door, leaving it to slam behind them, and started chasing each other round the garden. A minute later Ezra came out. He asked my mum if he and his friend Yossi could have some money to go and buy icy poles.

"Icy poles? In the middle of winter? Oh, all right, but take Hillel and Moishe with you and buy some for them, too. Anything for a bit of peace and quiet!" She hunted in her purse for some small change but couldn't find any. Then she realized she was out of notes too.

"Ditty," she said, "could you give Ezra money for some icy poles?"

For a second, I froze.

Any other time, I could have said yes.

Any other time, I would have said yes.

But she had to pick that day to ask me!

"Sorry, but I don't have any," I said.

In that instant, I knew exactly what she was going to ask me next.

"But Ditty, what do you do with all that money you earn?"

It was such an obvious, foreseeable question that I should have been expecting it. I should have been prepared.

My mum was waiting for an answer. My heart hammered in my chest, and for a second I thought I might throw up.

"I ... uh ... give it to tzedakkah," I said.

She looked surprised at first. Then her face relaxed into

a huge smile of approval, because there is no greater mitzvah than giving money to charity.

"Good for you, Ditty," she said. "Your father will be so proud when I tell him."

I turned away quickly, before she could see the hot flush of shame flooding my cheeks.

———

After lunch, I locked myself in the bathroom to sew the ribbons on my pointe shoes. It took me over half an hour, though I was sure my mother could have done it in two minutes flat. I pricked my finger on the needle and watched as a trail of blood trickled down toward my wrist. A tear escaped and I brushed it away, but I refused to cry. After all, maybe this was my punishment for telling my mother that the money I earned went to tzedakkah, though I doubted I'd get off with just a pinprick. I was sure there was a special place in Hell for liars like me.

Seventeen

•◆•

Pointe class was taught by Miss Moskowicz, who had taught Grade Five the year before. She was so tough that several girls had left the National because of her, or given up ballet altogether. Not me, though. I loved the discipline. I loved the fact that she was so demanding.

Miss Moskowicz did not believe that near enough was good enough. She expected you to pick up the steps the first time she showed you, and she glowered every time you got something wrong. She was the sort of teacher who could crush you with a word or a look, and she was incapable of giving anyone a compliment, however small.

Occasionally she said "Not bad" to Emma, in a grudging, resentful kind of way, but she had never said it to me or anyone else in the class. Naturally, I was determined to win her approval. If I could get a "Not bad" out of Miss Moskowicz, I'd know that I was doing okay.

One day, I was practicing *relevés* at the barre. I took a balance in fifth position, and all of a sudden I could hear Miss Moskowicz's voice ringing out from the center of the room.

"Very *nice*, Miss Cohen."

The other fifteen or so girls in the class all turned to stare. I was so stunned that I lost my balance and narrowly avoided falling flat on my face.

All the way home, Miss Moskowicz's compliment played itself over and over in my head. I floated down the street to the recollection of my moment in the sun.

Very NICE, Miss Cohen. The words became stuck in my mind, like a song I would never tire of hearing.

The combination of hard work and success had given me an appetite, and when I got home, I headed straight to the kitchen.

"How were the kids this week?" my mother asked me.

"Which kids?"

My mind was miles away, dreaming up additional compliments from the toughest teacher in town. *Fabulous, Ditty,* I imagined her saying. *You do that so beautifully.*

"The Riskin kids," said my mother.

The Riskin kids? What was my mother talking about?

Then I remembered. Just as my mother gave me a bemused look.

The *Riskin* kids. Of course! My alibi. I had forgotten all about them.

"What did you say their names were?" asked my mother.

What *did* I say their names were?

"Aaron and Talia." I made it up on the spot. "They're … fine. They're … pretty good kids, actually." Were there only two of them? And how old were they supposed to be? Had I ever mentioned their age?

"There are just the two of them, right?"

"Yep, that's right," I agreed. I decided there and then that the fictional Mrs. Riskin (a lawyer, I remembered now) was definitely not having any more.

As soon as dinner was over I went to my room and collapsed onto my bed, my head in my hands. My mum had almost caught me out. I was juggling too much—school, ballet lessons, a real job, and a fake one. It was hard keeping track of all my lies, and I couldn't be on my guard every second of every day. I had to relax at least some of the time.

I felt nauseous and my hands were trembling. What sort of twisted game was I playing? How much longer could I keep it up?

————

It was hours before I managed to fall asleep, and when I woke up, the first thing I remembered was Miss Moskowicz's compliment. It had given me such a sense of achievement. But it had gone to my head, and I was nearly caught out because of it.

What had my life been like before I started dancing? I couldn't remember. I must have filled the hours somehow, before I knew that ballet existed. Now, it had become such a huge part of my life that the thought of giving it up was devastating. Dance filled a void that nothing else could, but I was amazed that I had come this far without being found out.

During Mrs. Katz's maths lesson that morning, I opened a blank notebook and wrote the day's date, followed by the words *Riskins, Aaron, Talia.* I underlined their names and ruled a line down the center to form two columns.

While Mrs. Katz was writing an algebra equation on the board, I wrote out two lists that looked something like this:

—Riskins—

Aaron	Talia
6	4
fair hair	curly brown hair
blue eyes	hazel eyes
freckles	olive skin
lisps	good singing voice
likes: dinosaurs, footy	likes: riding her tricycle, finger painting
dislikes: chocolate	dislikes: playing with dolls
favorite food: ice cream, pizza	favorite food: meatballs, M&M's

I planned to study those lists harder than I'd ever studied for a test at school, so if questioned again, I would have the answers at my fingertips.

I glanced up from my lists to find the teacher scowling at me. "I didn't hear that, Ditty."

"Excuse me?"

"I asked you to tell the class what x equals."

"x?" I looked up at the board.

"You obviously haven't been listening. What *have* you been doing?"

"I ... uh ... nothing." I slipped the notebook under my Maths textbook and looked at the whiteboard. There were seventeen girls in my class. Why did Mrs. Katz decide that I should be the one to tell the class what x was?

"I've just spent ten minutes explaining this," she said. "Why do I bother? Leah, perhaps you could tell us ... "

By the end of the lesson I had forgotten how to work out what x equalled, but the name "Riskin" would stay with me forever.

Eighteen

· ◆ ·

One day, Sara was called out of class and sent to the principal. She didn't come back, and when it was time to go home, her schoolbag, which usually hung on the peg next to mine, was missing. No one seemed to know where she had gone.

As soon as I got home I sought out my mother, who was simultaneously mashing potatoes and spooning peas onto Gittel's plastic plate.

"Sara was called out of class today," I began, as I watched Gittel mashing peas with her fist. "No one knows what's happened to her."

Gittel threw a meatball at the wall. I wiped her hands and face with a damp paper towel, lifted her up out of her high chair, and stood her gently on the floor. "She just vanished," I added.

My mother sighed. "Ditty, Sara didn't vanish. She's sitting *shiva*. Her father died last night."

"*What?*"

It was the first time my mother had ever mentioned Sara's dad without calling him "that good-for-nothing father of hers."

"What did he die of?"

"I think he was sick."

"Sara didn't say anything about him being sick."

"I don't think she knew. Look, why don't you take the day off school tomorrow and spend it at Sara's? She'll be sitting shiva by herself, the poor girl. It must be awful being an only child."

"Isn't her mother sitting shiva too?"

"No, Ditty, you don't sit shiva for someone you're no longer married to."

———————

The next morning I arrived at Sara's just before nine. A few women were sitting around talking in subdued voices, but no one our age was there. Sara was sitting on a low black mourner's chair, her eyes red from crying. Her mum was sitting in a more comfortable armchair. She nodded at me when she saw me.

As custom demanded, I didn't greet anyone. I didn't touch Sara or say anything to her. I just sat down in a chair opposite and waited until she spoke first. After a few minutes,

Sara's mum went into the kitchen with the other women, and Sara and I were left alone.

"They told me my dad died."

"I know."

Sara's face crumpled up and tears began to flow. She mopped them up with a handful of tissues and blew her nose.

"I never saw him again, Ditty. Not once since we moved here. Why didn't he come to see me? Why didn't he care?"

I didn't know what to say at first. Then it hit me. "Maybe he was too sick to come."

"My mum never even told me he was sick."

"Maybe she didn't know either."

"Maybe."

She was quiet for a while.

"What if she did, though?"

"What?"

"What if my mum did know he was sick?"

"You mean, you think she would have kept it from you deliberately?"

Sara shrugged. "It's possible. I mean, if I'd known he was sick, I'd have wanted to go up to Queensland to see him. And she would never have agreed."

"Maybe she couldn't afford the airfare," I said.

"For one ticket to Queensland? How much would it cost?"

Neither of us knew.

"But at least that might explain why he never came to see you. It wasn't that he didn't care about you, Sara. He was probably too sick to come."

I didn't honestly buy my own argument. I mean, too

sick to even contact his own daughter? And how long had he been sick for, anyway? But I would have said anything if it helped Sara to feel better.

"Maybe," she said. "Or maybe my mum just didn't want him here. Maybe she wouldn't let him come." Angrily, she blew her nose again and sniffed. "She's not even sad that he's dead. She doesn't care."

Sara's mum came into the room and glanced at Sara. "All he ever did was make you cry," she mumbled. "I'll bring you another box of tissues. This one's almost empty."

I couldn't believe I'd heard right. Not that I wanted to defend Sara's dad or anything. It wasn't as if he was such a wonderful guy. Still, there was such a thing as respecting the dead.

"She seems mad," I said, after Mrs. Kesten left the room.

"I know. She's acting as if he got sick and died on purpose."

Sara's mum came back into the room carrying another box of tissues. She dumped it in front of Sara, then went back into the kitchen and returned a moment later with a tray of fruit. She offered it to me and I shook my head.

"I'll leave it on the table, then." She paused on her way into the kitchen. "Thanks for coming, Ditty. Thanks for being such a loyal friend to Sara."

———

That night I woke up thirsty and I knew I couldn't have slept for long. I got out of bed and tiptoed softly across the floor, careful not to wake Shayne and Gittel, who were both fast asleep. I walked silently down the hall toward the kitchen. There was a light coming from under the living room door, and my father and Reb Saunders were talking softly, even though their shiur must have finished long ago.

Rochel's name was mentioned, along with the word "shidduch." My breath caught in my throat and I froze. They were talking about marrying Rochel off. They were planning her future.

I don't know why I was surprised. Some of Rochel's friends were engaged and one or two were already married. I guess I hadn't thought about Rochel's age.

" ... too young," I heard my father saying, and then, "Ask me again next year."

I wondered what Rochel would say if she knew she was the subject of this conversation. Knowing Rochel, she probably wouldn't mind. Besides, she wouldn't think she was too young to think of marriage. She was sixteen and a half now, nearly seventeen, and plenty of people in our community— Reb Saunders included—didn't think that was too young to get engaged. I was glad my father didn't agree with them. Still, he was planning to wait just one more year ...

It hadn't been very long since my cousin Shoshi got married at seventeen, and from my twelve-year-old perspective, that hadn't seemed too young at all. In only a year and a half, my perspective had changed, and seventeen seemed very young indeed.

———

The next day, I went into Rochel's room and sat on her bed while she braided her hair. She had beautiful hair, and I thought she might as well enjoy it while she could, because she wouldn't be able to once she was married. No one would ever see her hair except for her husband. Husband. God! Husband! I couldn't bear to think about it.

"Do you want to get married?" I burst out suddenly.

"What?"

"Do you want to get married?" I repeated.

"You mean, ever?"

"Uh-huh."

"Of course I do. Why? Don't you?"

"When do you want to get married?" I asked, ignoring her question.

Rochel shrugged. "I don't know. Maybe in a year or two. Definitely before I'm twenty."

"Why before you're twenty?"

"Well, twenty's old, isn't it? I want to have kids by the time I'm twenty."

"What if you're not ready to get married before you're twenty?"

She shrugged again, as if the whole subject really wasn't that important. "Then I suppose I'll wait till Mummy and Daddy think I am."

I hated the way Rochel still called my parents Mummy and Daddy. I'd started calling them Mum and Dad when I was eight.

"What if they wanted you to marry a boy you didn't like, and you didn't want to marry him?"

"They wouldn't *make* me marry him. They'd find someone else."

"Wouldn't you want to pick the guy yourself?"

"No, not really."

"So you'd prefer that Mum and Dad pick him for you?"

"Yes. I trust their judgment."

"But you're the one who has to live with him."

"True, but they've been around longer. And they'd choose someone with my happiness in mind. They know me, right? So they'd choose someone who would suit me. It's only an introduction, Ditty. In the end, it would be my decision."

Rochel was so calm and accepting, I didn't know whether to pity or envy her.

Nineteen

Miss Moskowicz continued to pay me compliments almost every lesson, and it was clear that I'd become the new favorite. When I had trouble getting to sleep at night, I'd count Miss Moskowicz's compliments the way other people counted sheep. It was flattering, but it was stressful, too, because it meant that I had to push myself still harder in order to live up to her high expectations. And sometimes she praised me as a way of putting the other girls down.

"How long have you been dancing on pointe, Miss Cohen?" she asked one day, when we were in the middle of center work. It wasn't a genuine question because she knew the answer as well as I did.

"Six weeks," I murmured.

"You hear that, girls? Ditty has only been on pointe six

weeks, and look at those beautiful *échappées*. Look how well she lifts up out of her shoes."

Some of the girls struggled with the steps, forgot the sequence, or gave up too soon. Not me. I loved finding out what my body could do, how far I could push it, how much more I could progress each week.

Unlike the girls who complained that pointe work hurt their feet, I embraced it. It was a small taste of what it might be like to be a real ballerina, and each time I rose up onto my toes, I felt like I might actually touch the sky.

Miss Mitchell had been right the first time she saw me in class. I was built for ballet. It felt so right that it was hard to believe that Hashem didn't want me to do it.

Then one afternoon in Miss Mitchell's class, my foot fell in on itself after a series of *petit jetés* and I let out a small scream as I collapsed in a heap on the studio floor.

"Don't move," said Miss Mitchell, as she hurried over to assess the damage. She told Emma to demonstrate the next exercise and she helped me up and along the corridor to the office, where she asked Miss Johnson to ice my foot.

My ankle had begun to swell, but there was a strange numbness that had dulled the pain.

"Will you be okay, Ditty?"

I nodded, but I couldn't help wondering whether those few small jumps had caused real harm.

"Make sure you see a physical therapist as soon as possible. You'll probably have to stay off that foot for a while, but it can't be helped. It's always a mistake to work injured."

She went back to class then, and Miss Johnson handed me a glass of water.

"Is it bad?" she asked.

I didn't want her fussing over me. "I'm okay," I said.

Ten minutes later I was hobbling back down the corridor to get my schoolbag when the other dancers in my class spilled out of the studio and rushed over to see how my foot was.

"Ditty, how are you planning to get home?" Miss Mitchell asked me, close on their heels. "You usually take the tram, don't you?"

"Yes."

"Not on that foot, you don't. Come back into the office and ring your mother. See if she can come and pick you up. If not, I'll drive you home."

"I've got a mobile," I told her.

"Good. Well, let me have a word to your mother when she gets here."

I started to panic. "I ... don't think she'll be able to come. She'll be busy making dinner."

"But, Ditty, your foot! Look, I'll drive you home."

"No, I ... " I didn't want her to know my real address. I had given the office a fake one. "I'll be okay. My foot's not that bad. The tram stops right near my house."

In the end, we compromised. She insisted on driving me as far as the tram stop and I accepted, because by now my foot was beginning to throb.

Miss Mitchell's car was a small white Toyota, in pristine condition. Unlike our car, which was littered with empty packets of potato chips, lolly wrappers, and the discarded remains of stale bagels, this car was clean, crumb-free, and dust-free. No child had ever trailed greasy fingers on the dashboard, left a signature on the window when the car fogged up, or ground melted chocolate into the soft, cream leather seats.

Miss Mitchell turned on the radio to the classical channel and hummed along. In our car, no one would bother turning on the radio. There was always so much noise there'd be no point.

The ride in Miss Mitchell's car was over before I had a chance to really enjoy it.

"Ask your mother to give me a call, Ditty," she said, as she dropped me at the tram stop.

I told her that my mum might be too busy to call, and in a way that was true. She was busy. I suppose that's why I managed to get to the National at all.

Sometimes, I got the feeling that Miss Mitchell knew me better than my mother did. Right now she was watching me with a worried look on her face as I climbed slowly and carefully out of her car.

"Take care of that foot," she said. "I don't want to see you back in class till it's completely better."

My mother was cutting up an apple for Hillel when I walked into the kitchen and didn't look up, so she didn't notice I was limping.

Rochel did, though. "Ditty, what happened to your foot?"

"I'm not sure. I tripped."

Now my mother did look up. "Does it hurt?"

I nodded, and she could see I was biting my lip because of the pain.

"I think I need to see a physical therapist."

"A doctor, more like," she said. "It might be broken."

She took me to Dr. Herschel in Glenhuntly Road, whose office was always open until seven-thirty, and we waited about twenty minutes until I was called. My mum came in with me, and Dr. Herschel sat me down and examined my foot. It was still cold and damp from the ice pack.

"I see you've iced it already. Excellent!"

My mother shot me a puzzled glance. "When did you get a chance to ice it, Ditty?"

"Um … I was about halfway home from the Riskins when I tripped, so I stopped at Sara's to break the journey. Sara took care of it."

"You should have rung me, Ditty. That's why you've got a mobile. I don't like the thought of you walking on an injured foot. You could have made it worse. What if it was broken?" She turned to the doctor. "Could it be broken?"

"I doubt it," Dr. Herschel said, "though it's almost certainly sprained. But don't worry. There's an excellent physical therapist just down the road. He'll be able to treat it with ultrasound, and later with massage." He rang up to make sure I could get an appointment. Then he came back to check the swelling, which was starting to bruise.

After a while he removed the ice pack and wrapped my foot tightly in a bandage, telling me to ice it every hour.

"By the way, how exactly did you do this?" he asked.

I shrugged. "I was walking along the footpath, and I kind of … tripped."

"Walking?"

"Well, maybe I was running and jumping along the footpath."

"Ah!"

"Ditty doesn't walk, she bounces," said my mother.

"Well, no bouncing for a couple of weeks," said Dr. Herschel.

My mother insisted I take a two-week break from my "job" at the Riskins', so that I could stay at home and rest my foot. The two weeks seemed to last forever, and when at last my ankle had healed, I returned to the National with renewed dedication, more determined than ever to keep on dancing as long as I could.

Twenty

Once again, it was the Jewish New Year. Once again it was time for repentance. How quickly the weeks and months had flown.

Thinking over my actions of the preceding year, I realized that although I regretted breaking my promise to Hashem and deceiving my parents, I didn't actually believe that dancing was wrong. I knew there were some modern orthodox girls who danced. There might even have been some haredi girls who learnt ballet, too. There was nothing bad about dancing itself. It was just that in my community, it wasn't considered compatible with a haredi lifestyle. Still, the knowledge that I intended to maintain the deception made a mockery of the High Holidays and all that they stood for.

The day before Rosh Hashanah I rang Linda to wish her a Happy New Year. I didn't tell her how heavily she weighed on my conscience—she'd probably have laughed at me if I had—but she had told so many lies on my behalf. They were therefore my lies, lies for which I was responsible.

Since there was no point in praying for myself, I decided to pray for Linda instead. On Rosh Hashanah, I went to shule with my mother and sisters. I prayed for forgiveness, but as I mouthed the words, I knew my prayer was useless. How could Hashem forgive me if I didn't earn that forgiveness through doing teshuva? For the first time in my life, I left shule feeling worse than before I'd arrived.

A day or two before Yom Kippur, I was hanging out in the schoolyard with Sara. She'd been strangely quiet all day, and I was wondering what was up when she suddenly turned on me.

"It's gone too far, Ditty. You've got to stop."

"Stop what?"

"Learning ballet, lying to your parents … "

"I thought you were on my side," I exclaimed. "I thought you understood."

"I did. I do," said Sara. "It's just … I feel so bad. It's all my fault, you see."

"*Your* fault?"

"If I hadn't told you about my mother's TV, you would never have seen that ballet … you would never have known anything about ballet, you would never have started the lessons in the first place."

"I'm *glad* I did."

"It was all right at first," Sara continued. "I thought you'd take class for a month or so. You know, just to get it out of

your system. But you're still doing it, and it isn't a joke anymore. You act as if...as if ballet's your life."

"It *is* my life."

"You see? That's what I mean. It's taken over. You're ruin-
ing your life, Ditty. You've got to stop."

"Why?"

"What will happen if your parents find out?"

"What will happen if your mother finds out you watch
TV? What will happen if she finds out about those books
you read?"

"It's not the same."

"Isn't it?"

"*No.* I mean, I'm not saying I'm a saint or anything, but
it's not like my whole life is one big lie, Ditty. I'm not as bad
as..."

"Me?"

"I didn't say that."

"No, but you were going to."

We were silent for a while. I couldn't believe we were
arguing.

"I'm sorry," she said at last. "I don't want to fight."

"Neither do I."

"Still, I wish you'd quit ballet, or at least stop lying about
it."

"Will *you* stop lying to *your* mother?"

She squirmed and said nothing.

"Well, then. Neither will I."

"I'll pray for you, Ditty."

I didn't know whether to laugh or cry. Suddenly we were

playing Musical Prayers. I was praying for Linda, Sara was praying for me. Maybe if we all prayed for somebody else, somehow we'd all be forgiven.

I seriously doubted it, though, and by the time Yom Kippur arrived, I really didn't want to go to shule. But I knew I had to.

We ate dinner early, brushed our teeth, and walked to the small *shteibel* in Mayfield Street, a dilapidated old house where my father prayed at least twice a day on weekdays, and three times on weekends.

The shule was just as shabby inside as out. The only thing about it that was fairly new, and therefore looked somehow out of place, was the one-way glass dividing the women's section from the men's. It was intended to prevent the men from seeing the women and becoming distracted, but a thick, dark curtain covered the glass, as if no one quite trusted it to do its job.

The men's section was much larger than the women's, and had proper seating. The women's section was tiny, consisting of three meager rows of wooden benches.

Unlike men, women aren't required by Jewish law to pray with others, so most of the women in our community only attend services on major holidays and festivals, as well as weddings and bar-mitzvahs. I, too, had stopped going regularly once I turned twelve.

Even so, it was still so familiar to me. I knew every face, every nuance of the service, every prayer that was made, every song that was sung. I had always felt at home in shule, and I had good memories of it—sitting on my father's knee when I was still young enough to be allowed into the men's section, or crossing the room to talk to Mr. Klein, the lolly man, who sat in the front row across from my dad. If you went up to him and said, "Good Shabbos, Mr. Klein," he'd shake your hand and press a lolly into it. Hillel, Gittel, and Shayne still came home with pockets stuffed full of lollies every week.

No one would be eating lollies today. Not on Yom Kippur.

Extra chairs and benches had been brought into the women's section, and there were so many of us crowded into the tiny space we could hardly breathe. No one complained. All eyes were toward the curtain, everyone listening for the sound of the cantor's voice.

The first service was the Kol Nidre, which started with the words: *May all my vows be null and void...*

I had always thought this a strange way to begin the prayers on the holiest day of the Jewish year. Now, I understood.

A year had passed since I had vowed to give up ballet, and I had not kept my promises. The prayer suggested I wasn't alone. There must have been scores of vows that were never kept, countless promises that were thoughtlessly broken. By negating all our vows, promises, and resolutions for the year ahead even before we had made them, we would not be guilty of breaking them.

Besides, actions, not vows, were what counted.

That year, I did not make promises.

I looked around me at the other women and girls praying with *kavannah*, with intent, and a part of me envied them. They were apologizing for a whole range of sins they probably hadn't committed in the first place, whereas I could catalogue each lie I'd told, each rule I'd broken.

From my position at the end of the front row, I peeked around the curtain and through the one-way glass into the men's section. The men were rocking back and forth as they mumbled the prayers. Some of them had their eyes shut, and others were swaying so hard it looked as if they might fall over.

I found myself wondering what this scene would look like through Emma's eyes, through Miss Mitchell's eyes. To me, it had always seemed so normal, so comforting, so safe.

Now, it looked a little ridiculous. And I was starting to feel like I was an impostor, like I didn't belong.

There was a nostalgic part of me that longed to become again the little girl I used to be. There was something unbearably sad about knowing I couldn't.

Twenty-One

·◆·

My last ballet class of the year was over, and once again there were hugs and kisses and promises to stay in touch.

"Ditty," said Emma, "you've got to come to my place over the holidays."

I wasn't expecting the invitation, and I was about to turn it down. For one thing, I knew I could never invite her to my house in return. All my life I'd been told that Jews were different, that we could never mix, that there could be goyim living right next door but we'd still be worlds apart.

I'd never been inside the home of a non-Jew before. Actually, I'd never even been in the home of non-religious Jews. But I liked Emma. A lot. I could almost imagine being as close to her as I was to Sara.

"Go on, say you will," said Emma, when she saw me

hesitate. "I'll miss you too much if I have to wait eight weeks to see you."

That clinched it. I promised I'd go. And it made leaving the National for the summer just a little bit easier.

———

Once again, Sara and I ran a holiday program for the same girls as last year, plus a few more. It was the same week that Emma was away in Ocean Grove. She rang my mobile the day she got back, and I told her I'd visit the following week.

I tried to get Sara to come along. "You'd *like* her, Sara. She's really nice."

"I'm not saying she isn't. That's not the point, is it? She isn't Jewish, and it just wouldn't feel right. And Ditty, it's one thing being friends with her when you're learning ballet. But, I mean, going to her house!" She shook her head in disbelief. "Sometimes I wonder if you know what you're doing."

Sometimes I wondered the same thing. Still, my heart sank when she said she wouldn't come. I had broken the rules again and again, and Sara had always been my ally. I'd always assumed that when I mustered up the courage to venture outside the haredi world, I could take Sara with me.

Now I knew that I couldn't.

———

I was nervous the whole way there, though I couldn't say exactly why. I mean, what was I expecting? Swastikas on the walls? Statues of Jesus Christ or the Virgin Mary in the living room? The smell of pork roasting in the kitchen? (Not that I knew what pork smelt like, but if it did happen to be cooking, would smelling it somehow be the equivalent of eating it? Would it make my body *treif*?)

Emma lived in St. Kilda, not far from the National, in a semi-detached Victorian house painted terracotta. It was one of a row of similar houses all in different colors. I rang the bell and a minute later the door was flung open and Emma stood there, grinning.

"I'm *so* glad you're here."

Emma was tanned all over, her blonde hair long and loose, her face glowing. She was wearing a pair of pale blue shorts and a crimson top with shoestring straps, and her feet were bare. I was dressed in a calf-length skirt and a high-necked shirt. My dark hair was pulled back into a ponytail, and only my face and hands and lower arms were tanned.

What would it be like if I could click my fingers and change places with Emma? Would I dare?

"Come on in," said Emma.

I hesitated, then out of habit I pressed my fingers to my lips and reached up to kiss the mezuzah on the doorpost, only to discover there was no mezuzah there. Of course, why would there be?

I followed Emma inside. No one else was home, and the house was quiet and empty. It was a bit smaller than my house, but seemed bigger because only four people lived in it.

I took a long look around. There were no silver candlesticks on display and no books of Torah in the living room, but other than that it was just like—well, an ordinary house, I suppose. There were no crosses on the walls, no pictures of Jesus or Mary, nothing religious-looking at all.

"I thought you were a Christian," I said.

"I am. But I'm not religious. I don't go to church or anything."

"Ever?"

Emma shrugged. "Well, sometimes on Christmas. Come see my room."

Her room was pale pink and full of trophies. There were at least two whole shelves full of them, in different shapes and sizes.

"Wow! Where did these come from? Did you win them?"

"Uh-huh."

"Where?"

"Different places. Eisteddfods, mostly. I compete in ... oh, about three or four eisteddfods a year."

"And you always win?"

"No, not always." Her smile was somehow both confident and shy. "But often I do."

I picked up a statue of a slim figure, a dancer in a tutu standing on her toes. "What's this one for?"

"That was just last year. It was for the Open Classical."

"How about this one?" The trophy I was holding now was the biggest in the room, and it was really heavy. It must have been made of metal. It was a large, two-handled cup, and the words *Adjudicator's Choice* were printed at the bottom of the stand.

"That's supposed to go to the dancer with the most potential," said Emma, "but it's pretty subjective."

I was even more in awe of Emma than I had been before. "Wow!" I said again. "I wish I had your talent."

"You do," she said emphatically. "The only difference between you and me is that I've been dancing since I was three years old."

"How old were you when you did your first eisteddfod?"

"Four and a half. I competed in the Under Sevens."

"That's amazing. I would love to have done that."

"You still can," she said.

"No, I can't. I'm not four and a half anymore."

Emma laughed. "No, but you're not exactly ancient. Look, you can't change your past, Ditty, but you've still got your future."

"I hope you're right," I told her, "but it's not as simple for me as it is for you."

"Why not?"

Suddenly, I found myself wanting to tell her. I sat down on the end of her bed and for the first time ever, explained what it meant to be a haredi Jew, what the lifestyle entailed, and how our lives were dictated almost entirely by what was written in the Torah.

Emma listened incredulously. "God, that's so full-on," she said. "I'm not sure I get it, though. There's a Jewish girl in my year at school, and she doesn't seem to keep those rules."

"Most Jews aren't haredi," I explained. "But as far as my dad is concerned, there are only two types of Jews—good Jews and bad ones."

"And the haredi Jews are the good ones?"

"Exactly."

"What if you decide you don't want to be Jewish?"

"If you're born Jewish, then you're Jewish. You don't get to choose."

"Says who?"

"Says the Torah."

"But what if you don't believe in the Torah?"

"It's still the Torah that decides."

Emma was so easy to confide in. I swore her to secrecy and told her that four times a week my parents thought I was babysitting, and didn't know I danced.

"What would happen if they ever found out?"

"I don't know, Em. I'm too scared to think about it." And it was true. I had butterflies in my stomach just from having this conversation.

"I can't even imagine that," said Emma. "My parents have always been so proud of my dancing, I always took it for granted. I guess I never realized how lucky I am..."

For a moment we were silent, and I searched around for a lighter subject.

"Gorgeous earrings, Em," I said, admiring her simple gold loops with warm green stones.

"Try them on," said Emma, already starting to take one off.

"I can't," I said. "My ears aren't pierced."

"Oh, then try the bracelet that goes with it. They're a set."

She opened a jewelry box, the kind that plays music and has a ballerina spinning on the top when you turn the key.

"Here it is," said Emma, but my attention had been

caught by a thin silver chain with a tiny cross on the end of it. A shiver went through me.

"Try it," said Emma, fastening the bracelet around my wrist.

"It's beautiful," I murmured. Then I slipped it off and handed it back. I was still staring at the cross, not daring to imagine how my parents might react if they so much as suspected me of having a Christian friend.

Emma was saying something, but I barely heard. I followed her into the kitchen and she offered me crackers and cheese, and I told her I couldn't eat them because they weren't kosher.

"What's 'kosher,' exactly?"

I opened my mouth to answer her, but realized there was nothing I could say that would sound logical. "I can't explain it, Em."

Emma gave a theatrical sigh. "Never mind, Ditty. What *can* you eat?"

"I wouldn't mind an apple," I said, eyeing the fruit bowl on the bench.

She threw me one and I grinned as I cupped it in my hands.

"A perfect catch," said Emma, grinning back.

Twenty-Two

———◆———

At Beis Hannah, the days were already dragging, even though it was only the second week of the new school year. I sat in class and did the work assigned, but my mind would drift off and I'd stare out the window, practicing dance steps in my head. Mostly, I just waited for the day to end, counting the hours until it was time for ballet.

When I entered the National, my body felt light with a sense of relief, a sense of freedom. After ten minutes of barre work, stretching my legs and feet in familiar patterns, hands positioned lightly on the timeworn wood, it felt as if I had never left.

"Good for you, Ditty," Miss Mitchell said. "I'm glad to see you've remembered everything you learnt last year."

Of course I'd remembered.

Turn out from the hip joint, not the foot.

Make sure your knee is over your foot in a plié.
Keep your weight over the supporting leg when you balance.
Don't lift your shoulders.
Spot when you turn.

You could hurt yourself if you worked incorrectly, but there were no threats of punishment, no dire predictions. If you got it wrong, no one made you feel guilty, or worthless, or afraid. The rules were there to help you, and if you managed to follow them, the reward would be instant—you'd be able to dance.

It was simple. Rules were something I knew all about, but here there were no pangs of conscience, no mental anguish. There was nothing that could not be understood or demonstrated or proven. The rules made sense. They were rules I could keep.

In second term, the school curriculum was much the same as it was before, with one exception. Sports (and that included gymnastics, the one subject I really liked) had been replaced with community service, which meant that once a week we'd leave school at lunchtime to go and visit the residents of the Jewish nursing home around the corner.

Every Tuesday afternoon I'd find myself sitting beside old Mrs. Hoffshtetter's bed, listening to her dry, rasping voice informing me of the latest developments in her medical history while I did my best to nod and smile at appropriate times. I had this theory that if I did my share of mitzvos, maybe my family wouldn't disown me when they found out what I was really like. Also, it was a kind of penance. Maybe, at the end of the day, my good deeds would outweigh my bad ones.

Besides, it helped me put things in perspective. I mean, there's nothing like an old-age home full of people who lost entire families in the Holocaust to make your own problems seem trivial.

My own grandparents, Buba and Zaida Fineberg, had lived through the Holocaust, but it was something they never talked about. Buba died from cancer when I was eight, and Zaida died of a heart attack two years later. My other grandparents, Grandma and Grandpa Cohen, died in a car crash when I was six, so I'd never had a lot to do with old people.

"You can only beat Hitler by defying him," Mrs. Hoffshtetter said during one of my visits. "By surviving him despite the odds. By bringing more Jewish children into the world."

I'd heard this argument before—live as a Jew to avenge the deaths of our fellow Jews. But suddenly that seemed like the worst of all reasons to live as a Jew. If anything, it made me resent my Jewishness. Why should my future depend on the past?

But then, Judaism is all about the past. Our prayers are full of yearning for times long gone. We were supposed to long for the past, just as we were supposed to long for the future, for the Messiah, for the World to Come.

It was a strange way to live, and at that moment I knew that I didn't want to get to Mrs. Hoffshtetter's age and find

out that my life had been shaped by those no longer alive—
by the fact of their suffering.

As I walked back to school, I was quiet, thinking about
the Jews who had survived the Holocaust. Then I thought
of the six million who didn't and suddenly my feet felt
heavy, and every step became an effort. I felt like I was suffocating, even though the stale air of the old-age home was
already behind me.

The other girls in my class were laughing and chatting
and didn't seem to notice my darker mood. Esther Malka
Gordon and Leah Kaplan started a tedious discussion about
the finer points of *kashrus*.

"Did you know," Leah said, grabbing my arm and
attempting to involve me in the conversation, "that you
should really have separate salt shakers for milk and meat?"

"Why?" I asked. No point telling her I couldn't care less.

"Because you shake it over hot food. The steam rises,
you see, and gets into the salt."

The rest of the girls were following the discussion with
genuine interest, and it occurred to me, not for the first time,
that we didn't have much in common anymore. I couldn't
share my life with them. I couldn't share my *self* with them.
They didn't know who I really was because I couldn't tell
them.

I looked around for Sara and linked my arm through
hers. She'd heard the discussion and was trying to suppress
an irreverent giggle, and I could see she knew exactly what
I was thinking. I sent up a silent prayer of thanks for Sara,
the one friend who made school life bearable.

"What is the halacha regarding head-covering?" Mrs. Teitlebaum asked.

"You have to cover your head as soon as you're married," said Leah, "but you're allowed to show a *tefach* of hair."

"And how much is a tefach?"

"About two centimeters. Not very much."

"Exactly. Which is why it's best to show none at all."

Her eyes scanned the classroom for anyone who wasn't listening.

"And when and where do you have to cover it?" she asked. "Esther Malka, it's been a while since I've heard from you."

"Strictly speaking, only in the market place."

"And what is meant by 'the market place'?"

"Any place other than your own home."

"Does that mean you can leave your head uncovered any time just as long as you're at home?"

"No. It has to be covered whenever there are men around. And it's better to keep it covered all the time. You never know who might come to the door."

Mrs. Teitlebaum nodded, satisfied. "A married woman's hair represents her modesty," she continued. "How do we know this? Well, the Talmud tells the story of Kimchit, who was so modest that the walls of her house never saw her uncovered hair. Because of that modesty, all seven of her sons grew up to be *kohanim gedolim*... What's so funny, Sara Kesten?"

"Nothing. It's just... walls can't see."

Mrs. Teitlebaum glared at her. "Perhaps not," she said. "But Hashem can. Hashem sees everything. Including you. He sees you every minute of every day. And He knows exactly when you're being disrespectful. So I'd wipe that grin off my face if I were you."

———

That night, after my shower, I balanced on the edge of the bathtub, craning my neck to look at my reflection. I had never seen the whole of my body naked before, and I was curious. Mirrors did not encourage modesty, and there wasn't a single full-length mirror in our house.

The bathroom mirror started above the sink, halfway up the tiled wall. It was so small that even from here, perched at a distance, I couldn't see my entire body. And the angle was wrong. I couldn't get a frontal view.

I wasn't sure I liked what I saw. I wasn't used to seeing this much skin. And I was embarrassed by the curling tendrils of pubic hair, and the gentle slope of breasts above my rib cage. But I liked the smallness of my waist, the way my body curved down to my hips, and the slimness of my thighs.

"Ditty, are you still in there?"

The voice was Ezra's.

"Nearly finished." I stepped down off the bathtub and onto the bathmat on the floor.

The bathroom door was locked and there was no one around, but I had a horrible feeling I was being watched. And I remembered what Mrs. Teitlebaum had said. *Hashem sees everything. Including you. He sees you every minute of every day.*

I shuddered, filled with a sudden sense of shame.

Twenty-Three

It happened so fast. One day Rochel went out on a date with Zvi Aaronson. Three weeks later, she was engaged to be married. Had it really been over a year since I'd overheard Reb Saunders talking to my father? I was fourteen and a half now, and Rochel's wedding was scheduled to take place in six weeks time.

Rochel would be turning eighteen one week before the wedding. Zvi was nearly twenty. He was planning to help out in his father's shop and spend at least half of every day at the kollel, and Rochel would work, also in the shop, until she had babies.

Rochel was amazingly serene. Now that she was engaged, she had marriage lessons with a *rebbetzin*. She learnt about the laws of *nida* and *mikve*, the details of family purity, and about how to keep *shalom bayis*, peace in the home. During this time, she hardly ever saw her fiancé, but spoke to him daily on the phone.

"Rochel, aren't you scared?" I asked her.

"Scared? No. Why should I be?"

"You hardly know him."

"I'll get to know him."

"But..."

"He seems wonderful," she said, dreamily.

What if he's not, though? I wanted to ask. *What if he's not wonderful? What if he's not the person you think he is?*

A week before the big day, the Aaronsons came for Shabbos lunch. They had nine children, but three were already married and one was away studying at a *yeshiva* in Israel, so there would be seven of them altogether, as well as us. I counted out sixteen knives and forks.

"How many children do you want?" Shayne asked Rochel while we set the table.

"As many as Hashem will give me," said Rochel. "As many as Hashem decides."

My mother looked up from the napkins she was folding and smiled at Rochel approvingly. "It took me almost two years to get pregnant the first time," she said. "You don't know, until you try, just how awful it is when you don't immediately conceive. I was distraught when it didn't happen straight away. I was just desperate to have children."

I wasn't sure why my mother was so desperate to have

kids. I mean, I knew we were supposed to want them. And the stories in the Torah make you think there's no worse a fate than being barren, and maybe there isn't. But I could see how hard my mother worked. The shopping, the cooking, the laundry, the housework—it never ended. It seemed to me that any fun would stop the minute you had children.

"Do you think everyone feels like you did?" I asked my mother. "Or do you think some women might not want children?"

"Not want children?" My mother was shocked at the question. "Don't be silly, Ditty. All women want children."

I remembered how proud my cousin Shoshi was when we found out she was pregnant soon after her wedding. And suddenly it struck me that in haredi circles, the number of children women had was almost like a status symbol. As if there was nothing else a woman could do that would be worthwhile.

————————

All during lunch there was a noisy clatter of dishes around me, vying with the chatter of raised voices. It all sounded so pointless, so inane. I owed it to Rochel to muster up some enthusiasm, but I just couldn't get excited about the idea of my sister marrying a boy she hardly knew.

Suddenly I didn't want to be there anymore. I was desperate to get away. I thought of my friends at the National who danced on Shabbos, and wished I too could be practicing pirouettes or *grand jetés* in the studio, instead of sitting at home.

Rochel was married on a Tuesday, which is supposed to be lucky. She sat on a throne-like chair woven with flowers and the women came up to kiss her and wish her mazeltov. The men were in another room with Zvi, sorting out the details of the wedding contract. Eventually, they led Zvi in to check that the bride was indeed Rochel, and after that the ceremony began.

Rochel looked pale, because she'd been fasting, but beautiful. She was wearing a high-necked, lacy dress that was covered in tiny white pearls, and a veil to match. She had a sheitel on under her veil, because as soon as the ceremony was over she would be a married woman. She would never show her hair in public again.

After Zvi smashed the glass and everyone shouted "Mazeltov," the women and girls went into one large room and the men and boys into another. We danced a *hora* round the bride, while the noise of the men singing and dancing drifted through the open windows. Four women lifted Rochel's chair so high her head almost touched the ceiling. The chair tilted precariously and Rochel clung onto it, laughing, managing, even now, to look happy and serene.

I was standing with Shayne and Linda, watching her, when Aunt Rivka came up and complimented all three of us on our outfits. Linda was dressed in a stunning green, and for this one occasion my mum had indulged my desire for brighter colors. Red was out of the question, of course, but she had agreed to let Shayne and me wear a muted purple.

Our dresses were no less modest than usual, but the cut was smarter, the material richer.

"You all look lovely," Aunt Rivka said. Then she looked at me approvingly and said, "Ditty, you've developed such beautiful posture."

I'd been quite proud of my graceful posture, but now I slouched immediately, before my treachery was somehow discovered. For the first time in years, I was thankful for the modest clothes I had to wear, and the way they hid my developing muscles.

———————

The next morning I slept in, and when I got up the house was quieter than usual. Shayne and the boys were still asleep, and my father had already gone to work.

My mum must have been up very early, because she had washed the shirts the boys wore to the wedding and was already ironing them. She had the ironing board set up in the living room; you couldn't squeeze a thimble, let alone an ironing board, into our tiny, overcrowded laundry.

Gittel, still in her pajamas, was sitting on the floor with an assortment of dog-eared picture books spread out around her. They had once been Rochel's, then mine, and then Shayne's. They were Jewish books for Jewish children, with titles like *Malka does a Mitzvah*, *Devorah likes to Daven*, and *Bruriah makes a Bracha*. Had I ever liked those books, I wondered?

Classical music was playing softly in the background and my mum was humming along. She turned the volume up a notch, and Gittel got up and started to dance. I sat down with a bowl of cereal in my lap and watched her. There was something so carefree and happy about the way she danced that I felt a pang of envy.

My mother looked at Gittel and laughed, and she sounded so nostalgic as she said, "Oh, Ditty. She reminds me of you at that age. You were such an adorable child. You were the most active baby I've ever seen. You climbed out of your crib when you were just six months old. I lowered the base, but it didn't help. You still managed to climb out of it. Nothing would stop you."

My mother smiled at the memory. "One night," she told me, "when you were about one and a half years old, you disappeared. We looked all over the house for you, but we couldn't find you anywhere. Finally, we thought we'd better look outside, and that's where we found you. You were standing in the middle of the garden, dancing in the dark…" Her voice trailed off and I swallowed hard, not trusting myself to say a word because I was afraid I might cry.

I haven't changed, I wanted to say. *That was the real me.* Suddenly I felt a sharp pang of loneliness because the people I loved, the people who had raised and nurtured me, didn't have a clue who I really was. And although my whole life had somehow become an elaborate plot to deceive them, there was a part of me that resented the fact that they could be deceived.

There were tears in my eyes, but my mother was busy with the ironing and she hadn't noticed.

She was still chuckling at her memories. "You laughed when you saw us...you were having a wonderful time."

I tried to imagine it—the innocence, the feel of night, the absolute freedom.

I finished my cereal and told my mum I was going to Sara's, and that, at least, was true. I waved goodbye to Gittel and she blew me a kiss. And I no longer envied her, because I knew that one day she'd grow up too.

Twenty-Four

At three o'clock on a Tuesday, two weeks after Rochel's wedding, I was scheduled to do my first ballet exam—the RAD Intermediate. Luckily, Tuesday was the day we all left Beis Hannah at lunchtime to pay a visit to the nursing home, so at least I wouldn't be missed at school.

On the last Sunday before the exam, I went to see Mrs. Hoffshtetter so that she wouldn't miss out on her weekly visit, and when Tuesday arrived, I left school ten minutes earlier than the other girls. With any luck, they'd assume I was already sitting by Mrs. Hoffshtetter's bed. I was hoping and praying that no one would check. Only Sara knew the truth, and she had promised to cover for me if she had to.

I tried to ignore the fear that knotted my insides as I took the train to Flinders Street, then walked to an unfamiliar studio in Southbank, clutching a piece of paper with the address written on it. I kept checking and re-checking that piece of paper, even though I already knew the address by heart.

Miss Mitchell had explained that I would be examined with one other girl, about the same age and height, who attended a different dance school. I saw the girl arriving when I did. She was dropped off outside the studio by a blonde woman who got out of the car, hugged her, wished her luck, and drove off, promising to come back to collect her.

The girl smiled at me and introduced herself, and we walked into the building together. After that we didn't talk much, just concentrated on warming up.

It wasn't long before we were called, and we ran into the studio and took our places at the barre.

At first I was so nervous I thought I might throw up. But once the music started, my nerves began to melt away. There was comfort in the familiarity of the classical pieces, and in the repetition of exercises I'd done over and over and over again.

The examiner, an elderly lady called Mrs. Peters, smiled as she watched us, but turned serious every time she looked down at the paper on her lap and scribbled a comment.

Miss Mitchell had coached me so well that my body seemed to know just what to do. The movements flowed out of me, fluid and smooth. About halfway through the exam, I realized how much I was enjoying it.

Then it was over. So soon. We were already doing our final curtsy.

———

The day after the exam I was allowed to move up to Advanced 1, even though I wouldn't know my results for at least a month.

"How did it go?" asked Emma, who'd done the exam the week before.

"Okay, I think."

"Just okay?" She gave me a hug. "I bet you were brilliant."

In open class, the work got harder. We'd been doing triple *pirouettes* for a while now, but after the exam we tried them on pointe. For the first few lessons I stuck to doubles. Then one day I managed a perfect triple.

"Ditty," said Miss Mitchell, "did I just see what I think I saw?"

"It was a fluke," I told her.

"There's no such thing as a fluke." To prove her point, she made me do it over and over, but I knew she was watching and kept messing it up.

"It's only because you're not pulling up enough on your supporting leg," she said. "Try it again, Ditty. Don't throw it away in the middle."

So I tried. Again, and again. Finally I managed to do three triple *pirouettes* in a row. The other girls applauded and I couldn't stop smiling. Neither could Miss Mitchell. She caught up with me at the end of the lesson, just as I was leaving the studio.

"Well done," she said. "And, Ditty?"

"Yes?"

"I think it's time you started learning contemporary."

"When's the class?"

"Wednesday, straight after classical. It's only an hour. Do you think you can make it?"

I nodded. It would be easy enough to tell my mum that Adele Riskin had started working later on Wednesdays.

"Good. And there's another thing I've been meaning to ask you. Do you think you might be able to come to class on Saturdays?"

The question gave me a jolt. I'd told her before why I couldn't.

"I know it's your Sabbath," she continued, "and I respect that, but I'm not asking you to give up the entire day. All I'm suggesting is that you do one technique class and one production class. It's time you started performing."

"But...what if...what if I can't?"

She shook her head regretfully. "That would be a real shame, Ditty. You've got such talent, such potential. But ballet is tough, really tough, and if you want to get anywhere in dance you can't afford to take Saturdays off. And if you do end up dancing professionally, you won't have a choice."

Was that a real possibility?

"Do you think I *could* become a professional dancer?"

"I don't see why not. You've got everything going for you—the right build, the brains, the talent. And you work hard. You've made enormous progress. But if you want the chance, you've got to give it your best shot. And that means getting performance practice and coming to class whenever you can, including Saturdays. At least think about it, Ditty. Talk to your parents. You never know, maybe they'll let you."

The idea of my parents "letting" me was so ludicrous I almost laughed.

————————

That Friday night, Rochel and Zvi came for dinner, and I had to admit that Rochel was glowing. She and Zvi sat as close together as they could without actually touching, and when they were physically separated by more than a meter, they kept sneaking sickeningly love-struck glances at each other.

I guess when they decided to get married, they just made up their minds to love each other. Maybe it was as simple as that.

After my father made *Kiddush*, we all filed out of the dining room for the ritual washing of hands, and when we were seated at the table again, he made the bracha over bread, tore the challah into pieces with his hands, and passed it around the table. He was still chewing when he turned to Zvi, launching straight into the subject of Torah as he usually did.

"So, Zvi," he began, "what was the most interesting passage of Talmud you learnt this week?"

Zvi thought for a moment before answering. "We had a shiur about conflicting values."

My father nodded and waited for Zvi to continue.

"For instance," Zvi said, his voice quietly confident, "*emes*, truth, is a very important value, so important that our whole belief system is based on it. Yet our Torah of truth tells us that there are other, competing values, which are just as important, or maybe even more important, than truth itself.

For instance, the Talmud clearly states that if a woman has bought a new dress and asks her husband if he likes it, not only is he *allowed* to lie and say he likes it, even if he doesn't, he *must* lie. Why? Because shalom bayis, peace in the home, is an overriding value, more important even than truth."

I turned Zvi's words over and over in my mind, letting their full weight sink in. If peace in the home was more important than truth, I might finally have found a way to ease my conscience. If truth was not the ultimate value, maybe it was okay to lie.

———

Long after Rochel and Zvi had left, I lay awake, wondering if the lies I'd told had been morally necessary, or at least morally defensible. The arguments went round and round inside my head, until I finally turned my thoughts to Miss Mitchell's suggestion that I come to class on Saturdays.

I had thought about it quite a lot. In fact, I had to admit this wasn't the first time the idea of going to class on Shabbos had crossed my mind. But it would mean traveling on Shabbos, dressing inappropriately on Shabbos, engaging in an unsuitable activity on Shabbos. Could I really be contemplating such a serious sin?

Apparently, I could. I'd even worked out the logistics of it.

The truth was, it wouldn't be all that difficult. I was only expected to go to shule on major holidays and festivals. On a regular Shabbos, I was free in the morning, and since my bat-mitzvah, I had mostly slept in or gone to Sara's. Even if I went to shule, it didn't have to be the shule my father and brothers went to. No one would expect me there, so no one would comment on my absence. If I went to the National instead, who would know?

I could leave home at nine in the morning, dance from nine-thirty till twelve-thirty, no questions asked. It was a fairly safe bet I could get away with it, just as long as I was home by one, in time for lunch.

I knew I'd never become a dancer unless I took ballet seriously. *Really* seriously. But how could I? How could I even think about going to class on Shabbos? I would be crossing a line, invisible but nonetheless definitive. I would no longer be, in any sense of the word, an orthodox Jew.

Twenty-Five

• ◆ •

When I woke up, the sky was a brilliant blue. It was early spring, cold but sunny. Almost as soon as I opened my eyes I found myself thinking that I *might* go to ballet, even though it was Shabbos.

I hadn't made a definite decision, but I'd left my shoes in the changing room after my last class, just in case. Carrying anything in a public area on Shabbos was not permitted, so there was no way I could leave the house holding a bag.

While Shayne was still asleep and Gittel was already having breakfast in the kitchen, I wriggled into my regulation navy leotard and skin-colored tights. Then I slipped my Shabbos dress over the top and put on my knee-high boots.

In the kitchen, my mother was slicing cake for Hillel

and Gittel, the honey cake I'd baked on Thursday after I came home from ballet. She looked up as I came in and asked me if I wanted some. I shook my head and helped myself to a glass of milk, a cracker, and a piece of cheese instead. I mumbled a bracha without thinking twice about it, and then I told her I was going out.

"Have a nice time at shule," she said as I was leaving.

Luckily, our street was deserted. Instead of turning right toward our shule, I turned left and walked up Gordon Street toward the tram stop on Glenhuntly Road.

The main road was already quite busy. There was a fair bit of traffic and most of the shops were already open. Cafés were filling up with couples having breakfast, and there were people in tracksuits walking or jogging along the footpath.

My heart was racing and I wasn't sure whether I'd be able to bring myself to get on the tram. It wasn't too late to turn around and go back home.

I thought about doing just that. I thought about it as I crossed the road to the tram stop. I thought about it as the tram ground to a noisy halt beside me. I thought about it as I climbed on board. I hunkered down in the nearest seat and did not look at anyone. This was the first time I had ever been on a tram on the holiest day of the Jewish week, and it was a *chillul Shabbos,* a desecration of the Sabbath.

I was the lowest of the low. I should have been in shule by now, praying for world peace and the salvation of my wayward soul. Instead, I was riding a tram down Brighton Road, praying that no ticket inspector would ride the 67 route that day. I was all too aware of the inherent contradiction in the fact that I had not paid for a ticket because it was forbidden to handle money on Shabbos.

———

Miss Mitchell said she was really glad I'd decided to come. "I had a feeling you would. I knew your parents would let you in the end."

I spent the next few days in an agony of paranoia. What if someone had seen me getting on the tram, or getting off again? What if my parents discovered the truth? Or worse, what if I had gone too far this time and angered Hashem?

I was sure He understood my need to dance. I wasn't so sure that He accepted my need to desecrate Shabbos or to deceive my parents on the one day of the week when my behavior really should have been above reproach.

I could still remember when Linda told me she'd turned on the lights on Shabbos. I had been so shocked. Keeping Shabbos was one of the most important tenets of Judaism. I couldn't pretend that it didn't matter, that it wasn't important. But all Linda had done was turn on the lights. That seemed like such a little thing compared to what I had done.

———

About a month later, Miss Mitchell came into class beaming and carrying six large, tan-colored envelopes, which she handed out to the four girls and two boys who had done their exam.

"You all did exceptionally well," she said. "No one got below seventy, and there were a couple of very high distinctions—Emma with ninety-seven and Ditty with ninety-six. That's fabulous, girls. You two in particular should feel extremely proud. Especially you, Ditty. Ninety-six is excellent for anyone, but for someone who's been taking ballet for just over two years, it's really outstanding."

The news spread faster than I'd have thought possible, and by the end of the lesson everyone at the National knew my mark. I soon lost count of how many times my cheeks were kissed, my back slapped, and my palms high-fived, but this first official success was marred by the fact that I couldn't share it with my family.

———

Meanwhile, I had bought myself a ten-trip Met card, and kept on going to ballet on Shabbos.

It got a bit easier each time. There was a tug of guilt the moment I first stepped on the tram, but once I arrived at the National, the world outside just disappeared. That was the thing about dance. It filled me so that there was no space left for doubt or fear.

The National had become my refuge. There was no conflict there between who I was and who I was expected to be. If anything, I was admired or envied. And it was a relief to finally do exactly what was asked of me, and do it well.

Twenty-Six

·—◆—·

Now that I came to production class on Saturdays, I was given a small part in the end-of-year concert, a ballet of *Red Hiding Hood*. I was to be one of the dandelions that Red Riding Hood passes in the forest on the way to her grandmother's. There were twelve of us, all wearing short, lemon-yellow sleeveless dresses made of some kind of transparent material, wispy and ethereal.

As the day of the show grew closer, I became impatient. It was the first time I would ever dance on stage. The first performance was scheduled for a Friday night, and I told my parents that I was going to Sara's for Shabbos dinner and would be sleeping over. In reality, I'd arranged to stay at Emma's.

I spent the last few days before the performance in a

too-familiar state of fear. What if my mum bumped into Mrs. Kesten and said something about my sleeping over?

"Does she usually bump into her?" Linda asked me, when I rang her in a panic.

"No. Mrs. Kesten's always working. Even on Sundays."

"How important is this performance?"

"Really, really important," I said.

"Well then," said Linda, "you'll just have to take your chances."

———

Red Riding Hood was completely sold out, even before the show had opened.

On the night of the first performance, I stood warmed up and waiting, backstage. The audience were still shuffling to their seats, calling out across the theater to people they knew. Some of the dancers sneaked glances around the edge of the curtain, trying to catch a glimpse of their families and friends. No one I knew would be there that night, but Sara was coming on Sunday to watch me, as was Linda with her current boyfriend, Mark, whom I'd met at Linda's house the week before.

The large theater was packed to bursting, and for a second I could hardly breathe. But then the music started, and the next thing I knew I was out there on the stage. I didn't even have to think about the steps; my body just took over. I floated through my dance in a kind of ecstasy.

This was what it must be like to fly.

That was all it took. Just one performance and I was hooked. During the finale, when the entire school was on stage and we were taking our bows, the applause was thunderous.

"You were lovely, all of you," said Miss Mitchell when she came backstage. "And Ditty, you looked wonderful out there. I bet no one guessed it was your first time in front of an audience."

The atmosphere among the dancers was charged with excitement. It was hard to believe that I was actually part of this wonderful show, and it didn't seem to matter then that none of my family or friends were there to see me. I couldn't wait to repeat the performance the following day.

But later that night, as I lay on a mattress on the floor in Emma's room, I pictured my parents, and tears of self-pity stung my tired eyes. Why was I made to feel ashamed of something the other girls in my dance class could be proud of? How come they got to show off the very thing I had to hide?

———

On Sunday, before the final performance began, I peeped around the edge of the curtain at the audience. Sara was there, together with Linda and a boy I didn't recognize. They were sitting just right of center, about ten rows from the front.

Suddenly I felt unnaturally shy. It was one thing performing in front of strangers, but it was different knowing that there were people who had come especially for me.

My nerves kicked in, but they were good nerves.

Sara, Linda, and the boy who wasn't Mark were waiting for me outside the stage door when I finally came out, dressed in my street clothes, make-up removed.

Linda and Sara flung their arms around me and showered me with praise.

"I'm so glad you guys could come," I said.

"Ditty, meet my boyfriend, Gordon," said Linda.

I said hello and smiled dutifully, wondering what had happened to Mark.

———————

Two days later, the high I'd been on was starting to wear off, but everyone at the National was in good spirits, and Miss Mitchell was more relaxed than I'd seen her in ages.

"What did your parents think of the show?" she asked me. "What did they think of your dancing?"

"Oh, they ... didn't see it," I admitted.

"What do you mean? Weren't they in the audience?"

I shook my head. "No, they ... they had too much to do over the weekend. They couldn't come."

"That's a real shame, Ditty. They would have been proud."

"They're just really busy people," I said, suddenly wanting to defend them.

"Well, let's hope they make it next time."

Twenty-Seven

⬥

That summer, Sara and I ran our usual holiday program for Beis Hannah girls, only this year we ran it over two weeks, and earned double the money. I needed the cash to pay for the extra dance classes I'd taken on, but I was glad when the two weeks were over. I wasn't sure I deserved the job, and I felt hypocritical each time I had to lead the girls in prayer, or in Grace After Meals.

For the rest of the holidays I hung out with Sara and looked after Hillel and Gittel, reading them Bible stories or taking them to Harlston Park, where we climbed on the monkey bars and took turns on the slide.

Sometimes I went out with Linda. Ever since seeing *Billy Elliot*, we'd been going to the movies together every few months, but we never went to the Classic again. Instead, we went to the Jam Factory, where there was no way I'd bump into someone I knew.

In between trips to the movies, Linda lent me DVDs, so Sara and I spent a lot of time in Mrs. Kesten's bedroom.

When Emma came back from Ocean Grove, she sent me a text message: *Call me. E.*

I took my phone into the garden and rang her. She was full of stories of people she'd met and dates she'd been on.

"When can I see you, Ditty? Let's meet up at Luna Park."

I lowered my voice so I wouldn't be heard. "I'd love to, but I can't." Blonde, blue-eyed Emma was so obviously not Jewish I just couldn't risk it. Luna Park was too open. Too public. Especially during the summer holidays, when haredi families might be there.

"Well, how about a movie?"

We met at the Village Cinemas ticket box inside the Jam Factory and bought tickets to a romantic comedy, and after the film had finished we took a tram, then walked to Emma's house. I'd been back there a few times since my first visit the summer before, so it no longer felt strange.

We were both ravenous by the time we arrived. Emma offered me a sandwich, as she always did, and I declined, as I always did. The offer of food she knew I'd refuse had become part ritual, part joke.

"Have some fruit, then," Emma said.

The fruit bowl was overflowing. I took an apricot and a too-sour plum, but it wasn't enough. I hadn't eaten for hours. I murmured the bracha for fruit and took a bite. A spurt of apricot juice trickled down my chin as I watched

Emma eating crusty bread with avocado, sliced tomato, and cheddar cheese. I knew I could have another two, three, or even four pieces of fruit if I wanted them—Emma wouldn't mind—but I began to wonder what would happen if I ate a sandwich.

I remembered Linda once saying, in that cynical way of hers, that religion was made to control us. That had been nearly three years ago, when I was only twelve, but I could hear her voice in my head as clearly as if it were only yesterday. *Don't you realize it's all a kind of conspiracy, a kind of trick?*

Was she right? Was it worth the risk of finding out? I was as curious as I was hungry. "What's in the bread, Em?"

"Flour, vegetable oil, and a dose of poison. One bite and you die." She handed me the packaged loaf and I studied the ingredients, noting there was nothing listed that was actually treif.

"You know what? I think I'll risk it." I made myself a sandwich and started to say the bracha for bread, then caught myself and let out a burst of laughter.

"What's so funny?" said Emma.

It was ironic, making a blessing over non-kosher food. No, it was more than ironic. It was absurd. But how to explain it to Emma? I waved my hand in a "you had to be there" kind of way. Then I gobbled down the sandwich quickly, before I could change my mind.

It didn't taste any different from kosher bread, but for hours after eating it I felt queasy, the heaviness in my stomach a constant reminder that I had, for the first time in my life, eaten something that wasn't kosher.

My mother was alone when I got home. Shayne had gone to a party. Hillel and Gittel had gone to friends'. Pinny and Ezra were out, I didn't know where.

"What's wrong?" asked my mother.

I glanced at her and looked away. "What makes you think anything's wrong?"

"You don't look good. You're off-color and you're ... " She studied my face. "Where have you been, Ditty?"

My mum wasn't usually psychic, and this rare moment of intuition was freaking me out.

"Where have you been?" she asked again.

"Where do you think I've been?"

"If I knew, I wouldn't be asking."

I didn't reply.

"You know, Ditty," she said, "if you've done something you regret, it might help to get it off your chest."

"You're so nosy," I burst out. "Can't I have any privacy?"

My mother looked as though I'd slapped her.

"Okay, have it your own way," she said at last. "But Ditty, if you don't tell me what the problem is, I can't help you fix it."

"I didn't ask you to fix it. Look, you really don't need to worry about me," I added as I stomped away toward my room.

A new bed had arrived while I was gone. It stood where Gittel's crib had been, and the crib had disappeared. Gittel, who was nearly four, had long ago outgrown it. She wanted to sleep in a bunk bed "like Ditty and Shayne." It had already been decided that the new bed would be mine.

I'd been hoping I'd inherit Rochel's room once she got married, but that had already gone to Pinny, who was older. I didn't mind too much, because the boys' room was even smaller than ours.

Now I threw off my shoes and flung myself onto my brand-new bed, which my mum had already made up with a new set of lilac-patterned sheets. I lay on my back, staring up at the ceiling. After a minute I sat up, then stood, then jumped up and down on the mattress. It had been so claustrophobic sleeping on the bottom bunk. I'd had to watch my head every time I got up. Now I had all this empty space above me. It was pure luxury. I forgot about the squabble with my mother and ran out to thank her.

"You got the new bed," I said. I skipped up to her, eager to share my enthusiasm. I tried to hug her, but her hands hung limply by her sides. She was still smarting from my rudeness.

"I'm glad you like it, Ditty," she said. "Now go and lie down on it. Maybe when you've had a rest, you'll be better behaved."

I plodded back toward my room and lay on the bed, thinking about all the evil things I'd done that day, and the horrid way I'd treated my mother. I hadn't meant to behave so badly. It was just that I couldn't tell her where I'd been, what I'd done. Or what I'd eaten. She'd be so shocked if she knew, so disappointed.

And my dad? I didn't dare imagine his reaction.

But was what I'd done really so wrong? I could just imagine Linda's response if I told her. "Jeez, Ditty," she would say, "it's not as though you've joined a tribe of cannibals. I eat bread that isn't kosher all the time."

Twenty-Eight

I'd been back at school for over a month. Rochel was pregnant, Gittel had started kindergarten, and I was busy with my double life, sneaking off to the National after school and on Shabbos, adapting my anecdotes of the Riskin kids as Aaron and Talia "grew up" and became more entertaining.

Jazz dance had been added to my already heavy schedule (Miss Mitchell said it wasn't enough to learn ballet—I had to be versatile), which meant that Adele Riskin had started working late on Monday nights as well as Wednesdays.

We soon started rehearsing for the winter production. That year, like Emma, I was singled out for a solo. It was a *petit allegro*, full of small jumps and beats.

I threw myself into class and rehearsals, and came home too tired to do much except eat, shower, and collapse into bed. I still baked cakes on Thursday nights, but I was way too tired for conversation. There were no more whispered giggles in the kitchen as Reb Saunders gave his shiur to my father and his colleagues. Even my mum had stopped humming as she kneaded dough for challah. She looked on helplessly as I grew more distant from the family.

———

"Hormones!" Aunt Tamara declared. "Don't worry, Zipporah. All teenagers go through it."

"Rochel didn't," said my mother.

"Rochel was different. She wasn't like most teenage girls."

My mother sighed.

It was a Sunday afternoon and Linda and I stood frozen in the hall outside the kitchen, our mothers oblivious to our presence.

"It's natural for teenage girls to want their privacy," Aunt Tamara continued. "How else can they develop independence?"

"I'm not sure I want Ditty to be independent," came my mother's reply. "Not in the way you mean. I don't know what I'd do if she started to stray."

"Stray? What an old-fashioned way of putting it."

"You know what I mean."

"Maybe you should try letting go a little," said Aunt Tamara. "You don't need to know every little thing she does. Why not just trust her, Zipporah?"

The front door slammed. My father and Ezra were home from the kollel, and Linda and I dashed into my room before they could catch us eavesdropping.

"Why don't we just go in there and join in the conversation?" suggested Linda. "Let them know we heard every word..."

"No. Let's go outside."

I called out to my mum that we were going out and we left the house and strolled down the street, toward the park.

———

"I'm a mess," I said to Linda as I sat down beside her on a rickety bench. "There's this kind of battle going on inside me. I feel guilty, but it doesn't stop me. I just keep on doing these terrible things. And I'm scared."

"Of what?"

"That Hashem will punish me. That I'll pay a price in the Olam Haba."

"Oh, Ditty! Don't you think God's got better things to do with His time than punish *you*? That's the trouble with religious extremists. You overestimate your own importance."

"Don't you think Hashem cares?" I asked her. "Don't you think He watches what we do?"

"No, I don't," she said. "He has to, like, make sure the sun doesn't collapse, and keep the trees growing, and whatever else it is He does. And even if He wasn't busy running the world, what makes you think He'd care that much about little you? I mean, how many people are there in the world? Billions? Well, do you honestly think He can be bothered watching every single one of them every second of every day? Or," she added sarcastically, "is it just the Jews He's keeping an eye on?"

"How do you know He isn't?" I challenged. "I mean, He's omnipotent, isn't He? That's what makes Him God. He's—"

"What? A spy in the sky? Jeez, Ditty, is that what you think? That's such a childish belief."

"Millions of people believe it."

"Maybe billions. So what? That doesn't mean they can't be wrong."

I watched an ant as it scurried along the concrete paving by my feet and disappeared into a tiny hole. A dog barked on the grassy verge where the paving ended, and a baby cried. Linda was looking up into the branches of the plane tree above us.

If what Linda was suggesting was actually true, then Hashem had nothing to do with the ant, the dog, the baby, the tree. Nor did He have that much to do with me. Linda was not only challenging the core of our beliefs, she was challenging the way billions of people led their lives.

"My parents wouldn't lie to me," I said.

"No," Linda agreed. "Not deliberately. It's just that they've been brainwashed too. And anyway, the existence of God isn't the sort of thing you can prove."

"That's why we're supposed to believe."

"Believe *what*?" she asked. "If the Jews are right, then

everybody else is wrong. But if the Christians or the Muslims or the Sikhs are right, then the Jews are wrong. You know what I think, Ditty? Maybe they're all wrong."

I tried to close my mind to these blasphemous thoughts.

"My parents were right," I said at last. "You are a bad influence on me."

Linda burst out laughing. "I love you, Ditty. You know that." She put her arm around me and squeezed my shoulder.

"You really don't believe in Hashem?" I said in wonder.

"It's not that I don't believe in Him. I just don't think He'd punish you for something as silly or as petty as dancing on Shabbos, or eating the wrong kind of cheddar cheese. I mean, why would He? It's not like it's hurting anyone."

"But it would hurt my parents, if they found out about it."

Linda shrugged. "Their choice," she said. "It's called 'emotional blackmail.' Anyone can say they'll be hurt if someone doesn't do things their way. But there's nothing harmful about dancing, Ditty. I mean, compare dance to religion. How many wars have been fought, how many people have been killed in the name of religion, and how many in the name of dance?"

There was a certain logic to what Linda had said. But religion went beyond logic, beyond reason.

If my parents were right, if all our rabbis and sages and scholars were right, then I had sinned so badly I'd be spending an eternally wretched and miserable existence in the Olam Haba after I died.

But if they were wrong, and I believed them? Then I'd miss out on this world and all it had to offer.

Either way, I was doomed.

Twenty-Nine

I was standing backstage, warming up for the winter performance, shivering in my sleeveless costume. I peered through a hole in the curtain at the rows of unfamiliar faces, half wishing that my parents were out there, along with my brothers and sisters, aunts and uncles. I scanned the blur of faces for someone I might recognize, though I wasn't sure who I was hoping to see.

My hands were shaking. Maybe it was a good thing that no one in the audience would be watching me. I could think of the performance as a dress rehearsal, a practice run. I must have used the loo five times in the last half hour. I wasn't the only one. There was a queue that stretched right out of the bathroom and halfway down the corridor.

Emma came and stood beside me in the wings.

"Good luck, Ditty."

"Good luck, Em," I whispered back. Then we fell silent. The music had already begun.

I took a few steadying breaths while I waited for my cue, and when it came, I danced out onto the stage, my heart pounding.

After the first few steps, my nerves disappeared, and I gazed out into the blackness of the audience, projecting to the center of the very back row, imagining that every single person out there had come that evening especially for me.

When the show was over and I'd changed back into my everyday clothes, I stood in the foyer of the theater, waiting for Emma's parents to take us home. The other dancers were all being hugged and kissed and congratulated. Probably no one had even noticed me.

———

"What did your parents think of your performance?" Miss Mitchell asked me.

It was a few days after the final show, and we were about to file into the studio for the last lesson of the term.

"Oh, they didn't see it," I said. "They couldn't come."

The conversation was eerily like the one we'd had six months before.

"What, again? They couldn't come last time, either."

"They're busy people. They don't have time to watch concerts."

Miss Mitchell shook her head, looking so disappointed on my behalf it somehow made my deception worse.

"You know, Ditty," she added, "I'd really like to meet your parents. I think they should know how talented you are and how well you're doing. I've tried phoning them a few times but I can never get through. I think the office must have the wrong number. Give me the number before you leave, and I'll give them a call."

I froze, and Miss Mitchell saw the panic in my face.

"What's wrong, Ditty?"

"My parents . . ."

I wasn't sure how to continue.

"Your parents . . . what?" she prompted.

I took a deep breath.

"Don't know I dance."

The words tumbled out before I could stop them. Maybe I hadn't wanted to stop them. I'd always hated lying to her.

Miss Mitchell stared at me, with a kind of awed fascination.

"I think we'd better discuss this in the office," she said at last, and I followed her down the hall.

"All right, Ditty," she continued. "What's all this about? Why don't your parents know you dance?"

"I . . . I haven't told them," I whispered.

"Yes, but why haven't you told them? Don't you think they'd want to know? Don't you think they'd be proud?"

I shook my head. "No. They . . . they wouldn't approve."

"How do you know that?"

"We discussed it before I started. I asked if I could

learn ballet and they said no. They don't think it's suitable for Jewish girls."

"But, Ditty—all this time! You've been dancing for...what? Three years now?"

I nodded.

"How is that possible, Ditty? Where do your parents think you are? And how have you managed to pay for the lessons?"

"They think I'm babysitting, and I really do have a job babysitting. That's how I earn the money for classes."

Miss Mitchell was quiet.

"It's really not okay, Ditty," she said at last. "It isn't right to deceive your parents. I think you should tell them you've been taking lessons. Or, I could talk to them if you like. Maybe if they knew how much potential you have..."

"No. I'd be in so much trouble." Tears started welling up behind my eyes, and I tried my hardest to blink them back.

"But, Ditty, I feel like an accomplice, now that you've told me. I might even be breaking the law. You're still a minor."

"I'm fifteen," I said. "I shouldn't have to tell my parents where I am."

"What if you had an accident in class?" Miss Mitchell said, her expression stern. "What would happen if you had to be rushed to the hospital?"

I said nothing, thinking of the time I'd sprained my ankle and what a close call that had been.

"I don't like it," she said.

I gulped and whispered, "Neither do I."

She sighed and tapped her fingers on the arm of her

chair. "Oh, Ditty, what are we going to do with you?" She glanced up at the clock and noticed the time. "We'll talk about this later. Come on, we're late for class."

She didn't say a single word to me during the lesson. But I could see her watching me, a worried expression on her face. I tried to concentrate on my technique, but my legs were shaking. I was annoyed at myself for telling her, though a part of me was also relieved. But could I trust her? Would she keep my secret, or would she give me away?

She approached me as soon as the class was over. "I think I should contact your parents," she said, and I felt sick with dread. She couldn't, she just couldn't tell my parents. I wouldn't survive.

"But I won't," she added.

I didn't know I'd been holding my breath until I felt myself exhale.

"Thank you, Miss Mitchell."

"Don't thank me. I'm not at all sure I'm doing the right thing. Call it selfish," she continued, "but I just can't bring myself to give up on my most promising pupil. And as you said, you're fifteen years old now. I suppose you're entitled to your secrets. But I wish you'd tell your parents yourself, Ditty. Nothing stays secret forever. Sooner or later, they're bound to find out."

"If they do, they'll stop me from taking classes."

"Maybe they won't," said Miss Mitchell. "Maybe you should give them a chance."

"You don't understand. We're … they're very religious."

"A lot of the girls who dance here are religious."

"Yes, but we're *Jewish* religious."

"I know you are."

"Well, that's different."

"Why? Wouldn't God want you to use the talent He's given you?"

I didn't answer, though I'd often asked myself that very question.

Thirty

"What would you do if you lived in Nazi Germany during the Holocaust," asked Mrs. Honig, our Jewish History teacher, "and you were asked by a German soldier whether you were Jewish? Would it be okay to lie? Remember," she added, "telling the truth means you get sent straight to the gas chambers. What do you do?"

"You ask your rabbi," said Raisel Bromberger.

"Yes, if he is there to be asked. But he has already been sent to a concentration camp."

"I don't think you should lie," said Esther Malka, predictably. "I think you should stand up for your beliefs. Then Hashem will save you from the gas chambers."

"How do you know?" Leah challenged her. "How do you know what Hashem will do?"

Esther Malka shrugged. "If He doesn't, He'll reward you in the Olam Haba."

"You don't know that for sure," said Leah. "How can you second-guess Hashem like that?"

"It's a matter of faith."

"Come off it. Telling the truth to someone who would kill you because of it is just plain stupid."

"What if Hashem is testing your moral fiber?" asked Esther Malka.

"What if He's not?" Leah shot back. "What if He's testing the Nazi's moral fiber and you're just the guinea pig?"

"Girls! Girls!" said Mrs. Honig. "Let's put it another way. Do you owe the truth to people who don't have your best interests at heart? Are you obligated to tell the truth in a situation where you know the truth will be used against you?"

"I guess," said Raisel, "if you were attacked by a man in the street, it would be okay to lie and tell him you had a highly contagious illness." The entire class agreed—it would definitely be okay to lie.

"Maybe it would also be okay to lie out of kindness," I volunteered.

"What do you mean?"

"Well…" I hedged. "Suppose you lied to your parents because you knew the truth would upset them. I mean, let's say you'd done something they wouldn't like—"

"I beg your pardon, Ditty Cohen!" Mrs. Honig interrupted.

"Truth isn't an absolute value," I persevered, remembering what Zvi had once said about competing values. "It says in the Talmud that if a woman asks her husband whether he likes a dress she has bought, he has to lie and say that he does, even if he doesn't."

"You're right, it does say that," Mrs. Honig agreed, "but that refers to a very specific situation. We started with a question about lying to a Nazi whose stated mission is to kill you. There is an enormous difference, Ditty, between lying to survive, or even lying to preserve a marriage, and lying to avoid getting into trouble. Just as there is an enormous difference between lying to an enemy and lying to *your own parents*." She emphasized the last three words as if she had caught me out long ago, and her suspicious glare almost convinced me that she had.

"Every situation must be considered on its own merit," Mrs. Honig continued, "and our obligation is to do what is right in each particular situation."

But how do we know what is right? I wanted to shout. Is something right because your parents or your rabbi told you it is? Or can a thing be inherently, intrinsically right? Don't human beings have an innate sense of what is right, anyway? And if we do, why can't we trust ourselves?

I didn't say these things out loud; I didn't want to say anything else that might get me into trouble. Besides, it was all so complicated. I was getting a headache just thinking about it. I wanted to be out of that classroom, and when at last the lesson ended, I was the first to leave.

Thirty-One

In the spring, our neighborhood burst into color. Outside our house, the starkness of winter gave way to the lush greens of budding leaves and the rich deep yellow of acacia trees. Crab apples blossomed pink and white, half-forgotten rhododendron bushes fanned their crimson flowers, and Rochel gave birth to a baby boy. Propped up against the pillows of her hospital bed, cradling the small wriggling body against her chest, her eyes shone with a joy that seemed tender and fragile. My heart felt like it was bursting as I gently stroked the soft, silky skin and downy hair.

"How do you feel?" I asked my sister.

"Overwhelmed," she said, "and ... fiercely protective."

The shriveled face and screwed-up eyes of my tiny nephew gave no clues about his future. What sort of person would this little soul become? How much of his life would be determined by his parents, whose lives in turn had been determined by theirs? One thing I knew: his role as a Jew and his personal covenant with Hashem would begin in eight days time, at his circumcision, his *bris mila*.

On Saturday night, Shayne and I stayed up late, baking apple strudel, poppy-seed cake, and chocolate swirls. We got up early on Sunday morning to cut up fruit and arrange it on platters. The bris was scheduled for ten in the morning, but Jewish Standard Time meant it wouldn't begin till almost eleven. As we'd expected, the bell didn't even ring until twenty past ten.

Aunt Rivka was the first to arrive, with Uncle Solik and most of their children. My cousin Shoshi and her three small kids came five minutes later. Then came the men from my father's shule and kollel, as well as Zvi and Rochel's friends.

I was on door duty, directing the men to one room, the women to another.

Aunt Tamara, Uncle Yankel, and Linda were the last to arrive.

"We haven't missed it, have we?" asked my aunt.

"Wish we had," said Linda when I shook my head. "It's such a barbaric tradition. Mutilating the body of a tiny baby. And the kid gets no say in it."

"Don't start, Linda," said Aunt Tamara. But Linda's protest had already hit a chord. I had visions of a blood-soaked baby, his little life cut short as the *mohel* tried in vain to stem the bleeding.

Uncle Yankel tried to reassure me. "Don't worry, Ditty. It's just a tiny snip. It won't harm the baby."

The "tiny snip" was over almost before it had begun, and my nephew's name was now revealed. Asher Aharon. Asher for short.

———

"Don't you think it's immoral, though," Linda said later, as the two of us sat on the grass in our back garden, "imposing circumcision on a tiny baby? I mean, who's to say he'd even want to be Jewish?"

"I guess that if Hashem didn't want him to be Jewish, he wouldn't have been born into a Jewish family."

"Jeez, Ditty, that's such a fatalistic view. It's like what they believe in India. If you were born poor, then God must have wanted you to be poor. That's why they don't fight the caste system. That's why they let millions of people die of starvation in the streets."

"It's not the same."

"Why not?"

"People of all religions can be poor, Linda. It's a different issue."

"Not really. You're saying that God wants you to live the life you were born into. So if you were born Muslim, He'd want you to be a Muslim? And if you were born a Christian, He'd want you to be a Christian?"

"Yeah, I guess…"

"But Ditty, that's ridiculous. That's just like saying that if your parents happen to be criminals, then God would want you to be a criminal, and if your mother's a prostitute, then you were meant to become a prostitute. Or if your parents happened to be alcoholics—"

"No. Hashem would want you to rise above that…"

"Then maybe He'd want you to rise above religion, too."

———

It was hard to argue with Linda. She was flighty, sociable, and so interested in boys and clothes it was easy to forget that she was also smart.

"You've got to admit," I said, "that of all religions, Judaism is the most credible."

"No. Why have I got to admit that?"

"Judaism came first. The others followed."

"So?"

"So the Torah says that it's the only true religion, that nothing else can replace it."

"What makes you think that our Holy book is any more credible than anyone else's? You only believe in the Torah because you've been taught to."

"Maybe…"

"*Definitely.* You could just as easily be a Buddhist, a Scientologist, a Hindu… people manage to rationalize and justify all sorts of weird beliefs."

"Maybe, but Judaism is the only religion that doesn't

need any rationalizing. In every other religion," I argued, "the miracles were only ever witnessed by one or two people, and everyone else had to take their word for it. But six hundred thousand people witnessed the revelation at Mount Sinai."

"Who knows how many people were there or what they witnessed? It was so long ago. Anyway, what makes you think six hundred thousand people can't be brainwashed?"

"What makes you think they can?"

Linda gave her earring a twirl and gave this some thought.

"Mass psychology," she said at last. "Ever heard of Jonestown, Ditty?"

I shook my head.

"There was this Christian sect, the Peoples Temple, led by a guy called Jim Jones. Anyway, in the seventies he managed to convince his followers that God wanted them to kill themselves. So they did. Over nine hundred of them. The kids were killed too. Even the babies."

"They killed their kids?"

"Uh-huh. They thought God told them to do it."

"They shouldn't have listened."

"I agree, but no one says Abraham shouldn't have listened when God told him to sacrifice Isaac. We're always taught how wonderful Abraham was. We're supposed to admire his blind obedience, his willingness to do whatever God commanded. I bet none of your teachers have ever suggested he might have been wrong."

"Of course not, Linda. But that was different."

"Why was it different? Only because all your life you've been taught to admire that kind of faith."

"There *is* something wonderful about that kind of faith."

"Even if it makes you a murderer?"

"He wasn't a murderer. He didn't even kill Isaac, in the end."

"Only because, at the last minute, God told him not to. But he was going to kill him. He was about to kill him. And personally, Ditty, I don't think that's something to be admired."

"Aren't you ever envious of people who have that kind of faith, that kind of certainty? It must be so peaceful."

"Peaceful?" said Linda. "When it's responsible for Holy Wars and suicide bombings?"

"No, I'm not talking about people who are looking for an excuse for violence. I'm talking about people like Rochel. She's so at peace with herself and the world, because she truly believes."

"How nice for her!" said Linda. "Well, maybe you're right. Maybe faith really does make her feel peaceful, and maybe ignorance really is bliss. But given the choice, Ditty, I don't think I'd choose ignorance no matter how happy it made me. Given the choice, I'd rather have the truth."

Thirty-Two

One day, Miss Mitchell overheard me telling Emma that I had Friday afternoons off school.

"Why?" asked Emma.

"Because," I explained, "most of the girls would stay home anyway. They have to help their mothers get ready for Shabbos."

"Do you help your mother?" Miss Mitchell asked me.

I nodded. "I bake cakes and set the table for dinner. But usually I do the baking on Thursday night, and sometimes I set the table before I go to school on Friday morning. That way I'm free in the afternoon."

"In that case," said Miss Mitchell, "you could join the advanced students' *pas-de-deux* class. It's at three o'clock on Fridays. It's time you started dancing with a partner. I'll tell Miss Morris to expect you. You too, Emma, if you're free."

The National offered a full-time course to students who had finished school, and they were the only ones who had a *pas-de-deux* class as part of their timetable. They usually got the best parts in performances, too, and it was an almost unheard-of honor to be told we could join them.

The class was taught by Bill Kurtz and Toni Morris, who had both been principal artists in major dance companies overseas. I had seen glimpses of them demonstrating lifts to the older students, and I was always enthralled. The two of them moved so beautifully together it was almost as though each was an extension of the other.

It would be such a thrill to join their class, but it would be terrifying, too. I'd never even touched a boy before, let alone danced with one.

That first lesson, I was partnered with a guy called Brendan. He was gorgeous.

A shiver went through me as his eyes caught mine, and my mouth went dry. I tried to ignore him, but it was hard not to notice the large dark eyes and full lips, not to mention the long lean muscles and narrow hips. When his hands came to rest on the curve of my waist, his touch made me tingle all over.

Suddenly the floor seemed eminently worthy of my attention, as did the ceiling, the door, the Yamaha piano in the corner of the room ...

"What are you doing, Ditty?" said Miss Morris. "You have a partner. *Look* at him."

A flush of heat spread from my neck up into my face. I

forced myself to focus on the bridge of Brendan's nose, but I still couldn't bring myself to look in his eyes.

"Right, now put your hands on his shoulders."

My palms were sweating. How could I touch him? He'd know at once how nervous I was. I hesitated, but Miss Morris was watching. I swept my hands through first position and raised them tentatively toward his shoulders, allowing them to hover just above.

"He doesn't have an infectious disease," snapped Miss Morris. "You won't catch anything by touching him."

I could sense the heads of the other students turn toward me and I placed my hands on Brendan's shoulders, wanting nothing more than to sink through the floor.

At this point, Mr. Kurtz stepped in. "Ballet is all about creating an illusion," he explained. "You have to pretend you're in love."

Before I knew it, he had nudged me closer to Brendan, who smiled and started to lift me, higher and higher.

"Eye contact, Miss Cohen," Mr. Kurtz was saying. "It's all about eye contact." Brendan's eyes were on my face, and my skin was burning. "Look at him, Ditty. Look. At. Him."

Finally, I forced myself to do just that.

"Better," he said at last, as Brendan lowered me gently to the ground.

Thirty-Three

In the summer, Emma, Kirsten, and Frances went away to a holiday house that Frances's family had rented near the beach. By now, all three knew my secret, and though they wanted me to join them, they understood that I couldn't.

I thought of them wistfully during the weeks they were away, but I was too busy to mope. Two days a week I worked in the kitchen of a kosher catering company, and on other days, whenever I could, I did extra babysitting for the Kingsleys, who had recently had another baby.

Gittel was growing up now. She was already five. I spent whole days with her, teaching her some of the gymnastics I'd once learnt at school. I watched with satisfaction as she arched effortlessly into a backbend, or executed a perfect cartwheel, pigtails flying behind her as she spun through the air. I wished I could teach her basic ballet.

Gittel was so well-coordinated, I knew she'd make a fabulous dancer if only she had the chance to learn.

Sometimes I went over to Linda's and we hung out at her place or went to a movie.

"Wish I could dress like you," I said one day. I was peering into Linda's mirror, scowling. Linda, wearing three-quarter-length cargo pants and a stripy, sleeveless top, was sprawled out on her bed.

"You can," she said. She jumped up and rifled through her wardrobe, pulling out a cute pair of jeans she'd grown out of, as well as a gorgeous little top her last boyfriend had given her—two sizes too small and never worn. "Here. Try these."

The jeans were a bit loose, but I cinched them in with a belt. The top looked as though as it had been made to measure.

For once, as I wandered through the Jam Factory with Linda, queued for tickets, and rode up the escalator to the cinema, I didn't feel as though everyone was staring at me as if I was some kind of weirdo.

It felt good, not standing out in a crowd.

———

"I'm taking you shopping," Linda declared when the film was over.

The last time I'd gone shopping had been with Rochel, who was pregnant again even though Asher was only three months old. There was nothing in the maternity shops that was modest enough or cheap enough for her to buy. The whole experience had been a bore, so I wasn't particularly keen to go shopping again.

"I haven't got any money with me," I replied.

"Who needs money? I never said we were going to buy anything."

We crossed a side street and Linda pulled me into a small boutique, where two rows of overpriced dresses hung on racks. They were absolutely divine—low-cut, strapless and backless, and so flimsy they were barely there.

Linda grinned at me. "Come on. Let's try some on."

Most of the dresses were too big for me, but there was a size 6 that was perfect. It was bright red and hugged my body, leaving my back and shoulders bare. When I came out of the cubicle, even the sales assistant looks impressed. She gave me a pair of high-heeled shoes to try on with the dress and fastened a chain around my neck.

"Lovely! Take a look."

She turned me toward the mirror on the opposite wall, and I was stunned to see the stranger looking back. She looked grown-up and sexy. But I knew she was innocent, and a bit unsure.

Linda stepped out of her cubicle wearing a long, black, off-the-shoulder dress. She was struggling to do up the zipper in the back when she turned her head in my direction and did a double take.

"Omigod! Ditty! I didn't recognize you. You look am*aaaz*ing."

After that, trying on seductive clothes became my new holiday addiction. Sometimes I dragged Sara along to the boutiques that Linda had shown me, but she was always terrified we'd be caught.

One day, Sara and I went into a super-trendy, super-expensive shop in Glenhuntly Road and tried on evening wear. I came out of the fitting room wearing a sparkling, clinging, pale-blue halter-neck dress and high-heeled silver shoes. I grinned at Sara, then looked in the mirror, spinning around to admire myself from every angle.

Halfway through my second spin I looked out the window, and there stood Aunt Rivka. Her nose was flattened against the glass, and she was staring straight at me. My whole body went rigid with panic. I turned away and hurried back into the changing room, where I stayed until I was sure Aunt Rivka had gone.

When I got home, I found I'd been busted. It was the one week in the entire summer my dad was off work—he only ever had a week because of all the Jewish holidays he took mid-year—and he and my mother cornered me in the kitchen.

"Aunt Rivka said you were trying on clothes that weren't tsnius today," my mother began. "Clothes that barely covered your bottom, clothes that made you look practically naked. What were you thinking, Ditty?"

"It's not like I was thinking of buying them," I said. "I was only doing it for fun."

"Fun?" Coming from my father, the simple word sounded strange. "Are you trying to tell me that disregarding Hashem's commandments is something you consider enjoyable? Is this the way you invite the moshiach into our lives? Is this the way you prepare yourself for the Olam Haba? This world, Yehudit," he continued, "is nothing but a stepping-stone to the next world. The more we prepare ourselves in this world, the happier we will be in the Olam Haba."

Oh, I knew the theory. I'd heard it all my life—I'd even believed it—but it occurred to me now that no one had ever come back from the World to Come to tell me that it even existed, whereas I knew for a fact that this one did.

But offering that particular opinion would only make things worse, and my heart was sinking as I looked at my father, trying to remember the last time we'd had a real conversation.

Had we ever had one?

I tried to remember when we'd last enjoyed each other's company. There must have been a time, when I was younger, much younger, long before I started disobeying him . . . but we were so different now. My dad hated the secular world, and the more I learnt about it, the more I loved it. The more I loved it, the more distant I grew from my family. Especially my father. It seemed like I'd been avoiding him for years.

But I did remember—how, when I was Gittel's age, he'd held my hand when we walked to shule. How I'd sat on his knee once we got there. How he'd chucked me under the chin as he left for work in the mornings. All that had been a lifetime ago. It had been years since he had even touched me.

For a second I thought I'd start to cry for the loss of the relationship we used to have, a long, long time ago.

Now any contact I had with my father just made me feel wrong. I saw myself through his eyes, and disapproved.

I thought of Emma, and the way she and her dad chatted so easily together. I thought of Linda and her comfortable, easygoing relationship with Uncle Yankel. And I was envious.

"Yehudit!"

"What?"

"You will not go out of the house again for the rest of this week."

And that was it. I was grounded. For the first time in my life.

———

When I was allowed out again, I steered well clear of Glenhuntly Road. Instead, Sara and I took the bus to Chadstone—a shopper's heaven.

Sara tried on almost as many clothes as I did, but she seemed uncomfortable doing it. She shocked herself by even daring to put them on.

As we wandered the mall arm in arm, we passed a lady holding a tray of shortbread biscuits, offering them to passers by. I took one and bit into it.

Sara froze.

"Ditty! What are you doing?"

She knew I'd eaten non-kosher sandwiches at Emma's house, but I'd never eaten anything that wasn't kosher right in front of her.

"It's only a biscuit," I said, making light of my crime. "It's not like I'm eating lobster or ham."

"Would you?" she asked.

"Would I what?"

"Eat lobster or ham?"

"You mean, ever?"

She nodded.

"I don't know, Sara. I don't know what I'm going to do tomorrow, let alone what I might do in ten, twenty, or thirty years' time. It doesn't make sense, though. Me keeping kosher. I mean, I lie to my parents all the time. And I don't even keep Shabbos anymore."

"So?"

"So eating something that isn't kosher just doesn't seem so bad."

Thirty-Four

By the time I started Year Ten, I was getting used to dancing with a partner, and the *pas-de-deux* classes were becoming easier. I wasn't as self-conscious as I had been, and
when I allowed myself to relax, I enjoyed being lifted. In
a way, it reminded me of how it felt to be four years old,
sitting up high on my father's shoulders as he carried me
proudly down the street or danced in shule. When I was
partnered with one of the taller, stronger boys, it gave me
that remembered thrill tempered by a sense of security—a
feeling of literally being on top of the world.

The difference was that now there was a hint of romance
in the air, a tiny spark that made *pas-de-deux* class fun, excit-
ing, and a little daring.

But overcoming years of being segregated from boys
wasn't easy. Some of the lifts required my partner to place

his hands on my rib cage, my hips, my inner thighs. So although the work was becoming more natural, there were still times when I was embarrassed by the intimacy involved.

————————

One Friday afternoon at the end of winter, there was a new boy in Miss Morris's class. His name was Jason Brown, he was seventeen years old, and he had just moved down from Perth to audition for the Australian Ballet School. He'd decided to stay on in Melbourne for the rest of the year and take classes at the National.

Jason was in the open class on Tuesday, as well, and I saw him watching me, his eyes following my every move.

"Jason likes you," said Emma, as soon as the class was over.

"Yeah," Kirsten agreed. "Haven't you noticed that he can't stop staring at you? It's, like, so over the top."

I didn't admit that I'd noticed him staring, but on Friday I was partnered with him in *pas-de-deux*.

Jason was a superb dancer, and a better partner than any of the boys I'd danced with before. I admired his strength, his technique, and his artistry. He was even more gorgeous than Brendan. And I could tell by the way he looked at me that Emma and Kirsten were right. He did like me.

The following Tuesday, after open class, he asked me out.

"Out where?" I asked, as if this was the issue.

"Wherever you like."

No one had ever asked me on a date before, and the truth

was, I couldn't imagine going out with any boy, let alone one who might well believe in Jesus Christ or have an anti-Semitic family.

He was still waiting for an answer, and I squirmed uncomfortably.

"I ... have to go now," I said, and I hurried into the changing room.

"But will you think about it?" he called out after me.

"I ... yes, okay, I'll think about it."

Once inside the changing room, I shut the door and slumped against it.

"You're blushing," Emma playfully accused.

"No, I'm not."

"You so are."

"He asked you out, didn't he?" said Frances.

"Uh-huh."

"What did you tell him?"

The other girls in the changing room were listening but pretending not to, desperate, as usual, to be up-to-date on the latest gossip.

"I said I'd think about it."

"That means yes."

"No. Actually, I'm going to turn him down. I can't possibly go out with him."

"Why not?" said Emma. "It's only a date, Ditty. It's not like he's asking you to marry him." Easy for her! Her parents didn't mind her going out with boys. "I mean, you're ... what, sixteen? Nearly seventeen? So why can't you go out with him? It's *normal*, Ditty. What you guys do—never mixing with anyone of the opposite sex until three weeks before you marry some boy your aunt picked out for you—that's *not* normal."

Maybe I shouldn't have told her about our matchmaking system, because now she thought she was an expert. I had a sudden urge to stick up for my community, even if I didn't exactly share their old-fashioned beliefs.

———————

Jason was waiting for me outside the changing room.

"So, how about it?" he asked.

I liked his voice. It was low-pitched and kind of gravelly.

"I'm sorry. I can't."

"Why not?" He sounded upset.

"The thing is—I'm Jewish. And you're not."

"Actually, I kind of am."

"Kind of?"

"My father was Jewish."

"And your mother?"

"Italian."

"Jewish Italian?"

"Catholic Italian."

"Then you're not Jewish," I sighed. "Sorry. Fathers don't count."

"Give me a break!"

"It's true. You're only Jewish if your mother is Jewish."

"I didn't think you'd be such a racist, Ditty," he said, stepping away from me.

"I'm not a racist," I said, indignant. "Look, don't shoot the messenger. I didn't *make* the law."

"Whose law?" he challenged. "And why does it matter?"

I had to admit he had a point. I mean, I'd broken so many laws already. Why should I care about this one?

It wasn't something I could properly explain, even to myself, but I knew that I did care. I couldn't imagine going out with a non-Jew. I just couldn't. Judaism is more than a religion. It's a history, a heritage, an entire culture.

Going out with a non-Jew, even one as cute as Jason— especially one as cute as Jason—was the first step toward assimilation, and in our community, assimilation is the worst crime of all. It's the ultimate act of disloyalty, the worst possible betrayal.

———

"Have you ever wondered what it would be like not to be Jewish?" I said to Sara the following day.

"Not really. Why?"

We were on our way to school, heading toward the pedestrian crossing on Orrong Road.

"I think about it sometimes. I have this fantasy about disappearing, traveling to some remote part of the world. I could start my life all over again. Live as I choose."

"You'd still be Jewish," said Sara.

"Would I, though? Even if no one knew where I came from or who my parents were?"

"Yes," said Sara.

"No, I don't think I would. I'd be anonymous. There'd be no one to define me. I could go out with whoever I liked. As long as he was good-looking, of course."

Sara spun around to face me. "Who do you want to go out with, Ditty? Have you met some guy?"

We'd stopped at the crossing. The green walking man lit up and I grabbed Sara's arm and tried to steer her across the road.

"No," I said. "I mean, not really. Sort of. There's this guy at the National … it's not that I'd want to go out with him, exactly, it's that I'd want the choice."

"Did he ask you?"

"Yeah."

"Well, you can't."

"No. I know. But that's why I'm asking … haven't you ever wondered what it would be like to just *be*. To have the chance to connect with any other human being on the planet, just because you're both human?"

"Actually," Sara admitted, "I do have this one fantasy. I'm all alone on a desert island, and suddenly I discover that I'm not alone. There's this gorgeous guy, and he's walking toward me … " That was Sara. She was such a romantic.

"It's all those books you read."

"Yeah," she agreed. "But the thing is, Ditty, I know it's a fantasy. I know it's not real."

"But don't you want it to be?"

She didn't answer.

"Wouldn't you," I persevered, "want the chance to re-create yourself, to start from nothing?"

"I don't think that's even possible," she said.

"But if it was…I mean, if the whole world were destroyed, and you were the only person left alive, would you keep the Torah?"

"There wouldn't be much point, would there?"

"Exactly!"

"But there wouldn't be much point to anything."

"Not true. You could get to know yourself, find out who you really are."

"No, I couldn't. I'd die of loneliness first. And even if I didn't, I'd have no one to reflect back at me. I'd be completely lost. People are nothing," she said decisively, "without other people in their lives."

Thirty-Five

·◆·

I watched my nephew, Asher, as he grabbed the edge of the coffee table.

"Dit... Dit..." he said when he saw me. He pulled himself up to a shaky upright position, took a few steps, grinned, and then fell over. He got up and tried again.

"Asher," I called. I held out my arms and he fell into them, and I threw him up into the air and whizzed him around. He threw back his head and laughed. Then he grabbed a lock of my hair, twisted it around his chubby finger, and pulled.

"Let go."

He tugged harder, shrieking with delight. He looked so happy that it was impossible to feel angry.

It was Shayne's bat-mitzvah and our living room was crowded. Asher and I were attracting a lot of attention.

"What a life!" said Linda. "To be the only boy in a room full of women."

"Yeah, well, I'm not sure he appreciates it."

"I wonder what it'd be like to be the only woman in a room full of men," she continued. She looked meaningfully at the smoky glass doors that divided the living room from the dining room, the women from the men. "Do you think I should find out?"

"I wouldn't, if I were you."

"Oh, guess what, Ditty! I've got a new boyfriend. You've got to meet him."

"Lawrence? I met him last month."

"No, Ditty. Lawrence is old news. I'm talking about Paul."

I was about to make some scathing remark about her latest romance, but I didn't get the chance. Asher was pulling my hair with a strength I didn't think a one-year-old would have, and I let out a yell. I pried his fingers open and hugged him when he started to bawl.

"You'll be ready for a shidduch soon, Ditty," said Aunt Rivka, coming up to me with a knowing expression on her face. "You're so good with children."

"No, I'm not. And I'm nowhere near ready for a shidduch. I'm too immature."

"I'll keep my eye out for the right boy," said Aunt Rivka. "In fact, I already have a few in mind..."

"A few?" Linda winked at me. "I thought polygamy was against the law."

I struggled not to laugh while Aunt Rivka eyed my cousin with contempt.

"Mind your manners, young lady." She looked Linda up and down, trying to find fault with her outfit.

Asher let out another piercing scream. I picked him up and carried him into the kitchen in search of his mother. Rochel, eight months pregnant, was nowhere in sight. Instead, I came across my own mother, giving Shayne the standard meaning-of-your-bat-mitzvah speech, the same one she'd given me when I turned twelve.

"You are a link in a chain," my mother was saying, "and it's up to you to make sure that chain is never broken." When I was twelve, the word "chain" evoked an image of a pretty piece of jewelry. Now, the phrase "chained, bound, and fettered" came to mind.

My father emerged from the dining room where the men were sitting around a long trestle table. He was carrying two empty jugs, probably intending to refill them, but he caught the tail end of Shayne and my mother's conversation.

"Your mother is right," he said to Shayne. "Never forget who you are. Never forget your responsibility to the Jewish people."

"You don't need to tell me that," Shayne replied. "I know where I belong. I know who I am."

How does she know? I wondered. What makes her so

sure? I was four and a half years older than her and I still wasn't sure.

"Ditty, put these cakes on the table, will you?" said my mother. "What's wrong with Asher?"

"Nothing. He's just cross because I wouldn't let him pull my hair." I transferred Asher to one arm, balancing him on my left hip, and took the plate of cut-up strudel with the other.

I went back out of the kitchen and caught sight of Rochel, who was just coming out of the bathroom. "Looking for this?" I asked as I handed Asher over. He was rubbing his eyes and whimpering.

"Thanks, Ditty. I'll put him to bed."

I put the plate of cakes on the dining room table, moving silently among the men, who didn't acknowledge my presence. Then I went back into the kitchen to see if my mother needed more help. She handed me a tray of fruit, and as I carried it out of the kitchen I noticed that Aunt Rivka had cornered Pinny in the hallway.

Though Pinny was slightly taller than my dad, lately he'd begun to look a little stooped, probably from all the hours he spent learning Talmud, hunched over his books. The hair on his head was shorn so short you couldn't tell it was thick and black. But like all the men in our community, he never shaved his facial hair. His dark beard was trimmed and neat.

Now, his black hat tilted as he scratched his head, and his payos dangled by his cheeks. "There wasn't anything wrong with them," he was telling Aunt Rivka. "I just didn't want to marry them."

Poor Pinny! The pressure was on. Ten months older than Rochel, he was already twenty-one, and Aunt Rivka just wouldn't let up. Even my parents had started lecturing him about how it was time he settled down, always reminding him that it was a mitzvah to have as many children as Hashem would provide. Personally, I hoped he'd take a long time deciding. As long as Pinny was single, maybe Aunt Rivka would be too busy trying to arrange a shidduch for him to bother with me.

———

"Don't you want to get married?" I asked him later.

He was immersed in *Torah News*, and when he heard my voice he looked up, startled. We didn't often have these kinds of conversations. Pinny spent most of his time at the kollel, and I, too, was hardly ever at home. We had never been especially close. Most of the time, it felt as though we just happened to share a house, but when I saw him fending off Aunt Rivka I realized we probably had more in common than I'd thought.

"I wish she'd give it a rest," he said, lowering the paper. "It's not that I don't want to get married. It's just... it's such a huge decision, choosing the girl. It's the most important decision I'll ever have to make. You'll be next, Ditty, and you'll see what I mean."

"Oh, I do see. This one decision can mean the difference between being wildly happy and completely miserable for the rest of your life."

"Rub it in, why don't you?" he muttered crossly.

Thirty-Six

•◆•

The summer production at the National was over, and we were back in the studio for a final lesson. Miss Mitchell was issuing instructions, but I barely heard. I was trying to shake off the feeling of anti-climax that took hold of me after every performance season. It was always worse at the end of the year.

Most of the girls were already in holiday mode, flopping through their center work in a half-hearted way, their minds on pool parties, sleepovers, boyfriends, and long lazy days at the beach in exotic locations.

As for me, I was determined to make the most of this summer of freedom, in case it turned out to be my last.

"Make sure you do your body-conditioning exercises over the holidays, girls," said Miss Mitchell, "and keep up your stretching. I'll see you all back here at the start of next year—fit, supple, and ready to go.

"Have a nice break, Ditty," she said as I was leaving the studio.

"You too," I said, and hugged her goodbye.

———

Miss Mitchell's advice to keep in shape was never far from my mind. Each day, I got up early and walked to Elwood Beach, where I took off my trainers and tights and did a stretching routine on the grassy hill overlooking the sea. As the sun rose higher in the sky, I'd finish stretching, then hitch up my skirt and cross the sand to paddle in the cool, shallow water near the shore.

Some days I worked for the Kingsleys. Other days, I headed off to Sara's, and Sara and I would watch TV or dance to the Top 40 on the radio. We pretty much had the run of the house.

One afternoon, I kicked off my shoes, stripped off my tights, plonked myself down on the carpet in the Kestens' living room, and started to stretch, chatting idly while Sara looked on. I flexed my feet, pointed them, and reached out beyond them to the opposite wall. I folded my body into a corkscrew twist, then stretched my legs out into the splits. After I had done the splits three ways, I stood up and moved to the sideboard, placing one hand lightly on the glossy surface of the dark mahogany.

I was in the middle of a leg mount, using the sideboard

as a barre, when I looked up to find Mrs. Kesten standing in the doorway. Her jaw had dropped open in amazement, and she was staring straight at me.

"Ditty! Where on earth did you learn to do that?"

I was too stunned to speak.

For a second, I wanted to ask her what she was doing in the living room and why she wasn't at work. Then I remembered that it was her house, her living room.

"It's ... just something I've been practicing."

"Ditty's like, really flexible," said Sara.

"Yes, I can see that," said Mrs. Kesten.

It was only then that I realized I was still in the leg mount, legs bare, one foot flat on the floor in a turned-out position, the other stretched above my ear. But Sara's mum was actually smiling.

"Well, Ditty," she said, "you've obviously got a great deal of talent."

"Please don't mention it to my mother," I begged as I straightened my skirt. "My parents hate me doing this sort of stuff. They don't think it's tsnius."

A troubled look briefly crossed her face, but after a moment she nodded. "All right, Ditty. I won't say a word." She slipped off her shoes and nylon socks and trod barefoot across the cream-colored carpet. "Come into the kitchen and have a drink with me," she said. "I've just bought some fresh orange juice."

We followed her into the kitchen and I took a seat at the kitchen table.

"Are you okay?" Sara asked her mum. "How come you're home so early?"

"To see what you two get up to when I'm not here."

It was meant as a joke, but my laugh was strained.

"No, it was just so hot in the shop," she continued. "The air conditioner has broken and I couldn't get anyone to come and fix it."

Sara took three glasses out of the kitchen cupboard.

"Oh, don't pour me one," said Sara's mum. "I'll have a coffee." She opened the fridge. "On second thought, I won't have a coffee. We're out of milk."

"Ditty and I will go and get some," Sara offered.

"Thanks, girls. Sara, take some money from my wallet."

Mrs. Kesten started fiddling with the radio, and Sara opened her mother's handbag. She sifted through its contents, looking for the wallet.

Suddenly Mrs. Kesten's eyes flew to her handbag and she started to panic. "Wait! Sara, give me the bag."

"You just told me to take money for milk."

"I know I did. Never mind that. Give me the bag. I'll get you the money."

Too late. Sara had already fished out an envelope and was holding it up. Her eyes narrowed with suspicion. She looked at her mum accusingly, and then back at the envelope in her hand.

"What's this?"

"Nothing. Put it back and give me my bag."

"But it's for me. It's got my name on it." Sara ripped it open, pulled out the piece of paper inside, and started to read.

"Don't … " said her mother, but Sara already had.

At first she looked puzzled. Then pale.

"What is it?" I whispered.

"It's a letter from my...father. My...dead father." Her voice sounded oddly flat.

"I told you not to read it," said Mrs. Kesten.

"I don't understand. It's dated five days ago." Shock turned to anger as Sara glowered at her mother. "Is my father alive?"

Mrs. Kesten sucked in her breath and nodded, so slightly you'd almost miss it. "For all the good it ever did you. He might as well be dead. He's supposed to be, to you."

"To me? What are you talking about?"

"It wasn't my idea. I did what the rabbi wanted."

"The rabbi? Which rabbi? Why would he want me to think my father was dead?"

Mrs. Kesten folded her arms across her chest and turned to gaze out the window, refusing to meet her daughter's eye.

"Why do you think?" she said at last.

"I don't know," said Sara.

But I knew.

There is only one reason why, according to Jewish law, a person must regard a living family member as dead, go through the process of mourning, and never mention that person again.

"He married a *shikse*," said Mrs. Kesten, confirming my suspicion. "Your father married a non-Jewish woman."

"So you decided it would be better if I thought he'd died?"

"Not me. I told you, it was Reb Saunder's idea. He said it would be best for all concerned."

Sara was fuming.

"You lied to me!" she shouted. "I can't believe you would do that."

"Reb Saunders—"

"You shouldn't have asked Reb Saunders. He had no right to make that decision. And neither did you!"

Sara's outburst left a hot, sharp silence in its wake.

I fidgeted uncomfortably. "I think I should leave ..."

I don't think anyone even heard. Sara and her mother were still glaring at each other, their faces red, their bodies trembling. I slipped quietly out of the house and into the street.

———

My legs were shaking. The sun was hot but there was a chill in my bones. I rubbed my hands up and down my arms, but I couldn't get warm. Despite my wobbly knees, I ran all the way home. I burst through the door and into the kitchen.

My mother was standing at the sink, her head lowered over a pan she was scrubbing. She turned and looked up in alarm as I crashed my way into the kitchen.

"Ditty! What's wrong?"

I blurted out what had happened. My mum put her arm around me and made soothing, tutting noises. Damp patches of hair stuck to my forehead and covered my eyes, and she smoothed them back off my face.

"The poor girl," she said. "But," she continued, "her mother is right. A father who married out would be a terrible influence on Sara."

I backed away from my mother in horror.

"I . . . I don't understand. You're condoning it?"

"It's not that I don't feel sorry for Sara," my mother said. "I do. But it's better that people think her father's dead. If anyone knew he'd married a shikse, Sara's chances of getting a good shidduch would be completely ruined."

"So what?" I yelled. "Who cares about a stupid shidduch? And why should Sara's chances of getting a good shidduch have anything to do with her father? That isn't fair."

My mother shrugged. "I'm not saying it's fair, Ditty. That's just the way it is. Life's not always fair. It might be hard for Sara to accept right now," she added, "but one day she'll see that her mother was only doing what was best."

Was depriving Sara of a father who loved her really what was best?

"Think about it, Ditty. What could that madman offer a girl like Sara?"

"*Madman*? What makes you think her father is mad?"

"He'd have to be, wouldn't he?" my mother said. "Why else would he abandon the Torah and marry a shikse?"

"You don't even know him."

"I don't need to know him. I know enough to know that Sara's mum was only trying to protect her daughter. I understand why you're upset, Ditty. It's sad, but it's hardly Mrs. Kesten's fault."

I stared at my mother, uncomprehending.

"You honestly think the only reason a Jew could marry out is because he's insane?"

"Either that, or he's given into his yetzer hara, which is worse."

"But he—"

"Made a choice," said my mother. "When a Jew marries out, he cuts himself off from his people. It's as simple as that." Her voice was harsh, brooking no argument.

With a leaden heart, I realized that I didn't really know my mother. I wouldn't have thought she could be quite so uncompromising, quite so severe.

Suddenly, something inside me hardened, and I stormed out of the kitchen shaking with rage. There was something so intolerant about our community. What was their conviction worth if they had to be so ruthlessly shielded from anyone who didn't share it? What they did to Sara was heartless and cruel, and if that was my religious heritage, I wanted no part of it. I loved my family, but I could not, would not, believe what they believed.

The gulf between us now was greater than it had ever been. And I understood, finally, that if I could not accept their brand of religion, they would not accept me.

———

As I tossed and turned in bed that night, something niggled at the back of my mind. It was the recognition of my own similarity to Mrs. Kesten. I, too, had been lying. And for just as long.

She had lied to manipulate Sara, whereas I had lied to avoid being manipulated. I had lied to take control of my own life, not anyone else's. But I did understand her. She, too, was a victim of a harsh, uncompromising religion. Maybe she'd honestly thought she was doing what was best for Sara. Maybe she'd felt she had no choice.

When morning came, I dressed quickly and hurried over to Sara's. I stood on the doorstep and rang the bell. No one answered at first, but finally the door was opened and Mrs. Kesten stood there, looking drawn and disheveled. Her eyes were red and puffy, her head was uncovered (I had never seen it uncovered before), and her untidy hair showed gray at the roots.

I bit my lip and said nothing.

"Come in, Ditty."

She led me up the stairs and into her room. Sara was sitting cross-legged on the carpet, a mass of open envelopes around her, their contents spilling out in an untidy sprawl.

Mrs. Kesten was looking at Sara with such regret, such apology, that I wondered if she'd realized the enormity of what she had done.

"I'll leave you two alone," she said.

Mrs. Kesten stood silently in the doorway a moment longer, then quietly shut the door.

I crouched down next to Sara and she showed me the letter she was holding. "He's been writing to me every week," she said. "Can you imagine? Every single week. For years. And all this time I thought he didn't care ... " I hugged her and she started to cry. "I always wondered what I'd done to make him leave. Why ... why he didn't want to see me—"

"But he did."

Sara nodded. "He did."

"Wait." I went to get her some tissues and she blew her nose and wiped her eyes.

"He never knew I didn't get the letters. He wouldn't have understood why I never replied. He kept on hoping..."

"At least your mum kept the letters..." I offered.

"Yeah." Sara sniffed. "She said she thought she might give them to me one day, when I was older. I was really mad at her, Ditty. I just kept shouting at her and then I was so exhausted I went to bed. We had a really long talk this morning, though. She stayed home from work especially, and she gave me the letters. It must be the first time in history my mum has missed a day of work."

For a moment I sat there quietly, just stroking Sara's hair.

"What will you do now?" I finally asked. "About your dad, I mean. Will you write to him? Phone him?"

"Of course. I'll write, I mean. Then I can plan exactly what to say. It's so weird, Ditty. Discovering I've got a father, after all. I don't even care that much if he's married to a shikse. He's still my father and I want to see him. I want to know what he's like."

"What does you mum think?"

"She hates the idea. But I'm saving up for a ticket to Queensland. She won't be able to stop me."

Thirty-Seven

· ◆ ·

"I hope you haven't developed lazy feet over the summer, girls," said Miss Mitchell. "Stretch that back foot, Frances. More. Yes, that's it!"

Getting back into ballet after the two-month break was harder than I thought it would be. It was only our third lesson of the year, and my muscles were aching.

"Andrea, keep your weight well over the supporting leg. Soften the arms, Emma. Right, that's better."

The barre exercises were long and complicated. After a demanding *rond de jambe*, we had to take a balance in *attitude* on demi-pointe and hold, hold, hold...

My shoulders tensed as I drew my working foot up the supporting leg, took it into a high *développé* to the side, and pivoted into *arabesque*, lifting the leg into an *arabesque penchée*.

"Relax the shoulders, Ditty. Remember to breathe. Right, let's see that *adage* again, girls. Watch your placement, and your pelvic alignment in particular... Good. Ditty, perhaps you'd like to show the class..."

I demonstrated the exercise and then the others were asked to repeat it.

"Thank you, girls," said Miss Mitchell. "Well done, all of you. And Ditty, I'd like you to come and see me in the office before you leave."

———

I looked around the office while I waited for her. A large timetable took up the whole of the wall behind me, and the other walls were covered with photos from ballets the school had produced in previous years. A few neat piles of papers, probably late enrollment forms, were stacked up on Miss Johnson's desk, but Miss Johnson herself had already left.

"Oh, good! You're here." Miss Mitchell swept in and took the chair behind the desk. "I thought it was time we had a talk about your future." She waited for me to speak, but I wasn't sure what I was meant to say.

"Is this what you want to do?"

"This?"

"Dance, Ditty. Do you want a career in dance?"

I had never asked myself the question in so many words. I had dreamed of dancing professionally. I'd worked toward it. But I'd never actually admitted it.

"Yes," I answered. It was the first time I'd dared to say it out loud.

"Because if you do, you should think about auditioning for the Australian Ballet School. The auditions aren't for another six months, but you'll need to apply much sooner. How old are you now, Ditty?"

"I'll be seventeen next month."

"Then it's definitely time to apply. If you leave it another year, it might be too late."

"Do you really think I've got a chance of getting in?"

"Of course I do. I wouldn't suggest it if I didn't. I think you need the challenge. And ABS is a magnificent school. If you do get in, it will almost certainly guarantee you a career in dance."

My heart skipped a beat when she said that, but the practical side of me was already dealing with the obstacles. "Isn't ABS expensive?"

"The senior school is subsidized by the government, and you might be eligible for a scholarship. You can certainly apply."

"What if I don't get in?"

"Well, there are always other options. But don't even think about that now. Stay positive. Stay focused. And most importantly, believe in yourself. But, Ditty?"

"Yes?"

"Have you told your parents yet?"

I swallowed hard, and shook my head.

"Oh, Ditty! I wish you would. If I were your mother,

I'd want to know. What do your parents want you to do after you finish school?"

"Get married. Have kids."

"What, right away?"

"Pretty much. They'll try to find a match for me at the end of the year. This is my last year at school. Beis Hannah only goes up to Year Eleven."

Miss Mitchell looked almost as shocked as she had when she first found out I was dancing without my parents' knowledge. "But don't you want to finish Year Twelve? Don't you want a higher education?"

"I've never really thought about it."

"But Ditty, this is your future we're talking about. You must have thought about it."

"No, I ... " The fact was, I hadn't even considered the idea. No one in our community ever did.

"Does ABS offer higher education?" I asked her now.

"Of course it does. And you can finish your Year Twelve studies while you train. This is really important, Ditty. Dance is such an unreliable career, so you've got to keep your options open. It's absolutely essential to get a good education."

"My parents don't approve of secular education."

"Well, Ditty, you'll be eighteen next year. It won't be up to them, will it? You'll be old enough to make up your own mind."

"My parents won't think so."

Miss Mitchell shook her head and frowned. "With all due respect to your parents, Ditty, it should be your decision.

It's time you told them who you are and what you want out of life. It's time you stood up for your convictions."

———————

Sitting at the kitchen table that evening, I was reliving my conversation with Miss Mitchell. If only I could tell my mother what Miss Mitchell thought—that I was good enough to audition for the Australian Ballet School, that I had a realistic chance of getting in.

I wished I could tell Shayne, too, or Gittel. But it wouldn't be fair to burden them with secrets they would struggle to keep. *One day*, I promised myself. One day I'd tell them.

I was in the bathroom braiding Gittel's hair when the doorbell rang, and a moment later I heard Aunt Rivka's voice, gushing loudly.

"…wonderful news for Pinny," she was saying. "She is an exceptional girl. And her family? Such yiches! Apparently, they can be traced all the way back to the *Vilna Gaon*."

"Are you going to meet her?" I asked Pinny later, as we sipped hot chocolate at the kitchen table after the younger kids had gone to bed.

"I suppose so," he sighed. "I know I should get married. But I hate the way Aunt Rivka goes on and on about the girl's family. It's almost as if the family matters more than the girl herself."

"The family does matter," my mother interrupted. "With any shidduch, it's always the family you look at first."

"Not very fair, though, is it?" I said. I was reminded of Sara and my blood boiled.

My mother stood her ground. "If you don't look at the family, what else is there to look at? A seventeen-year-old girl?"

———

"Ditty, are you insane?" Sara's reaction was not the one I'd been hoping for.

"I only said I'm going to audition. It doesn't mean I'd have to go, but I want to know if I'm good enough, if I stand a chance..."

We were on our way to school, dawdling as usual.

"Even if you did get in, your parents would never let you go. They'd probably ground you for the rest of your life."

"Or until they managed to marry me off." I winced at the thought.

"ABS is full-time, isn't it?" said Sara.

"Yeah."

"So it's not like you'd be sneaking off for a couple of hours after school. You wouldn't be able to keep it a secret."

"I know."

"I just don't see how it could work."

"Thanks for the vote of confidence."

"I'm sorry. I'm just trying to be realistic."

We walked on in silence.

"Maybe I *could* keep it a secret," I told her, after a while.

"No, Ditty. You couldn't."

"That's what you said when I first started dancing, and it's been nearly five years."

Sara let out a long, audible breath. "I still find that hard to believe, even though I know it's true."

"I know. I can hardly believe it either."

Thirty-Eight

• ◆ •

That term, Emma and I were both picked to share the title role for the winter performances of *Giselle*. Each of us was to dance the lead in two of the four performances, and we'd be dancing other, minor roles in the remaining two. Kieran McKenzie and Adam Wade were to share the role of Prince Albrecht, the male lead. I was paired with Kieran. Emma was to dance with Adam.

One day Jason Brown came to watch our rehearsal. He had been accepted into ABS and was dancing there full-time, but every now and again he came to visit his friends at the National. I didn't stay and talk to him after the rehearsal finished, like some of the others. For one thing, I didn't have time. For another, we hadn't hit it off too well the previous year. I couldn't forget the things he'd said. I unpinned my hair, brushed it out, changed into my school uniform, and headed for the tram.

Jason caught up with me just before I reached my stop. "Hey, Ditty," he grinned. "You did a great job there, in rehearsal."

"Thanks," I said. If he wanted to put the past behind us, I too was prepared to forgive and forget. "What's it like at ABS?"

"Fantastic. It's a really amazing school. Are you going to audition?"

I nodded. "Probably."

"Hope you get in."

He was watching me intensely, and I looked away, embarrassed.

"How about a coffee?" he asked.

"Sorry, I have to get home."

"I didn't mean now. How about Sunday?"

It had been over six months since he'd first asked me out, and given my reaction, I had to admit it was pretty brave of him to ask me again. He seemed taller and even more charismatic than when I'd last seen him, and I wished I could say yes.

I tried to imagine what it might be like to date him, but somehow the image that came to mind was that of Sara sitting shiva for her dad. And I realized that even if I could get my head around the thought of dating a non-Jewish guy, I couldn't do it to my parents. If I ended up marrying out of the faith, my whole family would regard me as dead. Not that a date meant marriage, but still ...

"I'm sorry, I can't. It's not that I don't want to—I thought I'd explained."

"Explained what?" he asked. "That you discriminate against people just because they're not Jewish? I was hoping you'd changed.

"Jason. I ..."

"Jase," he interrupted me. "Call me Jase. At least pretend to be my friend."

"All right, Jase. I'd like to be friends with you, but I can't go out with you."

At first he looked offended, then angry. "Then I guess I was right the first time," he said as he walked away. "You are a racist."

"I'm not," I called out after him, bristling at the accusation. "I hang out with Emma all the time. And she isn't Jewish."

———

Saturday morning classes became increasingly demanding as the four of us—Kieran and I, Emma and Adam—endlessly rehearsed the *pas-de-deux* dances, as well as our solos.

One day, in late autumn, I slipped and skidded along the floor. I panicked briefly, but luckily I wasn't hurt.

"God!" I said as I picked myself up and dusted dirt off my tights. "Imagine if that happened on stage."

"It probably will," said Kieran. "All dancers have accidents. Did you know that Kathleen Gorham fell over on stage the first time she danced a principal role?"

"Thanks, Kieran. That's *so* reassuring."

The following week we rehearsed on stage, and this time it was Emma who slipped. She twisted her ankle when she fell, and let out a cry. The rest of us rushed over to her, and I knelt beside her and put my arm around her shoulders. Emma was trying to put on a brave face, but she was biting back tears.

"Don't crowd her," said Miss Mitchell. "Emma, let's take a look. No, don't move. Kieran, go and get the ice pack. Now."

I watched as Miss Mitchell pressed the ice to Emma's foot. "We'll get you straight to the hospital and have it X-rayed."

"I'll come too."

"Thank you, Ditty, but that won't be necessary. You're needed here. You stay and rehearse. One of the other girls can come with me. Kieran, go and find Kirsten. I think she's rehearsing with Mrs. Moskowicz in Studio Four."

Emma had to take six weeks off dance, but at least she knew her foot would heal. It was too late for anyone else to learn the part, though. That meant I'd be the only female lead. It was a huge responsibility, and I was so sad for Emma. We'd been in it together. Rehearsals wouldn't be nearly as much fun without her.

That Sunday I visited Emma at home. She was hobbling around her house on crutches, trying not to put weight on the injured foot. I gave her a hug and a bunch of flowers.

"I'm so sorry, Em."

Emma sighed. "I just hope it's better in time for the ABS auditions."

———

When I got home, my parents and Pinny were in the kitchen with an American couple and their pretty daughter.

"Mazeltov, Ditty," said my mother when she saw me. "Come and join us for a *l'chaim*. It's such good news."

I didn't have to ask what she was referring to. Pinny had finally agreed to a shidduch. Maybe they'd worn him down in the end, or maybe he saw something in Beila Devorah Newman that he hadn't seen in any of the others. Either way, he'd made up his mind.

I said mazeltov and sat down at the kitchen table. I tried to smile. My father poured a small measure of cherry brandy into a glass the size of thimble. Apart from Shabbos wine, he had never served me alcohol before. I took a tiny sip and grimaced.

Gittel skipped into the kitchen, already hand-in-hand with Beila Devorah's younger sister. A bunch of other kids were playing in the garden.

"So how do you feel about it?" I said to Pinny, after Beila Devorah and her parents had gone.

"What does it matter how I feel? It's the right thing to do."

"Is it?"

"You know it is. Look, don't try to make me regret my

decision. It's not as if I have a choice. And neither do you," he added, seeing the skeptical expression on my face. "You'll be next, Ditty. So you might as well get used to the idea."

———————

"I suppose he's right," I said. "He's nearly twenty-two."

It was Wednesday morning. Sara and I were on our way to school, Pinny's impending marriage to Beila Devorah still on my mind. "Maybe he really does want to marry her. She's very pretty."

Sara still hadn't said anything, and it was only when I really looked at her that I realized she was a million miles away.

"Sara?"

"Sorry. What?"

She stopped walking and turned to face me. "I've been thinking about my dad, reading his letters," she said. "He's not the ogre Mum said he is. The thing is, all this time I thought he was dead, and it made me think, one day he *will* die. I want to see him now, Ditty. I don't want to waste any more time."

"What does your mum say?"

"She thinks I should wait till the school year is over, but I won't wait, Ditty. I'm going to see him, with or without my mother's blessing."

"Have you booked a ticket?"

"Not yet. I'm still fifty dollars short, but I'll earn the money. I'll scrub floors, clean windows, whatever it takes."

Unlike me, Sara didn't have a part-time job, and before she started saving for a ticket to Queensland, she really had given most of her money to charity.

"Won't your dad pay for the ticket?"

"Maybe, but I don't want to ask before I've even met him."

"Well, no need to scrub floors or clean windows," I said. "I'll lend you the money."

"Really?"

"Of course."

"Thanks, Ditty. But it means I won't be here to see you in *Giselle*. I feel really bad about that."

"Forget it," I said. After all that Sara had done for me over the years, the least I could do was be supportive in return. "You can watch it on DVD when you get back. It's more important that you see your dad."

———

Sara left the following Sunday, when her mum was at work. She didn't tell her mother she was leaving, but left her a note, so that by the time Mrs. Kesten read it, it would be too late to stop her.

That morning I took the train into the city with her.

"How long will you be staying with your dad?" I asked her.

"I don't know, Ditty. It depends."

"On what?"

She didn't answer. The airport bus had already arrived and she was climbing on board.

"Good luck, Sara!" I called.

She waved madly at me. Then the bus turned a corner, and a minute later she was gone.

I stood on the footpath a while longer, overwhelmed by a sudden rush of loneliness. For years now I'd spent more time with Sara than with anyone else, and I hadn't anticipated quite how desolate I'd feel without her. I was used to living in two worlds—the Jewish world and the world of ballet—and I managed in both. But Sara was the only person who was part of the first, yet knew about the second.

There was Linda, of course. But Linda wasn't really a fixture in either of my worlds, though she flitted easily between them, just as she flitted in and out of my life. Linda was like a genie to be summoned when needed—unlike Sara, who was an almost constant presence.

Thirty-Nine

It was the day after Sara had left. I had just been rehearsing at the National, and my mum accosted me the minute I walked in the door.

"Did you know that Sara was going to Queensland?"

I nodded. I'd been expecting the question. Sara's departure was all the girls had talked about that day in school.

"The whole community's gossiping about it," said my mother. "She didn't even let her mother know."

"Yes, she did. She left her a note."

"That's hardly the same, is it? Why didn't she just tell her mother she was leaving?"

"I guess she didn't want a confrontation. She knew her mum would try and stop her."

"It was so thoughtless of her," my mother said. "So irresponsible, and so dishonest."

"Not nearly as dishonest as her mother pretending her father had died."

I had to say it.

My mother looked at me harshly. "Mrs. Kesten is a single mother. She's done her best. She doesn't deserve to be treated so badly. I'd hate to think a child of mine might be plotting and scheming behind my back."

Not wanting another argument, I left the kitchen before my mum had finished talking. I thought of Sara, and wondered how she was getting on with her dad. I wished I could call her, but Sara didn't have a phone, and I didn't know her father's number.

———————

With Pinny's wedding date set, Aunt Rivka set her sights on me. I told her I was still too young, that I wasn't interested.

"You want to wait till you're old? Trust me, Ditty. Seventeen is not too young to start thinking of a shidduch. It's the perfect age."

"Let her finish school first," said my mother mildly. "She's only got six months to go."

Aunt Rivka snorted. "Well, don't blame me if someone else gets the best offers first. I know for a fact that Leah Kaplan has already met two fine, good-looking students from the yeshiva. And Esther Malka Gordon is meeting a lovely boy next week—he's coming here especially, all the way from Israel."

"Well, goody for them!"

"What's wrong with you, Ditty? It's you I'm thinking of."
Aunt Rivka turned to my mother. "What's wrong with her,
Zipporah?"

My mother sighed. That deep, resigned sigh I'd heard
all my life. "Ditty seems to have her own ideas," she said.
"Not that she ever tells us what they are."

————————

Giselle was scheduled for the long weekend of the Queen's
Birthday, and because Monday was a public holiday, the
usual Friday night performance was going to be replaced
by a Monday night one. Tickets had been on sale for over a
month, but still the show was nowhere near ready.

Giselle is a beautiful ballet, but a sad one. Betrayed by
Albrecht, Giselle dies of grief. The Wilis, the ghosts of jilted
lovers, sentence him to death for his disloyalty, but Giselle
protects him with her love. In doing so, she prevents herself
from becoming a Wili and is finally able to rest in peace.
Her story always reminds me that no situation is so bad that
it can't be redeemed.

"Wilis on stage, please!" said Miss Mitchell. "Where are
the Wilis?"

A dishevelled group of twelve-year-olds traipsed onto
the stage and arranged themselves in some kind of order.

"You're supposed to be in a line, girls. A straight line. Not
a semi-circle. Not a zigzag. A simple line. Who's supposed to
be standing here? Why are there three Wilis still missing?"

The dance of the Wilis had been choreographed by

Miss Percy, who usually taught the younger grades. Now she put them through their paces while Miss Mitchell stood at the side of the stage, alternately tapping her foot with impatience and sighing with frustration. Miss Moskowicz sat in the audience, her critical eye alert for error.

"Point your feet, Amanda Jones."

"I can't, Miss Moskowicz. The doctor says I have flat feet."

The Wilis ran through their dance three times, and then they were shepherded off the stage. They sat in the first three rows of the audience while Miss Mitchell, Miss Percy, and Miss Moskowicz lectured them on all the details they still had to work on.

In the meantime, Kieran, Adam, and I commandeered the stage, and Mr. Kurtz and Miss Morris barked instructions at us as we polished our dances.

"Kieran, that lift won't work unless you get closer to Ditty in the preparation. We talked about that. Remember?"

Over the next week, the pressure was mounting. Extra rehearsals were timetabled at the last minute, on top of our regular production classes. There was so much work still to do and so little time to do it that we were all exhausted.

Among the staff, stress levels were higher than I'd ever seen them and tempers were frayed. Even Miss Mitchell, who was generally so unruffled, seemed more tense than usual, which was understandable given that she had to oversee the whole production.

"You've got to work harder," she told us all. "You've simply got to."

Our final dress rehearsal was at two o'clock on Friday, the day before the first performance. The dance teachers were all on edge, their nerves contagious. Somehow, the most graceful dancers looked stiff and clumsy. There were last-minute injuries, mostly minor ones, and some of the dancers did the unforgivable—forgot their steps.

"We will not leave this theater," said Miss Moskowicz, "until we get it right."

I looked around the theater nervously. It could take all afternoon, all evening, and all night to get it right. And that was time I didn't have. It was almost Shabbos. Coming home late just wasn't an option.

What *was* the time, anyway? There was no clock in sight, and in the artificial light of the theater, it was impossible to judge the time.

A surge of panic left me short of air and I missed my cue. I looked up to see Miss Mitchell throwing a puzzled glance in my direction. What would she think when she discovered that her leading lady had to leave?

"You can't keep them here all evening," said Miss Percy. "They won't get it right if they're too tired to concentrate."

Thankfully, Miss Mitchell agreed. At last, the rehearsal ended and no explanations were required.

I changed out of my costume, hung it in the office, grabbed my bag, and dashed out the door. I ran all the way to the tram stop, only to see the number 67 receding into the distance. It would be at least another ten minutes before another one came.

When it did, I stood by the door, ready to leap off when it reached my stop. Why was this particular tram the slowest one in all of Melbourne? I willed it to go faster, but the tram crawled slowly along its track.

Finally it reached my street. I jumped off and broke into a run, and a minute later, 46 Gordon Street came into view. I longed to flop down onto my bed and give in to sleep. But it was nearly Shabbos. I had to get ready. Fast. Soon there'd be dinner with the family. The luxury of sleep would have to wait.

Ignoring my aching muscles, I pushed myself the last few steps and burst in the door.

Forty

• ◆ •

"Hi, I'm home!"

There was an eerie silence in the hallway. The house seemed empty and all the doors were closed.

"Mum?"

There was no answer.

"Shayne? Ezra?"

Still no answer.

But I knew the house was not deserted.

The kitchen door swung open and my parents were standing in the doorway, their faces grim.

"It's about time you got here, Yehudit," said my father.

"Where is everyone?"

"Your brothers and sisters have gone to shule."

"All of them? Shayne and Gittel too?"

My father gave a single, brief nod. "Nearly ten minutes

ago. We have been waiting to speak to you. We did not want them to be here when we did."

"Why not?"

"We will ask the questions, Yehudit. You will answer. In here." He pointed to a seat at the kitchen table. "Sit."

I sat down in the chair he'd indicated. Then he and my mother took seats opposite.

I held my breath and waited.

"Aunt Rivka saw you today," my father said. "She was in Barkley Street at two o'clock, and she saw you."

Barkley Street! My stomach lurched and for a second I thought I was going to be sick. "Saw me... what?"

"She saw you go into a ballet school at the back of the National Theatre."

"She *followed* me?"

"She tried to catch up with you. She wanted to talk to you, but you were walking too fast."

I hung my head. I could not look either one of my parents in the eye.

"Was it you? Or was Aunt Rivka mistaken?"

There was no point in claiming Aunt Rivka was mistaken. My parents clearly knew the truth. And I was so sick of lying.

"No," I whispered. "She wasn't mistaken. It was me."

"And what were you doing there, Yehudit, at the ballet school?"

My voice was shaking as I told them. "I take ballet there, and contemporary dance and a little jazz, but mostly ballet."

"And when did you start learning these things?"

"I've taken classes for a long time."

"How long?" This was the first time my mother had spoken.

I hesitated.

"How long, Ditty?"

I let out a sigh. "Actually, a really long time."

They were still waiting for a proper answer.

"Do you remember that I once asked you if I could take ballet lessons?"

My father looked confused. He didn't remember. My mother did, though. "But Ditty, that was years ago. You were only about…"

"Twelve. It was a few months after my bat-mitzvah. I was twelve when I asked."

"And we said no," my mother reminded me.

"Yes."

"And you started lessons anyway?"

I nodded. "Not right away, but soon after."

"When we had forbidden it?" My father had abandoned all attempts at speaking calmly and looked as if he was about to hit me. "How dare you, Yehudit!"

I knew he wouldn't hit me, because the Torah forbids it, but there was a part of me that wished he would. Then this whole awful confrontation would be over.

"But that's five years," said my mother, stunned. "You lied to us for five whole years?"

I nodded, shamefaced. "It was the only way I could learn ballet."

"You weren't *allowed* to learn."

"Exactly. And I had to...I mean, it was just so important to me."

"I don't understand, Ditty. How did you even find the time for ballet lessons? You were always working, babysitting for the..." She stopped talking as the truth dawned on her.

Tears stung my eyes and spilled down my face. "I'm sorry I lied," I managed to say. "But you wouldn't have understood the truth. You *don't* understand it."

"What is it that we don't understand, Yehudit?" asked my father.

"That dancing is so important to me..."

"*Important*? More important than obeying your parents and keeping Hashem's commandments?"

"You see? You *don't* understand."

"What I do understand, Yehudit," said my father, "is that you were put on this Earth for a reason, to be the best Jew you can be, to do mitzvos, to—"

"Bring the moshiach into the world. Yes, yes, I know all that. I just don't believe it. I don't believe it anymore."

My parents were shocked into silence.

Gradually, I became aware of the clock ticking and my own heart thumping.

Eventually my father found his voice again. "Enough! Enough of this heresy, Yehudit. You will stop all this nonsense immediately. You will do teshuva, and you will never lie to us again. You will never go to the ballet school again."

"Your father is right," said my mother, as if the matter was settled. "Hashem will forgive you. We'll forgive you too, won't we, Yitzchok?"

My father nodded slowly, solemnly.

"And Ditty," my mother continued, "if you give up dancing now, no one need know. Aunt Rivka won't tell anyone. We won't tell anyone. You can still get a good shidduch, Ditty. It's not too late."

"You still don't get it." My voice was trembling as I spoke. "I don't want a good shidduch. I don't know if I want to get married at all. I want to dance. Ballet's my life. And I'm really good at it. There's a performance tomorrow night and I'm dancing the lead."

"No, Yehudit. You are not."

"I have to. I can't let them down."

My father was looking at me as if I'd gone completely mad. "You expect us to allow you to turn your back on everything we have ever taught you?"

"I'm not asking for permission," I said, through my tears. "I'm too old for you to tell me what to do."

"No one is ever too old to live according to Torah. And as long as you live under my roof, Yehudit Cohen, you will do as I say."

By now I was crying so hard I couldn't answer.

"Go and get ready for Shabbos," said my father. "I am late for shule."

———

It was silent at the dinner table. My mother still looked awful, and she seemed to have shrunk.

Even though no one was talking, my brothers and

sisters seemed to know exactly what was going on. I could feel their eyes on me, accusing. No one was making eye contact with anyone else. Even Gittel, usually so animated, looked subdued.

In between courses, my father tried to sing zmiros, but his voice cracked and he couldn't continue. And I realized the extent of the hurt I'd caused him.

I'd seen my dad angry before. I could deal with his anger. But I wasn't prepared for his pain. He looked old and broken, and I wished I could turn back the clock and freeze time for... how long? The truth had to come out. Eventually. I'd always known it would.

There was a heavy pressure building up inside me, and I couldn't sit there with them a moment longer. I didn't wait for Grace After Meals. I got up and went to bed. No one stopped me or questioned me.

After I'd left the table, stilted conversation started up. I could hear the murmur of voices, though I couldn't hear what it was they were saying. A long time later, Gittel and Shayne came in.

"Ditty?"

I kept my eyes shut and my breathing measured, feigning sleep.

Forty-One

•—◆—•

The clock on the wall said five past nine. I knew that at some point I would have to get up. I would have to face my parents and my family. But I could hardly move. I felt trapped. In this body. In this house. In this room. I didn't know how much longer I could fight. I was sick of life feeling like a battle.

Then I remembered. Tonight was my first performance of *Giselle*, and my father had forbidden me to go. He had forbidden me to leave the house.

But Miss Mitchell was depending on me and I couldn't let her down. Besides, this was the role of a lifetime.

The thought of dancing *Giselle* made my heart beat a little faster, and I let the music flood my mind. I could hear it as clearly as if it were there in the room with me, and I visualized my own transformation into Giselle. I saw myself dancing her steps, feeling her joy, her shock, her pain. And

I knew there was no way on earth I would miss this performance, or this morning's rehearsal.

I got out of bed and went into the bathroom. I could hear my parents talking in the kitchen. My father had warned me that he would stay home all day to make sure I didn't leave the house. I wasn't sure I believed him, because he'd never missed shule before, especially on Shabbos. But he'd been in the kitchen when I went to the bathroom earlier, and he was still there. Getting out of the house today would not be easy. And I'd be in even more trouble when I got home, but I'd go crazy if I thought about that now.

I closed the bathroom door quietly. I brushed my teeth, splashed cold water on my face, and toweled it dry. Then I tiptoed back into my bedroom, put on my tights and my leotard, and pulled my Shabbos dress over the top.

My parents were still talking softly in the kitchen. I tiptoed out of my bedroom and toward the front door. Just three more steps and I'd be out of there. Two more steps and the front door would close behind me and for a while, at least, I'd be free.

One more step and—

"Where do you think you're going?" said my father.

I stopped for a moment, but I didn't answer him. I took that final step toward the door. I would come back later, much later, after he'd calmed down. After they'd both calmed down. But who was I kidding? They would never calm down.

"Stay where you are." His voice was a command. "If you leave now, if you set foot outside that door, you are not to come back. Do you understand, Yehudit? *You are not to come back.*"

―――――――

My father is waiting to see what I'll do now, and I hate him for putting me in this position, for making me choose between my family and my future. I don't want to choose. But he was never one for idle threats, and I know he won't change his position, now that he has made it clear.

I hesitate for the very last time. Then memories start to flood my mind, and it seems like every one of them has led to this particular moment, and I know with absolute clarity what it is that I must do. I step out into the morning air, closing the front door quietly behind me.

"Ditty, no!"

My mother's cry, filled with anguish and despair, almost makes me change my mind. But I know that if I give in now, I will never be free. I manage to propel myself away from the house and onto the footpath. Then I walk down Gordon Street in the direction of Glenhuntly Road.

―――――――

My mother's cry haunts me all the way down Brighton Road. It's not until I get off the tram at the corner of Carlisle Street that I realize I left home without really thinking things through. Where will I live? Where can I go?

Walking down the street, I feel as if a million eyes are

watching me and strangers are talking about me in hushed and scandalized tones. *There she goes, Ditty Cohen, unwanted scum of the universe. Even her own family doesn't want her.*

By the time I arrive at the National, I'm shaking uncontrollably. Miss Mitchell catches sight of me and turns pale.

"Ditty, what's wrong?"

I burst into tears. Before I know it, her arms are around me and my whole body is heaving with sobs.

When I've calmed down a bit, I tell her everything, beginning with what happened when I arrived home yesterday and ending with this morning's ultimatum.

"We'll sort out your living arrangements after we get *Giselle* out of the way," she says. "But don't worry, Ditty. In the meantime, you can stay with me."

A rush of gratitude overwhelms me. Miss Mitchell cares. She always has.

I survive the morning by staying focused on my part in the production, refusing to think about anything else. During the lunch break I hang out with some of the other dancers, but I don't join in their conversation. I don't want to talk about what has happened in the last twenty-four hours. Not yet. I'll go nuts if I think too much about it. So I sit quietly trying to eat the cheese-and-salad sandwich I bought at the Milk Bar across the road, but not managing to get much of it down.

The other dancers tuck into their salads and sandwiches, their pies and pasties. They talk about fashion and the latest movies and who's dating who, as well as the usual dancer talk of diets, eating disorders, and food. And they tell jokes and laugh. And though I can't really concentrate on any of it, it's kind of reassuring to know that for some people, everything is normal.

While Frances talks about the fight she had with her mum yesterday, I notice Miss Mitchell leaving the building. She comes back nearly an hour later and hands me a Target bag. In it are six pairs of underwear, a pair of pajamas, two T-shirts, three pairs of socks, and a toothbrush.

"We'll see what we can do about the rest of your wardrobe on Tuesday," she says. "What's wrong? You look as if I've robbed your grandmother."

"I don't think I can pay for all of that."

"I didn't ask you to. Don't insult me, Ditty." Then she gives me a hug, as if to compensate for the harshness of her tone.

The rest of the day passes in a daze. I don't feel any of the anticipation I usually feel before a performance. But as the theater fills up, the excitement of the other dancers starts to rubs off.

And then, quite suddenly, it's time. The music begins and Giselle's friends amble across the stage. Then comes Hilarion, the gamekeeper in love with Giselle, proudly holding up a dead pheasant.

Now it's my turn. To capture Giselle's innocent joy, I remember the soaring feeling of being on a swing when I was small, before I'd told a single lie. And later, when Giselle goes mad, the emotional turmoil of the last twenty-four hours is all I need for a very convincing portrayal.

The applause warms me. Out there in the audience, there are people who like what I do. People who accept me. People who approve of who I am.

Forty-Two

Going home with Miss Mitchell feels weird. I've only ever seen her as my ballet teacher, only ever thought about her existence in relation to mine. There is a huge part of her life I know nothing about.

Her flat is like her car and like Miss Mitchell herself—small and clean and tidy. On the wall in the living room there are framed photos of her in lead roles when she was younger. A lot younger.

She points to the phone almost as soon as we're inside. "Ring your parents, Ditty, just to let them know you're safe."

"I don't want to ring my parents."

"They're probably worried sick about you."

"If they are, they'll ring my mobile. But they won't ring. You'll see." I don't tell her that I've put my phone on silent, just in case, because I don't think I could face talking to them right now.

I go into the bathroom and change into the pajamas she bought me, while she makes up a bed on the living-room couch.

"I know you've got a lot on your mind," she says when I come back, "but you look too exhausted to think straight. I suggest you go to sleep now. We can talk in the morning."

————

I sleep deeply and don't wake up till ten. Miss Mitchell spoils me. She makes me toast and muesli and cut-up fruit. It's not until I start to eat that I realize how hungry I am.

Miss Mitchell has peppermint tea for breakfast and a single slice of toast with jam. We eat in companionable silence, until she notices me staring at a photo on the wall behind her. A younger Miss Mitchell in a wedding dress standing beside a man who has his arm around her, looking at her adoringly while she looks into the camera.

"We were married for two years," she says. "Then he died of cancer."

I don't know what to say.

"We wanted children, but we were not blessed. Maybe we left it too late. I was already well into my thirties when we married."

The telephone rings and she goes to answer it.

"Yes, wasn't it?" I hear her saying. "A fabulous performance. I know … no, not yet. We've still got three more performances to get through. Who? The girl who danced the lead?" She smiles at me as she speaks. "Yes, she was excellent... thank you, Margie." She puts down the phone and comes back to the table. "What with all the drama yesterday, I think I forgot to tell you how wonderful you were. It's such a pity your parents..."

She rethinks what she was about to say. "You know, Ditty, your parents are angry now because they've only just found out. Anyone would be angry. I know I would. But if you apologize, if you explain how much your dancing means to you and how determined you are to succeed, maybe they'll come round."

"I did apologize. I tried to explain."

"They must have felt very hurt, nonetheless. Still, you're their daughter and I'm sure they'll want you back."

"No. They won't. Not unless I agree to live by their rules, and I won't. I won't do that, and I don't want to lie about it anymore."

Miss Mitchell sighs. "I hate to think of you abandoning your family altogether. Is there anyone else in the family you could live with? An aunt? A grandmother? A family friend?"

All our friends and relatives are just as religious as my parents are. There's Linda's family, but even though they're not as religious as mine, I doubt they'd want someone who doesn't keep Shabbos living in their house.

"No, I don't think so," I say.

"Well, you won't be alone, Ditty. I'll always be here for you. And everyone at the National will be supporting you. We'll make sure you're okay."

The rest of that day and the next passes in a blur of class, rehearsal, and performances, and before I know it, it's Monday night and the last show is over. I take my final bows, and one of the younger students runs on stage and presents me with flowers. The applause is deafening, and though I'm still in a daze, I can't stop beaming.

Backstage, there are hugs and kisses all round as students and teachers leave the building in a flurry of coats and bags, some with homemade costumes flung over their arms. Apart from the caretaker, Miss Mitchell and I are the last to leave. She opens the door for me and I go through it ahead of her.

Pacing up and down the path in front of the door, her breath making little puffs of cloud in the cold night air, is Linda. It's so good to see her. She's waiting for me to come out, and as soon as she sees me, she rushes up and flings her arms around me, crushing me so tightly I can hardly breathe.

"Omigod-Ditty-I-can't-believe-you-ran-away-from-home-your-mum-is-freaking-out-she-hasn't-stopped-crying-and-my-mum's-been-trying-to-calm-her-down-she-says-you-have-to-stay-with-us-you-have-to-come-home-with-me-right-now-otherwise-she'll-kill-me-where-have-you-been-staying-all-this-time-you-haven't-been-an-swering-your-phone." She stops to take a massive breath. "Your-mum-says-if-anything-happened-to-you-she'd-never-forgive-herself-but-you-were-so-amazing-tonight-just-like-a-real-ballerina-what-are-you-going-to—"

"*Stop*! Calm down." I've never seen Linda like this before

and I want to reassure her. "I'm okay, Linda. It's not like I've been living on the street. I've been staying at Miss Mitchell's, and I can't come back to your place tonight because I've still got some stuff there. But tell your mum I'll come over tomorrow. And Linda, I didn't run away. My dad said that if I left the house, I couldn't come back. Even if I wanted to go home, it's too late now. My father doesn't want me..."

As the meaning of these words sinks in, my voice begins to crack. If I say another word, the floodgates will open. I'm determined not to cry.

Miss Mitchell has been watching all this time. She seems confused but kind of relieved, and I realize it's time for introductions.

"This is my cousin—Linda."

"Susan," says Miss Mitchell, extending her hand. "Susan Mitchell."

"Miss Mitchell is my ballet teacher," I say, as if Linda didn't know, as if I haven't been talking about her for the past five years.

"Great to meet you," says Linda, sounding almost normal again, if a little breathless. "You must be an amazing teacher. Ditty was fantastic, wasn't she?"

"Yes, she was," Miss Mitchell agrees.

Watching the exchange between my cousin and my teacher, I can't help noticing that there is something very different about Linda tonight. She just doesn't seem like her usual self.

Then it hits me. Gone are the jeans, the tight-fitting tops, the nose stud, the eyebrow ring, and the outrageous hair.

Beneath her duffle coat, Linda is modestly dressed in a loose-fitting, high-necked jumper and a skirt that billows out below her knees. She's wearing sensible boots, and looks like the sort of person even my father would welcome into his home with open arms. What's more, there is no Ben/Mark/Gordon/Lawrence/Terrence/Paul hovering around her.

"Did you come on your own?" I ask her.

Linda nods. "I wanted Sam to come, but..."

"Who's Sam?"

"My new boyfriend. You've got to meet him, Ditty. But anyway, he couldn't, because he's, like, really religious and he won't watch girls dancing."

"Tell me more," I said. Anything to take my mind off my own problems for a while.

Linda shivers and pulls her coat more tightly around her. "Not now. It's freezing cold, and it's late. I'll tell you tomorrow." Her eyes narrow with suspicion. "You will come tomorrow, won't you, Ditty?"

"Of course. I'll come around three."

"Okay, then. See you tomorrow."

Forty-Three

• ➤ •

The sun filters in through a crack in the curtains and I glimpse a patch of blue outside the window. For a split second, my spirits soar. Then I remember. *Giselle* is over and I'm still camping on Miss Mitchell's couch because I've been kicked out of my house. My heart plummets to the pit of my stomach, and I close my eyes and huddle deeper under the covers.

It must be Tuesday. There is no ballet this week or next because holidays at the National coincide with school holidays, and most schools broke up on Thursday. Not mine, though. Our holidays almost always start a week or two before or after everyone else's. But I won't be going back to Beis Hannah. By now, everyone at school will know I'm no longer living at home, and I won't be able to look anyone in the face. In any case, I don't suppose my father will continue to pay the fees.

I told Miss Mitchell this last night. I also told her that I'm destined to be penniless until I can find another job, because by now it must be common knowledge that I've turned my back on Torah. There's no way the Kingsleys will want me babysitting their kids, contaminating them with my blasphemous ideas.

Miss Mitchell listened calmly and didn't once interrupt. She's a good person to have on your side in times of crisis. In true Miss Mitchell style, she told me not to worry. She said she'd have a think about everything I'd said, sleep on it, and in the morning we'd try to work out what I should do.

I'm glad I'm not going back to Beis Hannah, but I don't know what I'll do instead. I reach for my phone to check the time. It's almost eleven. My mother will be busy doing laundry now; Ezra, Shayne, Hillel, and Gittel will all be in school, and Pinny at the kollel. Rochel will be in the park, feeding her baby mashed banana or pushing him on the swing.

I don't know when I'll ever see any of them again. I suppose I could go round to Rochel's—I haven't been forbidden to go there—but Rochel is probably the last person I want to see. She won't be on my side. She won't see past the heartache I've caused my parents. I can't say I blame her.

I swing my legs off the couch and sit up. On the coffee table is a note from Miss Mitchell.

Dear Ditty,
Gone shopping. Make yourself at home and help yourself to
breakfast. Will be back by twelve.
Love, Susan.

Susan. I try to imagine myself calling her by her first name. In my head she's still Miss Mitchell and always will be. I wander into the kitchen, still in my pajamas. There is sliced whole-grain bread in the bread bin on the kitchen bench, a bowl of fruit on the table, skim milk, orange juice, and yogurt in the fridge, and a few boxes of cereal in the pantry. I look through drawers and cupboards for a bowl and spoon and help myself to a small serving of Wheet-Bix with milk. But even though my stomach is rumbling, I hardly get anything down.

I wash my bowl and spoon and go into the bathroom to shower. Then I check my phone to see if there are any more missed calls. There are six from Emma, but none from my parents. I'm both relieved and disappointed—more disappointed than I care to admit.

I find Emma's number and she answers on the very first ring.

"Ditty? At last. You haven't been answering your phone. You were brilliant last night. I'm sorry I couldn't get backstage. You were a fabulous Giselle."

"Thanks, Em. I…" My voice starts to crack and suddenly I'm drowning in a wave of self-pity.

"What is it? What's the matter?"

"My parents found out about my dancing."

"Oh God! Was it bad?"

"Awful. They said if I left the house, I couldn't come back."

"Jeez, are you serious?"

"Yes. I've been staying at Miss Mitchell's."

There's a long silence on the phone.

"Em? Emma, are you there?"

"I'm here. I've just been thinking. It must be really weird staying with Miss Mitchell. Why don't you come and stay at my place?"

I'm grateful that she's asked me, but I can't help worrying I'd be in the way. "What if your parents don't want me there?"

"Why wouldn't they? I'll ask them, okay?"

I give my nose an angry blow.

"Don't cry, Ditty."

"I'm not," I say, blinking back tears. "But I hate feeling like a charity case."

"It won't be for long. If you get into ABS, you'll be able to share a flat with some of the interstate students."

"*If* I get in."

"Well, you've got a really good chance."

The door opens and Miss Mitchell comes in loaded up with shopping bags, her hair slightly windblown. I ring off and help her carry her bags into the kitchen. She doesn't comment on my red eyes and blotchy face. She just smiles at me and absentmindedly pats her hair into place.

"You know, Ditty, I thought we'd talk about your future today, but I've changed my mind. I think you need to take a week or two just to rest and process what you've been through, what you're still going through. You're exhausted and you must be feeling very confused. So take your time. Don't make any rash decisions."

She puts the kettle on and makes us tea. Then we sip it in silence, each of us wrapped up in our own thoughts. Miss Mitchell takes forever to finish hers, gazing quietly into the distance.

"What about that aunt of yours?" she says at last. "Didn't you promise to visit?"

I nod.

"Come on, then. I'll give you a lift."

———————

When Aunt Tamara hugs me, tears prick my eyes and spill over. She hugs me harder. "Ditty, Ditty, we've all been so worried about you."

For some reason I don't understand, her kindness makes it harder for me to stop crying. She grabs a handful of tissues from the box on the table and passes them to me. I blow my nose, wipe my eyes, and blow my nose again.

"We?" I manage.

"Your mother, Uncle Yankel, and I."

"My mother? She hasn't even called to find out if I'm still alive," I say. "Did she know I was coming here today. Did you tell her?"

"Of course I did," says Aunt Tamara.

"Then why isn't she here? If she were really worried about

me, she'd be here. She'd want to know where I've been and what I'm planning to do."

Aunt Tamara guides me over to the couch and sits me down. "She does want to know, and I promised I'd tell her."

"That's not the same."

"Maybe not, but your ... " She stops talking and shakes her head. "Your father has forbidden your mother to see you."

Any shred of remorse I may have felt for the pain I've caused my father evaporates in a burst of anger. "Why does she have to listen to him?" I cry.

"You know what he's like, Ditty, once he's made up his mind, and your mother has never been very good at standing up to him."

"Why not? *I* did."

"It's different for you. Even if you hadn't just left home, you would have been married soon. You wouldn't have been living under your father's roof much longer. But it's not like that for your mother. She has to live with him."

"But why does he have to be so narrow-minded?" I say.

"I doubt he sees it that way. His one aim in life is to raise good Jewish children, and he thinks he's failed. He's probably angrier with himself than he is with you. And I'm sure he'd jump at the chance to have you back, if you decided to fit in with the rest of the family."

"Fit in? You mean, give up dancing and become the person *he* wants me to be? Well, I won't. I won't do that."

Aunt Tamara sighs. "I didn't think you would, Ditty. But have you thought? Have you really thought about what you're doing?"

I bite my lip and don't reply.

"Because you're giving up on your family. You do realize that, don't you, Ditty?"

"No, I'm not. I'm not giving up on my family. They're giving up on me."

Aunt Tamara sighs again, a deep, frustrated sigh. "The thing is," she continues, "you can't dance forever. What will happen when you're too old to dance? Or if you get injured? Dancers get injured all the time. What then? What will you have when you don't have dance?"

"I'll have my freedom."

There's a lot of bravado behind the words and in the tone of my voice, but I'm not as certain as I sound. I pick up my bag and get up to leave.

"Where are you going?"

"Back to Miss Mitchell's, I suppose."

"Your ballet teacher? Don't be silly, Ditty. You're staying here. I'll make up the pull-out bed in Linda's room."

"Really? You want me to stay here, with you?"

"Of course." Her voice is kind, her face a more peaceful version of my mother's.

"For ... for how long?" I ask.

"As long as you like. As long you need to."

I'm beginning to realize that Aunt Tamara is my strongest ally.

"Do ... do you think I'm making a mistake?" I ask her, daring to question what I've done.

"I can't answer that, Ditty. I can't tell you how to live your life."

"But what do you *think*?"

The creases on her forehead deepen as she tries to formulate her thoughts.

"I don't know, Ditty," she says at last. "But some people have a vocation in life, and from what Linda has told me, maybe you're one of them."

I'm alone at the Fishers'. Aunt Tamara has gone shopping, Uncle Yankel is still at work, and Linda isn't back from university yet. I have the house to myself. Minutes turn into hours, and still there's been no word from my parents or anyone in my immediate family.

I'm mulling over the conversation with my aunt when my phone rings. It's Miss Mitchell, wanting to know whether I need a lift back to her place. I thank her and tell her that I'll probably be staying at Linda's for a while, and she seems pleased for me, glad that I haven't abandoned all of my family, and that not all of my family have abandoned me.

I turn on the TV, the first time I've ever done this at Linda's house. After ten minutes or so, I realize I haven't taken in a word that's been said. I turn the TV off again and stare out the window. I sit there staring until Linda comes home.

Forty-Four

For the next few days I do nothing but sleep, getting up only for brief, unscheduled meals. I don't want to do anything. I can't do anything. I'm worn out, inside and out. I can't even think. Not about the future and not about the past. My mind and body have gone on strike.

A sort of emotional numbness has come over me, and I'm not sure what feelings lie beneath. Right now, I don't even care.

Sometimes people talk to me and I can't answer. I hear, but I can't respond. It's too much effort. I lie on the bed for hours at a time, forgetting where I am. There is the occasional opening of the bedroom door, a snatch of distant conversation, a hushed murmur of voices.

There's a light touch of a hand on my wrist. A woman's touch. I hear a woman's voice saying, "Give her time."

"Thank you, doctor." That second voice was Aunt Tamara's. I don't have the energy to acknowledge her, to reassure her. My eyes are closed, my face to the wall. I hear Linda when she comes in at night and leaves in the morning.

Aunt Tamara, Uncle Yankel, and Linda have been treating me like an invalid—taking care of me but giving me space. Maybe I am a sort of invalid, though I can't say exactly what's wrong with me.

Sometimes I find myself crying. I don't know why. I don't feel sad. I don't feel anything. The tears come of their own accord, like a sneeze or a nosebleed.

Miss Mitchell has rung and left messages for me. So has Emma. Not Sara, though. I wonder if she even knows where I am. I'm too tired to wonder for long, or to think much about her. I'm too exhausted to ring anyone back.

I slip in and out of consciousness, wondering, in some small, dimly aware part of my mind, whether my mother will come. She doesn't, but I'm too listless to care.

———————

Somehow it's Sunday, the day before classes at the National are due to resume, and I discover that time has tricked me. In my cocoon of a world where one slow day was like another, it wasn't clear where one day ended and another began.

Strangely, now that those long, timeless days are over, it seems they went by quickly after all.

Time has returned and life has begun to gain momentum. I make an enormous effort and return Miss Mitchell's calls, apologizing for not having called back sooner. She sounds worried about me. She says she wants to see me, and Aunt Tamara says she's welcome any time, so I ask her over. She says she'll come at eleven, and that's precisely when the doorbell rings. Eleven. On the dot.

I invite her in and introduce her to my aunt, who mumbles something politely and then leaves. The conversation feels oddly unreal at first, as if I'm a spectator, watching Miss Mitchell talk to me, watching my own responses, waiting to see how this film unfolds.

Miss Mitchell tells me that classes are starting tomorrow; she hopes I'll come. I tell her I don't feel like dancing. Don't think I *can* dance. Not sure I'll ever be able to dance again. She hugs me and says, "Ditty, I know things aren't easy for you at the moment, but you might find that dance is just what you need. Oh, I almost forgot. I brought you these." She opens her bag and takes out an envelope, lifts the flap to reveal a stack of photos—snapshots of *Giselle*. "These will have to do until the DVD is ready." She holds one up in front of me. I look at it, and a miniature version of myself looks back. But I feel removed from it, as if it's got nothing to do with me.

"I'm having that one enlarged."

"It's a good photo," I say.

"Well, you were a lovely Giselle."

Out of politeness, I look through the rest of the photos, though I can't motivate myself to feel interested. Most of the photos have me in them, but it's like looking at a stranger.

The photos were all taken during the final performance, when Kieran danced the male lead. There's one happy one of the two of us together, before Giselle discovers she's been betrayed.

"Ditty, I've been meaning to ask you..."

"Yes?"

"How about helping out with the younger students at the National? The four- and five-year-olds? Those classes are very large, and Miss Percy could do with an assistant."

"Really?" My tone is disinterested. I can't pretend.

"Really." Miss Mitchell's voice is full of enthusiasm. "It wouldn't be full time, of course, just a few afternoons a week, but in return, you could take class in the morning with the full-timers. We could waive your tuition fees and pay you a small sum of money. It wouldn't be much—but at least it would replace that babysitting job you've lost."

I'm not even sure whether I'll have the strength to leave the house—I haven't set foot outside the door since the day I arrived—let alone help teach a class of four and five-year-olds, but I know it's time I made the effort. Besides, it's such a generous offer.

"So, how about it?"

"I'll try, but I don't know if..."

"Good, that's settled, then."

———

After Miss Mitchell leaves, I'm on my own. Aunt Tamara and Uncle Yankel have gone to a funeral, and I noticed

Linda slipping out during Miss Mitchell's visit. I make myself a sandwich and think of Sara, wondering if her reunion with her dad was everything she hoped it would be. I still don't know how to contact her, and I'm not sure what I'd say if she called me.

Emma calls instead and tries to lure me out of the house. I explain that this is my final day of hibernation, and promise to see her in class tomorrow.

My aunt and uncle return at five. Aunt Tamara is busy in the kitchen and Uncle Yankel retreats to his study with a cup of tea. Then Linda comes in.

"You look better," she says. "How do you feel?"

"Okay."

"Good, because there's something I've been dying to tell you."

She waits until I'm forced to ask what it is. When I do, she looks smug. "It's about Sam," she says.

"Who?"

"Sam. You know, my boyfriend. I told you about him."

Maybe she did, now that I think about it.

"What about him?"

"He's not just my boyfriend, Ditty. We're unofficially engaged."

As if the events of the past few weeks haven't already been weird enough, this information adds a whole new dimension to weirdness. A job offer from Miss Mitchell, and now this. All in one day.

Things are happening so fast. Linda engaged? Is this a joke? I'm not sure how I'm meant to react.

"I'm serious, Ditty."

It turns out that she is. She goes on to tell me that no one knows about their engagement except for their parents. And now me.

"You'll meet him soon. He's coming for dinner."

———————

A couple of hours later, all five of us are sitting at the kitchen table and I'm eyeing my cousin's latest heartthrob. I still can't believe that Linda, Miss New-Boyfriend-Every-Month, is actually engaged, and to a boy who is so religious he won't watch women dancing.

How did this happen? When did this happen? How come I'd never heard of this guy until the night of my performance?

Sam is the stricter variety of modern orthodox. He's in his final year of Law at Melbourne University, where Linda is doing Arts with a major in drama.

Aunt Tamara places a bowl of vegetable soup in front of me, and as I blow on it I watch Linda and Sam surreptitiously, looking for clues. They're sitting side by side at the table, grinning at each other. By the time the meatballs and rice are served, I'm staring at them outright because I realize that no one is looking at me anyway. In fact, I don't think I've ever felt more invisible.

"When did you two meet?" I ask.

"Five weeks, four days, and seven hours ago," says Linda, still gazing into his eyes.

My mouth drops open.

"We're getting married in December, when Sam finishes his course."

Uncle Yankel beams at Sam and pours him some wine. Aunt Tamara piles more food onto his plate without even asking if he wants it. I sit there tongue-tied while the four of them make plans for the future. We remain at the table for hours, and Sam stays till midnight.

"So, what do you think?" asks Linda after he leaves. "Isn't he amazing!"

I don't know what to say. He looks like just an ordinary guy to me. "You haven't known him very long."

"I don't need to. He's the *one*, Ditty."

"How do you know?"

Linda shrugs. "I just do. I've never been more certain of anything."

"Why didn't you say anything before?"

"I didn't want to rain on your depression."

"Was I depressed?"

"What do *you* think?"

Maybe I was. I don't want to dwell on my own frame of mind. I'd rather think about Linda's.

"I thought you didn't want to be religious," I say as I lie down on the pull-out bed. "You always said it was a bunch of lies."

"Did I?"

"Uh-huh. How short is your memory span? You said you didn't believe in any of it. Six weeks ago you were all over that other boyfriend of yours and you were wearing jeans…"

"And now I'm turning over a new leaf. No more tight tops or mini-skirts. No more body piercing. And no more boyfriends."

"When did you make this decision?"

"The day I met Sam." She laughs, and I laugh with her.

"But seriously," I say, "are you going to try to talk him out of it?"

"Talk him out of what?"

"Out of being so … religious."

"No. Why would I? He has the right to believe, just as I have the right not to."

"Does he know what you really think?"

"Of course he does. And he doesn't mind, as long as I'm willing to lead an orthodox lifestyle."

"And are you?"

"For Sam? Of course."

"But what about all that stuff you said about brainwashing, and Hashem not caring what we do?"

"Honestly, Ditty, I don't think it matters whether I believe it all or not. Living an orthodox lifestyle won't be such a hardship. I was brought up with it. I'm used to it. It's not like I don't know what I'm letting myself in for."

"I don't think I could ever go back to that kind of life. It would be like going back to jail."

"It's different for you. You're a dancer. You can't be religious and a dancer. But I don't have your passion. And I definitely don't have your courage."

"I always thought you had more guts than anyone," I say.

"I didn't. Not really. I never risked anything like you did. There was never anything at stake. My parents never really minded what I did. I think I'd have been turned off religion forever if it had been shoved down my throat. But it wasn't like that for me. My parents gave me a choice. Yours tried to force you."

"You don't think what I'm doing is wrong?"

"No."

"I thought you might be disapproving, you know, now that you're 'religious' again..."

"Ha! That would be really hypocritical."

Then Linda gets this dreamy look on her face and says, half-joking, "The only thing that bothers me about becoming as observant as Sam is that I'll have to wait another six months before I can touch him."

"Yeah...but then you'll have the rest of your life to touch him."

"True," she says. "I hope we have lots of sex before we have kids."

"Kids?"

Linda yawns. "Sam wants five. He wants..." She falls asleep mid-sentence, and I never do find out what else Sam wants.

An hour later I'm still awake. I lie watching the shadows move across the bedroom wall. Then I glance at Linda, who is snoring, and I smile. She's lying on her back, one arm flung across her forehead, the other hidden by a quilt that lies diagonally across her body, its corner trailing on the floor. Linda asleep looks just like the old Linda. She might have ditched the nose stud and the eyebrow ring, but she's still the Linda I always knew.

Forty-Five

• ◆ •

I wait till I'm sure the house is empty. Then I walk quickly up the concrete path to the door. Once inside, I look around. The house is as familiar as an old pair of gloves, but it's unfamiliar, too.

I creep silently along the hall and into my room. The bunk bed has already been replaced by a single one, and Shayne's pajamas are folded on the pillow of the bed that used to be mine. I try to swallow the lump in my throat. How quickly this room has forgotten me.

I open the wardrobe. Luckily, my clothes are still where I left them—some hanging, some folded on shelves. I reach in behind a pile of jumpers, where a hidden stash of dance magazines is still wedged between the spare blanket and the back of the cupboard.

I pull the mags out. Then I take the other items I've come

for—my underwear, my winter coat, a pair of boots, a few shirts and jumpers. I stand on tiptoe to reach my secret wardrobe that lives at the back of the topmost shelf, the shelf that Shayne and Gittel are too short to reach. I pull out wrinkled jeans, a mini-skirt, a sleeveless top.

I don't know why I feel like a thief. These are my things— I'm entitled to take them. I bring in a large trash bag from the kitchen and stuff my belongings inside it. It's time to leave. I take a quick look around the house, peeking into every room.

Nothing much has changed, but Rochel's room is empty now. I still think of it as Rochel's room even though Pinny moved into it after Rochel left home. Now that Pinny is leaving, it would have been my room. How ironic! I would have finally had a room of my own.

It feels strange to be here in the middle of the day. It's ten to one now, and my brothers and sisters are at school, my father is at work, and my mother's out shopping. She always shops on Mondays. It's a safe bet that I can get out of the house again without anyone knowing I've come and gone, but I can't help feeling nervous. It's irrational, I know. But I've been forbidden to come here, and I feel uncomfortable. I have to leave.

I carry the bin bag through the front door and put it on the ground.

Goodbye house. Goodbye home. Just thinking the words brings tears to my eyes. I shake my head, trying to avoid this unwanted emotion. I can't afford to sink back into depression, into the emotional fog that clouded my world those first few weeks after leaving home. I have to be strong.

I start to lock the door when I hear a familiar voice behind me.

"Yehudit!"

What the hell is my father doing here? My hand trembles as I fumble with the key in the lock, and I turn to face him.

"Have you come to your senses? Have you come back to Torah?" There is an odd mixture of hope and resignation in my father's voice and eyes.

I shake my head slowly, deliberately, my whole body quaking beneath his gaze.

"I can't believe you're doing this," he says.

There's no point in arguing. We will never agree.

I drop the key and bend down to retrieve it.

"Leave that key." His voice is harsh and unyielding, his face once again an impenetrable mask.

I don't say a word. I don't ask him what he's doing home in the middle of the day, or how he's been. I leave the key where I dropped it, just as he instructed. Then I fling the trash bag over my shoulder like a sack, and flee.

Emma, Kirsten, and Frances all crowd around me. They're actually fighting over me—each of them has invited me to stay at their place.

We're standing in Chapel Street, right outside the entrance to Gloria Jean's. The four of us have agreed to meet here, one Sunday each month. It's the only way we can keep in touch, since Frances has just given up ballet and Kirsten, too, will be quitting soon. She says she has to study for exams.

I tell them that I'm fine at Linda's, that my aunt and uncle have been wonderful. But it's a relief to know I can stay over at their houses on the weekends. I've decided to move out of the Fischers' every Friday afternoon, and move back in again on Saturday night or Sunday morning. Even though none of them have asked me to do that, it just wouldn't feel right to stay there for Shabbos when I don't observe it.

"What was it like at Miss Mitchell's?" asks Kirsten. "I bet her flat was really clean and tidy, nothing out of place."

"You're right, it was."

Kirsten laughs. "I could never have stayed there. I would have been too nervous to breathe."

"Oh, but she's been fantastic to me…"

"She's coaching you every day now, isn't she?" says Frances.

"Twice a week. Just until my audition at ABS next month. And I'm doing class with the full-timers every morning."

"You two will get in for sure, though, won't you?" Frances persists.

Emma and I roll our eyes at this. Her ankle is better now, and she'll be auditioning, too.

"Unless you have a crystal ball," Emma says, "nothing is sure."

We go inside, place our orders, and settle ourselves in a corner of the coffee shop that's furnished with the kind of comfy but worn couches and armchairs that people usually have at home—easy to sink into and hard to get out of.

Our order is called, and Kirsten goes over to the counter and brings back a tray of cappuccinos. I blow on mine, skim the froth off the top, spoon it into my mouth, and lick my lips. It's sweet and delicious. My taste buds are starting to perk up again after weeks of barely tasting anything. This simple enjoyment is one I no longer take for granted.

"Ditty," says Kirsten, "can I ask you something weird?"

I look up and nod.

"Are you still Jewish?"

I smile at the question. "Of course I am. I'm just not religious, if that's what you mean. I guess I'm Jewish the way you guys are Christian. You know, you swap presents on Christmas but you're not religious."

"Actually, Ditty, I don't consider myself a Christian," Frances says. "Christmas presents don't have much to do with it. It's really just a question of belief."

"Well, I was born Jewish, so as far as I'm concerned, I always will be. For me, it's not a question of belief. It's just a fact."

"But you don't look so Jewish anymore," says Kirsten. "Not now that you've stopped wearing those awful clothes."

I laugh at her bluntness. "You mean I don't look haredi."

"Right," she says. "You look so much better when you're wearing jeans."

"So, what's it like helping out at the National?" Frances asks me.

"Great! The kids are really sweet. They're so..." Suddenly I get all choked up and I can't continue.

"What? What is it, Ditty?"

Thinking of the kids at the National reminds me of my brothers and sisters. Especially Gittel, with her wide smile and cheerful nature. And Hillel, his *tzizis* dangling, scruffy shirt hanging out over pants he can never keep clean. Their faces are still clear in my mind, but I'm scared the day will come when I'll forget them. They'll grow up, and change, and one day I might not even recognize them if I pass them in the street... I wonder what they'll think of me when they're older, old enough to understand...

"I miss my brothers and sisters," I say.

"You still can't see them?" Emma asks.

"Nope. I went to visit my older sister, Rochel, and she wouldn't let me in. She told me I've ruined my younger sisters' lives. That because of me, it will be really hard for them to get a good shidduch when they're older."

"Oh, that's crap!"

"It's probably true."

"Even if it is," says Emma, "it's not your fault. It's not your fault that some people are so narrow-minded that they judge others by what their sisters do."

"Maybe, but my family doesn't want anything to do with me now. My older brother, Pinny, got married last week, and I wasn't even invited to the wedding."

"Did you want to be?" asks Frances.

"Frances!" says Emma. "What sort of a question is that?"

But Frances isn't fazed. "Well, did you?" she asks again.

I picture my family and the easy sense of camaraderie among them. I'm hit by a pang of nostalgia so sharp that it winds me. It seems a lifetime ago. I try to imagine myself at

Pinny's wedding, and all I can see is everyone pointing fingers at me as if I'm some kind of criminal.

"Maybe not…" I concede.

"Well, then…"

"Yeah, I see your point, but…"

"But what?"

"It hurts," I say.

———

After I leave my friends, I find myself thinking about my dad, wondering if he'll ever change. I have to doubt it. Religion is the center of his life. He's passionate about it, and it leaves no room for anything else.

There's something to be said for religion, something that maybe a lot of people overlook. For some people, it's a great way to enhance their self-esteem. Religion will take anyone. Even if you're not particularly smart or particularly talented, and there's nothing you're especially good at, you can be "good at" religion.

My father is good at religion. So is Rochel.

I'm just not.

To be good at religion, you have to really believe.

Can you force yourself to do that? I'm trying to figure out the answer when my phone rings.

"Ditty?" I recognize the husky voice of Jason Brown. He must have heard I've left home.

"Hi Jase." It actually feels quite good to hear from him.

We chat for a while, and I'm thinking of the first time I saw him, how good-looking he was, and what a wonderful dancer.

Then I remember how he reacted when I turned him down. Was I being racist? I really don't think so, but I can see why he might have felt that way. Yet even though our conversations ended badly, he'd never held a grudge against me. I have to admit, he's pretty nice … he's also the best partner I've ever had, and I imagine the two of us at ABS …

"So, how about it?" he's saying now. "One date, Ditty. Coffee. A movie. It's your call."

A few months ago, a date with Jason was unthinkable. But things have changed. My family has disowned me now, so who would I be hurting?

"Okay," I say.

Forty-Six

•◆•

I'm sitting on the pull-out bed in Linda's room one evening, sewing ribbons on a pair of pointe shoes, when Aunt
Tamara knocks on the door.

"You've got a visitor, Ditty. And before you get your hopes
up ... no, it's not your mother."

"Then who?"

"Why don't you come and see?"

I follow Aunt Tamara down the stairs and into the living room.

"Omigod! Sara!"

We throw our arms around each other, shrieking and
jumping up and down.

"So, did you meet your dad? What was it like?"

"Offer your friend a drink, Ditty. And something to eat,"
Aunt Tamara interrupts. She puts a bottle of Vanilla Coke on

the table, along with two glasses and a plate of biscuits. "I'll get out of your way now," she says. "I'm sure you two have plenty of catching up to do."

Sara swallows a mouthful of Coke and takes a bite of one of Aunt Tamara's homemade biscuits. "It was weird, Ditty. I mean, my dad seemed happy to see me, but..."

"What?"

"He's got this whole other family now. I've got a four-year-old sister and a two-year-old brother."

"You're kidding me!"

"Nope."

"Your dad didn't mention it in any of the letters?"

"Not a word. He said he thought it was better not to, in case it upset me."

"Why did he think it would upset you?"

"They're goyim, Ditty. They're not even Jewish." I see the pain in her eyes when she says this and I wish I could say something that would make her feel better.

"Your dad's wife didn't convert after they got married?" I ask softly.

Sara shakes her head. "She's Catholic. Can you imagine? She cooks bacon for breakfast. But she tried. She made a little kosher kitchen for me in the laundry, with paper plates and plastic cutlery, and she bought me kosher food. But it was weird. I felt so out of place."

"I bet."

"I could never live like that," she says. "I could never do what my dad did. Give up on Judaism. Chuck it all away like that. I just…couldn't. I wouldn't know myself if I did. It's so much a part of me," she continues. "It's in my blood."

In my blood. I've heard that before. But is it true? Could Judaism really be in our blood? Is it in our DNA? It couldn't really be genetic, could it? Because if it was, then how could Sara's dad have thrown it away?

"I guess that's why I came back," Sara continues. "My dad said I could stay with them as long as I liked, but it just didn't feel right. I'm sorry I didn't call, Ditty. I just…I didn't know what to say. But I really missed you."

"I'm really glad you're back," I say. "So, what's he like, your dad?"

"Laid-back. Calm. Nothing like my mum. I'll still be in touch with him," she adds. "He's promised to come to Melbourne to see me."

"But your mum…"

"She'll let him see me now because I gave her a scare. She thought she'd lost me. Oh, and before I forget, she told me to give you this."

She opens her bag and pulls out a DVD. I take it from her and cringe when I see the cover. It's the movie *Billy Elliot* that I lost all those years ago. Which means that the secret Sara and I have studiously kept from Mrs. Kesten all these years is not so secret after all.

"I don't believe this!" I murmur. "Your mum…"

"Found it in her room, where you left it."

"I can't believe I was so careless."

"She knew that we knew about the TV. She knew we watched it."

"But why didn't she say anything?"

"She said she couldn't very well tell us to stay away from it when she watched it herself. She wanted to return the DVD sooner but she couldn't, not without letting on that she knew."

"Wasn't she angry?"

Sara shrugs. "If she was, she's over it. She wants to see you."

"Why?"

"Don't know. But I said I'd ask you to come over."

"Maybe she wants to tell me off. Maybe she wants me to stay away from you."

"Maybe you're just being paranoid."

I laugh, but I can't help feeling apprehensive as we walk back to Sara's house. Mrs. Kesten opens the door with a smile on her face, and I soon realize I have nothing to fear.

"Thanks for the DVD. I ... I'm sorry I went into your bedroom without permission," I stammer. "It was an invasion of privacy."

"Yes, it was, but I understand, Ditty, and I've forgiven you." She's looking at me with such compassion that I realize I may have underestimated her. "I know things can't be easy for you," she adds.

"I've left home. Did you know?"

Mrs. Kesten nods. "Of course. Everyone knows. I can't say I was surprised, Ditty. I knew about your dancing."

"You did? But ... how?"

"When I came home from work that day and saw you with your foot practically on the ceiling ..."

"I was only stretching."

"You call that stretching? With your foot so beautifully pointed and that perfect posture? You'd obviously been trained. It's all right, Ditty. I understand. I'm sure you'll make a beautiful dancer."

Forty-Seven

• ◆ •

As the weeks pass, I try to process all that has happened in the last few months—or, to be more precise, the last five and a half years. I don't know if I've fully come to terms with any of it yet and, to be honest, I don't know if I ever will. I still wake up some mornings expecting to find myself lying in my bed at home, with Shayne asleep on the top bunk opposite and Gittel stirring in the bunk below. Then, when I remember where I am, a familiar sinking feeling takes hold of me and I have to force myself to shrug it off.

Still, most days I'm okay. The confrontation with my parents, the thing I'd dreaded for so long, was every bit as bad as I'd feared. But I didn't die. The world didn't end. And I've learnt something about who I am—I'm stronger than I knew I could be.

I feel oddly serene. Maybe this feeling won't last, because

the truth is, I just don't know where the future will take me. Maybe there will be moments of panic or fear, moments when I question whether what I did was right, but at least everything is out in the open now.

———

One day I wake up feeling calm and energized. I'm hoping the day will be a good one.

Linda wakes up, sees me, and grins. "So, how are you this morning?"

"Good," I say, just mildly surprised that this is actually true.

"Big day, today, huh?"

Oh my God! It's the day of my audition. My nerves kick into place instantly, but they're good nerves. I jump out of bed.

"Make sure you have a hearty breakfast," says Linda.

My stomach's flipping like pancakes. Pancakes! Ugh! "I don't think I could eat a thing."

"You can't dance on an empty stomach."

"Yes, Mum." And I'm quiet for a moment, thinking of my real mum, wondering when, if ever, I'll see her again.

My audition is at eleven, along with the other dancers whose surnames begin with a letter from *A* to *K*. Emma, whose surname begins with *W*, won't be auditioning till one, so there's no point in going together. Instead, we wish each other luck over the phone.

Aunt Tamara offers to drive me to the station, and from there I take a train into the city. When I reach the Australian

Ballet building in Kavanagh Street, some boys nearly collide with me as they come through the door and I remember that the boys' audition class began at nine. It must be over now.

The butterflies in my tummy are still beating their wings as I take the lift up to the fifth floor, where the ABS has its offices and studios. When the lift door opens, I step out and come face to face with Kieran McKenzie.

"Hey, Kieran! How did it go?"

"Scary," he says. "But I made it to the finals."

"Congratulations! When are they?"

"Tomorrow at three."

"Well, good luck."

"Thanks." He kisses my cheek. "Good luck to you too, Ditty."

I wave to him as he gets into the lift, and then I take some deep calming breaths before going to register for my audition.

I am assigned a number—23—which I'm to pin onto the front and back of my leotard. I sneak a glance at the other girls who will be auditioning with me. They are thin, with well-toned muscles, straight backs, and slightly turned-out feet.

I try not to think about the fact that there are so many aspiring dancers and so few places. Instead, I visualize myself showing up for class here next year, and then being chosen for a coveted role. I'm so involved in my fantasy that by the time I reach the dressing room, I'm already being offered a place in the company.

I change into my ballet shoes, brush my hair and put it up, and apply just a little make-up.

"Ditty! Is there a Ditty Cohen here?"

Outside the changing room, Miss Mitchell is waiting for me. She's standing there calmly, as if she could wait all day.

"I just came by to wish you luck," she says.

A second later I'm enveloped in her warm embrace, which is solid and grounding and real. It seems like the only thing that is, because I can't quite believe I'm here, about to audition for the best, the most prestigious ballet school in the country.

"Just give it your best shot," says Miss Mitchell. "You deserve to be here. You've earned your place." Somehow she has read my mind. "Best of luck, Ditty!" she adds, and then she's gone before I have a chance to thank her.

Her words have given me the extra dose of courage I need. I've come this far, and if I could get through the last five years, and more importantly, the last two months, then I can certainly get through the next hour and a half.

"Okay, girls," says the lady in charge, "please line up in order of the numbers you've been given. Right. Now follow me."

We run into the studio and take our places at the barre. A panel of four judges sits at a table at the front of the studio, and every member of the panel is an ex–principal dancer. It is they who will decide who will be accepted into the school. Adrenalin rushes through my body, but my head is clear. The class begins.

I dance to vindicate my past. I dance for my future.

The audition is over so quickly it feels like time has accelerated. Then it slows right down to a relentless crawl while the panel goes off to deliberate. It's scary to think that my future is now out of my hands. Despite my bid for freedom and the right to choose, in the end it is not me, but a panel of judges, who will determine my fate.

Fate, chance, destiny, other people—all have a say in how my life unfolds. I know that now. I will never be completely autonomous—no one ever is—and there are no guarantees. In the end, the control we have over our own lives is tiny. Tiny—yet huge.

"Girls, the panel has made its decision. If I call your number, you will need to back here for a final audition tomorrow at ten."

Twenty-three, twenty three, twenty-three…

I repeat it like a mantra, like a prayer.

The waiting is almost over. I have done all I can.

EPILOGUE

—Three Years Later—

The dressing room is humming with activity. I push one last hairpin into my bun and use liberal amounts of hair spray to hold it in place, squeezing my eyes shut as I spray.

"Ditty! There's someone to see you."

"Who?"

Emma shrugs. "She didn't say."

I weave my way through the other dancers and out into the corridor.

I see her straight away, but I don't recognize her at first. For a split second she just looks old and unfamiliar. Then her features rearrange themselves into the mother I remember.

"Ditty!" She opens her arms and I fall into them. She bursts into tears as her arms close around me, hugging me tightly. I cry too, and minutes pass before either one of us can speak.

"I couldn't stay away," she says at last. "I had to see you. Aunt Tamara told me you'd be dancing tonight. I had to come..."

"You're...you're here for the performance?"

My mother nods and wipes her eyes. "I can't believe my daughter has just signed a contract with the Australian Ballet.

I lied to your father," she continues. "He doesn't know I'm here."

She's battling with her conscience and I feel for her. I know what it's like.

I look at her more closely. The lines on her face are more pronounced than I remembered, the skin more withered.

"I understand now, Ditty," she says. "I understand how you can want something so badly it makes you tell lies." It's her way of saying she forgives me. And if she can forgive me, then I can forgive myself.

"Thank you," I whisper.

And we're crying again. She takes a wad of crumpled tissues from her coat pocket and hands me one.

"How's everyone at home?" I ask her.

"Baruch Hashem, I can't complain. Rochel's baby is adorable and her other three are growing up nicely. Pinny's wife is pregnant again, and Ezra is going to study for a year in Israel before he gets married."

"And the others?"

"Shayne still misses you. She talks about you ... when your father's not around."

"And Hillel? Gittel?"

"They're children. They're still at school."

"Do you see Sara?"

My mother nods. "It hasn't been easy for her. She had a hard time finding a shidduch. Most of the boys lost interest as soon as they found out that her father married a shikse. But in the end it all worked out. She's getting married soon."

"I know."

Sara and I still talk occasionally on the phone, but our lives are so different now, we hardly ever see each other anymore.

Just then, Julia from make-up interrupts us. "Ditty, you'll have to finish getting ready now."

"Right. I'm coming."

I turn back to my mother.

"Where will you be sitting?"

"Row J, with Aunt Tamara, Uncle Yankel, and Linda."

"Will I see you after the show?"

She nods. "Now that I've seen you once, I don't think I'll be able to stay away. Good luck, Ditty."

I watch her as she opens the stage door and disappears behind it. Then I hurry into the dressing room to reapply my make-up, now streaked with tears.

———

The conductor stands up and a ripple of applause goes through the audience. Then the overture begins, the curtain rises, and time seems suspended while I wait for my cue. Before I know it, I'm taking my position on the stage, looking out into the black sea that is the audience. Somewhere out there is my mother.

She's watching a small spotlight that grows, larger and larger, until it floods the entire stage. Soon, the magic of ballet will unfold before her eyes.

She has never been to a ballet before. Will it capture her imagination as it did mine?

I lift my arms and rise up onto my toes. I look out in the direction of row J and I swear I can make out her face. She is leaning forward in her seat, her eyes on the stage.

Look at me, I silently plead. And she does. She looks right at me.

A moment later I am moving through space. Spinning. Twirling. Dancing.

In the light.

GLOSSARY

Am Yisrael: the nation of Israel

Baruch Hashem: Blessed be God

bashert: ordained by Heaven

bracha: blessing

bris: short for *bris mila,* lit. (literally) "covenant"

bris mila: circumcision/circumcision ceremony representing a male Jew's covenant with God

challah: braided rolls or loaves of bread traditionally used on Sabbath and festivals

chillul Shabbos: desecration of the Sabbath

daven: pray

emes: truth

goyim: non-Jews, lit. "nations" (other than Israel)

halacha: Jewish Law; a particular Jewish law

haredi: ultra-orthodox, lit. from the Hebrew word "hared" meaning "anxious" (The Torah is such a serious matter that one is anxious to keep its strictures.)

Hashem: God, word used to denote God, lit. "the Name"

hilchos Shabbos: the laws of Sabbath

hora: a dance that is traditionally performed at Jewish weddings and bar-mitzvahs

kashrus: the state of being kosher, pertaining to foods that are allowed to be eaten

kavannah: intent, esp. the proper intent in prayer

kedusha: holiness

kiddush: sanctification, the blessing over wine mostly made on Sabbath and festivals

kohanim gedolim: High Priests

kol isha: the sound of a woman's voice singing, lit. "a woman's voice"

Kol Nidre: the name of the prayer that ushers in the Day of Atonement, lit. "All My Vows"

kollel: a place where Torah is studied by men of all ages, including married men

l'chaim: toast, lit. "to life"

mazeltov: congratulations, lit. "good luck"

mezuzah: small parchment containing holy script generally fixed to the doorpost of Jewish homes as a symbol that God is protecting them

mikve: ritual bath

mitzvah: commandment, good deed

mitzvos: plural of *mitzvah*

mohel: a man who is trained and authorized, in accordance with Jewish Law, to perform a circumcision

moshiach: messiah

nida: time of the month where a woman is "impure" or "unclean"

Olam Haba: the World to Come

payos: side locks

reb: rabbi

rebbetzin: rabbi's wife

Shabbos: the Sabbath

shalom bayis: peace in the home

sheitel: wig

shema: a prayer declaring the oneness of God

shidduch: match, the pairing of two people as a couple

shikse: non-Jewish woman (derogatory)

shiur: lesson on Torah, lit. "lesson"

shiva: fig. sitting in mourning, lit. "sitting" (Mourners traditionally sit on low stools or on the floor for seven days after the death of a close relative.)

shofar: a ram's horn (traditionally blown on the High Holidays)

shteibel: small house (generally old and dilapidated) that has been converted into a *shule*

shule: synagogue, Jewish place of worship

tefach: a type of measurement

teshuva: repentance

treif: non-kosher, intrinsically unfit for eating (rather than through a lack of proper supervision), fig. unsanctioned, unclean

tsnius: modest, modesty

tzedakkah: charity

tzizis: fringes or tassels attached to garments (usually undergarments) worn by Jewish males as a reminder of God's commandments

Vilna Gaon: The Genius of Vilna (This was the title given to Rabbi Elijah ben Shlomo Zalman, a renowned Torah scholar and one of the most influential Jewish sages in modern history.)

Yamim Noraim: High Holidays, High Holy Days

yeshiva: a school where boys learn Torah and Talmud

yetzer hara: evil inclination

yiches: good family connections

Yiddishe: Jewish

zmiros: traditional songs that honor the Sabbath
   and other holy days

ABOUT THE AUTHOR

While Robyn Bavati never did become a professional dancer, she's thrilled to have fulfilled her dream of becoming a writer. *Dancing in the Dark* is her first novel. Robyn has taught creative dance in schools and worked as a shiatsu therapist. She is married, lives in Melbourne, Australia, and is the mother of three grown-up children.